Two-Gun
& Sun

Caitlin Press Inc.
8100 Alderwood Road,
Halfmoon Bay, BC V0N 1Y1
www.caitlin-press.com

Printed in Canada
Edited by Marnie Woodrow
Typset by Vici Johnstone
Cover design by Derek von Essen

Caitlin Press Inc. acknowledges financial support from the Government
of Canada and the Canada Council for the Arts, and from the Province
of British Columbia through the British Columbia Arts Council and the
Book Publisher's Tax Credit.

Library and Archives Canada Cataloguing in Publication

Hutton, June (Heather June Hutton), author
        Two-Gun & Sun / June Hutton.

ISBN 978-1-927575-95-6 (paperback)

        1. Cohen, Morris Abraham, 1887-1970—Fiction.
2. Sun, Yat-sen, 1866-1925—Fiction. I. Title. II. Title: Two-
Gun & Sun.

PS8615. U88T86 2015   C813'.6   C2015-904040-X

TWO-GUN & SUN

—A NOVEL

JUNE HUTTON

CAITLIN PRESS

For Tony
for the idea

"*Two-Gun Cohen* is essentially a piece of historic fiction. Each page, like many of the stories that he relayed to the press over the preceding thirty years, contained inaccuracies and outright falsehoods."

Daniel S. Levy, author,
Two-Gun Cohen, a Biography
—commenting on the Charles Drage version of Cohen's life, as told to Drage by Cohen himself

CONTENTS

III—LA FANCIULLA

APRIL 1, 1923

HONG KONG—Preparations are underway to launch yet another campaign against China's notorious warlords, according to a representative of Generalissimo Sun Yat-sen.

Mr. Morris Cohen, a former banker and financier from Montreal who currently serves as bodyguard to the national leader, told travelers and news correspondents gathered in The Hong Kong Hotel lobby that his first priority is a rail line to cross the country to facilitate the movement of goods and troops. The second, is to straighten out China's finances.

Furthermore, teaching the troops to box and shoot will be Mr. Cohen himself, once a sergeant with the Canadian Railway Troops in Europe during the Great War. In his new capacity he will be given the title of Acting-General. "It'll be a force such as China has never seen," he said.

Accompanying Mr. Cohen was by all accounts a handsome woman who declined to be named, simply insisting to all who asked that she was here for the drama and that no, she was not "the betrothed of Mr. Morris Two-Gun."

Recently he earned the name Two-Gun Cohen for the second pistol he packs as added protection, and because it was in the Wild West of North America where he first met the national leader . . ...

I—BLACK MOUNTAIN

In the Wild West of
North America

Midnight, and no stars, no moon. I stood alone on the deck, gripping the rail, waiting for a glimpse of this town that would be my new home. The rusted prow cleaved the bank of fog in two, grey foam folding rapidly to either side as the ship motored up the inlet, a dizzying presence that pressed against my face, rendering me sightless. The stink of it was up my nose, a mix of outhouse and crushed barnacles and rotten eggs—and damp, too. Hair that I had combed flat and clamped in place with my silver pin had gone haywire, I could feel it, had absorbed the wet and sprung to life, unwinding and loosening from the knot, coils of it dangling over my ears, tapping onto my shoulders and the back of my neck to drip and dance and bounce back up to drip again. One lock fell over my nose, a russet curl I snuffed away as a horse might. If I were made of metal I'd be hearing the bolts and screws clattering to the ground as I came undone.

The midnight ship, blinded as well by the fog, came upon the wharf so suddenly its sides ground and shrieked against the wood and its engines reversed, sending a shudder up the sides.

Hands clenched on the railing, legs braced, I rode each pitch and roll. I was not about to get tossed overboard, but if I had been I was prepared, my travel outfit a split-skirted, leggings style of get-up, lavender-grey to take the dirt, the one sensible piece of clothing I owned. I could ride a horse in it if needed, swim to shore if I had to.

The ship settled at last, rolling gently in its own wake. Lights flickered on down below, and the mist seemed to thin. I breathed in, then out, as though I were swimming.

There would be no one on shore to meet me. That was how I'd wanted it. Who would meet me anyway, except a stranger, and I saw no purpose in that. I had been eager to leave home, the stifling prettiness of the orchard, the suffocating heat, the long distance to town, the likelihood that I would die there without ever having lived. It was in

15

that very orchard, at the very moment I was inspecting the branches of budding fruit, looking over my shoulder, bear scat in the grass and any shadow the possible bulk of a bear that, far away in Black Mountain, Uncle died. I learned this only later. At the time, I never thought the shadows could be him, come by one last time to say farewell before leaving for good. A foolish thought, but it soothes me now. At the time, all I thought was: bear. It was too early for them, but it had been an early spring.

And there it was: Uncle was dead, and I was here to take over. He could have picked one of my brothers to run the newspaper, but his Last Will and Testament named me, the only girl, his only niece. Still, I almost said no, sitting in the lawyer's office back home, our horse, Ruby, tearing and chewing at grass outside the window while I listened to the details and contemplated a life in some desolate mining town on the coast. The bank agreed to a small loan for start-up costs if I could guarantee results in one month. If not, it would seize the newspaper, already in arrears.

I said yes, for all of the above-noted reasons.

Whistles and shouts erupted from the ship's crew. A rope was tied and the men began to fling crates onto the boards below. The lights that marked the edge of the wharf revealed two dark figures emerging from the swirling mist. I squinted. Chinese, one with his hair in a single braid down his back, like the old coolies who worked on the rail beds. They rummaged through the pile, unmindful of the falling freight, neither dodging nor ducking as parcels landed all around them.

I watched intently. My leather bags were in that pile.

One of the ship's crewmen materialized next to me.

Miss, he said.

Sinclair, I said, Lila.

He didn't introduce himself, but he must have been a navigator of some sort because he hung over the railing, barking directions about the crew, the ship, the ropes, the lowering of the gangplank, the moving of cargo.

I'm going down now, I told him.

He wrenched his grizzled head around. We're not done yet, miss.

I grabbed the rope railings anyway and lurched down the descending gangplank, its tip still inches above the wharf. I jumped and landed neatly on the boards below. Everything I'd thought essential to my new life here I'd packed in those bags. Clothes. A black, beaded evening bag that was all I could recall of my mother: her arm, and the beads sparkling from it. Favourite photos and books. A whisky bottle, full, so it wouldn't slosh around and give me away.

The handle of one of my leather cases jutted from the side of the pile and I ran for it.

That one's mine, I shouted.

I seized the handle and pulled.

There's another just like it, I said.

My words were wasted on the scavenging men. They were arguing back and forth in their language, flinging other people's goods aside while they searched.

The navigator must have followed me down because he pushed past me, now.

You two, he said. Watch it. Let the lady find her things!

Their digging had unearthed my second bag and the navigator plucked it for me. I grabbed it from him and clutched it against my chest, triumphant, but the one with the braid was equally victorious. He pulled out a package, long and slender like a rifle, and raised it high above his head. It was only then that I saw his face, his dark brows curved as though surprised, and a wide mouth that also curved downward, and realized that he was young, my age. He wedged the package under his arm and, with the other man behind him, vanished into the grey air.

It was a moment before I found my tongue.

They just up and took it, I said.

The navigator squirted tobacco, then wiped his chin. Most likely theirs, he said. Had Chinese writ all over it.

His stained fingers directed me to turn from the cargo pile. A luminescent mass had appeared behind us, undulating in the mist and growing closer. Could there be such a thing as fireflies in fog? Surely one extinguished the other. Pinpricks of light bounced madly in the air, as though whatever was holding them up perambulated on wheels over rough ground, while amongst the lights gleamed metal heads bobbing along with every bump as though each would snap right off. But strangest of all were the outstretched limbs that groped the fog, reaching perhaps, searching.

People! I declared.

Come to get their freight, too.

Are those miners' helmets on their heads?

Hats, helmets, he said. All fashion of headgear worn in Black Mountain. But strapped onto each is a light such as the miner's wear.

Here's one for you, courtesy of the General Store.

In his other hand, I noticed only now, dangled a strap.

You can settle your account later. Just say where you got it.

I dropped one bag and took the offered strap by my fingertips.

If the ship docked in the daytime we wouldn't need these, I said.

Every hour that calls itself day is dusk in Black Mountain, he said. Dirt and smoke from the coal mine for starters, and the fog, and them hills, particularly the largest. It's why the name. Throws the whole place in shadow. Sometimes you'll need the light, sometimes you won't.

I haven't heard any fog horns.

You won't, miss. It's always socked in to some degree, so why bother?

His eyes dropped to my wrist where I'd wrapped the strap of the lamp.

Wear it like they do so's it frees up your hands for carrying. I could have one of the boys assist you.

No, I said. I'll be fine. Thank you.

I took up the second bag and waded amongst the citizens, their pale beams piercing the grey, probing the pile for their things, not a hello from a single one of them.

Behind me, now, waves chopped as the vessel slipped from the dock. I let go of the handle and turned to wave uncertainly—was the navigator even looking?—and the light at my wrist danced crazily. Yes, I might have strapped the lamp onto my head, but I didn't want to look like one of them.

I struggled up the empty road, shoulders burning from the strain of the two heavy bags. In a short while I'd be glad of that bottle, but at the moment I cursed the bloody weight, I cursed my suffering self for dragging it along, I cursed my Christly insistence that I could make the walk unassisted. The lamp continually slipped behind my hand, my sleeve blocking half the light, making me stumble. In my pocket were the directions and they were straightforward enough: Walk down the road to the building at the end. I hadn't factored in the weight of my things, or the length of the road, or the dark.

I came to a standstill. Those Chinese hadn't worn headlamps.

Men sneaking about in the dark, carrying rifles, wouldn't want lights blazing. They could be around the next corner, for all I knew, ready to shoot me. I forced myself to keep walking, and quickly. The navigator didn't seem concerned about them. No business of mine, was the implication. Steal from their own if they want. Break their necks in the dark. Shoot themselves in the foot.

A golden light burned in a shop window just ahead, outlining the bent head of a dark-haired woman, busy stitching. I could use a friend, here. Before I could approach she reached up and pulled down the blind, done for the night I supposed. I was close enough now to see the words painted on the glass: *The Bluebell Shop ~ Dressmakers, Hats, Gloves, Alterations*. I could also see my own rumpled reflection. I would come back another time, when the shop was open and my outfit was pressed.

A scrum of wranglers whooped just ahead, the light of my lamp gilding them, their own lights bobbing on their hats as they strained and sweated and pulled on ropes, boot heels churning in the dirt to steady some lumbering beast lost in the dark. Between their dancing legs and the rows of buildings behind them, all corrugated tin, I caught a glimpse of an image, flickering like a moving picture show, of a black-haired man in white, hands tied behind his back, prodded along by a posse. I waded into the mist only to find the cowboys roping nothing more beastly than a boulder, and the man in white, gone, swallowed up by the grey.

Just ahead, at last, loomed a two-storey tin box with a wooden false front and veranda, a sight so welcome I didn't stop in at the hotel restaurant that appeared to be open, spilling green light onto the black dirt. I wasn't hungry after a ham and cheese sandwich on the ship. All I wanted now was a swig from my bottle. I walked past the hotel and up the steps onto the veranda, dropped a bag and fished in my pocket for the key, all the while studying, in the dim, grey-green light, the empty frame screwed to the tin siding by the door. Ragged strips of old news fluttered from its edges, all that was left from the front page, the torn masthead that left off the last two letters, *The Black Mountain Bullet--*

I liked that, *Bullet* instead of *Bulletin*. Fast. As though news could be shot from a gun barrel right into the minds of its readers. Not tomorrow, but soon, soon.

I slid the long key into the lock, turned it, and kneed open the door. I used an elbow to flick on the switch next to the doorframe.

Light fell onto a sheet of paper that had been slipped under the front door. I snatched it up and read quickly. It had the bold print of a wanted poster but announced, instead, the upcoming performance of Puccini's opera *La Fanciulla del West*.

Here, in Black Mountain. I'll be damned.

There was a whole series of names under the title, and a swirl of colours, velvet curtains or something. I clapped it under my arm—I'd have a closer look later—and picked up my second bag, edging through the doorway, kicking the door shut behind me. A hallway led to stairs and the promise of a bedroom above. To my right, a front counter where I set down the intriguing poster; to my left, a darkened doorway. I stepped over and slid my elbow up that doorframe, too, until it hit the switch and light flooded the room.

And there it was, confronting me in a way I'd never anticipated. Pipes bent in half, studded with bolts, clamps that bit into congealed grease and rust, drooling brown at the edges. I let my leather bags drop to the floorboards in a double thud of astonishment, reckless of the fragile contents.

The old printing press was bolted to a raised platform reached by three steps. A regal setting for a tangle of metal dredged in dust. It twisted itself up into the likeness of a huge creature from one of my brothers' action books. Incredible and awful at once.

Surely a month was not enough. Had anyone from the bank even stood in this doorway?

An oval brass side plate gleamed like a single eye, daring me to unlock the limbs of this contraption. The press filled the room all the way to the ceiling, was twelve feet high at least, and must have set the walls shaking once, a deafening resurrection that marked the start of each news day. Now, corroded and jammed with crud, the monstrosity was made stillborn by neglect.

Dare accepted.

Hanging from a hook on the doorframe was a pair of ink-stained coveralls. I slung them over my shoulder and carried my leather bags out into the corridor and up the stairs, flicking more light switches with my elbows as I climbed.

At the top of the staircase I turned and looked down the long, narrow room that was half the width of the space downstairs: a bathtub set in the middle of the floor, its claws gripping the raw boards, and a toilet, mercifully in its own closet, door agape, fitted next to the staircase. A bachelor's room, not even a sink, just a hole in the blue-painted boards where one had been intended. At the far end, underneath the window, was a bed. I didn't feel the need for sleep, not now. I wanted to get back to that press. I tossed my jacket onto the bed and stepped into the pair of coveralls. I unbuckled one bag, pulled out the bottle and took a long swig, then corked it and dropped it back in. I smoothed my sleeves and looked down at myself, dressed like a garageman.

So I was. So what?

I buttoned up as I clomped down the stairs.

An instruction booklet lay face down on the top step of the platform, its corners rounded from constant thumbing. Some comfort there. I wasn't the only one who'd puzzled over these parts. I flipped through the pages, circling the platform as I read.

⋆⟶⟹

Heat and oil had made slick work of the bolts and nuts and screws, the wrench I'd dragged over to get a grip, my fingers around it a useless knot, equally wet. I was sprawled on the floor of the raised platform, elbows up and spine grinding into the boards. A balled-up greasy apron propped up my head but still, more bits of brown frizz had worked their way free from the knot and hung in my eyes, and I scraped them away with my knuckles.

I was no stranger to machines. My big brother Will had a cantankerous Ford, and I had worked beside him, loosening and tightening bolts, steam billowing from gnarled pipes of lead. But this was different, more like two trucks clamped one on top of the other, maybe three, its insides of another nature entirely.

As I worked, I composed a letter to my brothers.

> *Dearest boys,*
> *The voyage was rough but arrived here without*
> *incident shortly after midnight. Don't tell father*
> *that —*

No, scuttle that. I should just say the voyage was several hours' duration. I didn't want their sympathy.

> *And now here I am working on Uncle's printing machine.*
> *I will write again soon.*
> *—your loving sister, Lila*

No. Just: *—Lila*

With the heel of my hand on the wrench, the weight of my body behind it, I shoved. Too hard. The bolt squawked, then gave, and sent the wrench flying.

I cursed the godforsaken grimy tin walls and sat upright, barely missing a metal bar overhead. That was it. I was done. Pale light shone in the windows now, just as the navigator had said it would. Day one of my new life and a wasp of anxiety buzzed from rib to rib inside me. A month to get the newspaper out. I fought a sense of welling panic, the fear that I might have tackled too much, was attempting the impossible and therefore was doomed to failure. And then the fear of succeeding, of feeling this beast leap to life under my fingers. What then?

Someone in town must know about my uncle's printing machine, who ran it, and where I could find him. I rolled to my feet.

With a rag that reeked of kerosene I rubbed furiously at my stained fingers and knuckles, squeezing through the cramped back shop as I worked at my hands, past the drawers of type, shelves of ink cans, stacks of paper. Newsprint smudges from Uncle's thumbs blackened the doorknobs, window sills and tin walls. Against the back wall, a washtub streaked black and full of jars of putty knives and rags and solvent. Above it a battered metal mirror, where I checked my face for streaks of black, then stuck my head under the tap to rinse my mouth. Uncle had a tin of denture powder on the shelf. I sprinkled some onto my finger and rubbed it over my teeth, rinsed again, and dried my face on my sleeve.

Hanging from a bolt in the wall next to the sink was a calendar. It had 1922 neatly printed over a painting of an orchard not unlike ours back home, and I could see why Uncle had picked it. I tore off the May, June, July and August pages from the pad at the bottom. A pencil had been tied to the bolt, and I grabbed it up to strike through September 1, yesterday, and September 2, today. I spun around and left the pressroom, the pencil clattering against the wall behind me.

Next, my coveralls. They slid into a heap around my ankles and I shook one foot and then the other to step out of them, smoothing as I did so the lavender-grey pleats of my travel outfit, even more rumpled than before. I was ready.

The opera poster still lay at a crooked angle on the counter. I'd pin it up later. The front office was the only room in the building where anything could be pinned. Its walls had been framed in wood and then finished with lath and plaster. It could use some brightening, though, because the white paint had yellowed over the years.

I felt along the shelves underneath the counter, finding trays of rubber bands and bundles of envelopes, pencils and paperclips. I took up one pencil and stuck in into the sharpener screwed to the countertop, cranked the handle five times and pulled it out. Perfect. The sharpener in my old classroom used to chew the pencils to bits. On the second shelf I found a ledger, and behind it, at last, the thing I had been looking for, a notebook. Spiral-bound, brown cover, the inside pages a series of calculations, my uncle's attempts to tally income and expenses and find a balance in his favour. I had the same habit and made a mental note to stop it. This was like finding someone's love letters, all their emotions and fears laid out for the finder to examine: my uncle's frantic discovery that he was nearing bankruptcy, each series of sums tallied hopefully, and then crossed out angrily. I tore out the scribbled pages and tossed them into a wooden box full of other scraps of paper.

Then I lifted the hinged counter and dropped it with a bang behind me.

Outside I was struck by the sensation of plodding through a dust storm. I could barely make out the wooden sign in my neighbour's darkened window: General Store. The navigator was right. A low-hung sky of dark grey turned mustard grey about the edges where the sun must be trying to burst through. Feeble as the daylight was, I could see what I had missed last night. No need for a lamp. To my left, thick black trunks of chimneys belching smoke. To my right, a strip of simmering walls of black metal pipes and roofs. Soot-stained windows that glowered dully. I turned in quick circles, trying to take it all in, trying to decide where to start seeking information. Leaning corrugated metal shacks and rotting logs, heavy iron pipes running between them, down low and up high, gave the whole place the look of a furnace room with the lights turned off. The road sign told me that this was Zero Avenue. Fitting. A nothing street. Not a leaf. Not a tree. The mountain that the navigator told me about rose through the mist, with a long tail of hills that whipped around the town.

Some towns are marked by the cry of gulls or the clanging of streetcars. But this one's music was a constant rumbling of coal carts along the tracks that skirted the tops of the hills.

At my feet its dank centre, strewn with boulders, hunks of cement, buckets on their sides.

Black motorcycles roared out of the fog, their silver-snouted sidecars squealing around me as I tried once, then twice, to dodge them and cut across the road. I had no idea these were taxis, that the black-booted thugs in goggles and tight leather caps were, in fact, the taxi drivers. Uncle never mentioned them when he came to visit. His talk was all about the newspaper. I didn't see a single taxi last night. I realized what they were only when a man across the way flagged one down. And I noticed him only because he was relieving himself against the side of a tin building, a saloon by the looks of the swinging doors, and waved with his free hand, turning his spray into the street.

In two long strides I had leapt out of his way, too.

I pressed on, past the only building of any substance, the bank all stone and equally grey—at once the wasp was back in my guts, reminding me of my deadline. I pushed the thought away. Before me was the only promise of elegance in town, a skeleton of iron girders that formed a square frame and, lying on the ground beside it, a matching skeletal dome that one day might top the structure. Right now, there wasn't a single worker on the site.

I stepped off the boardwalk to cross the road at the corner, and very nearly put my boot into a black hole. I leapt back, heart pounding, hand at my throat, reeling around to confront the first person I saw. What was this doing in the middle of the road? Why wasn't it blocked off? A child could fall in. I could bloody well fall in.

But all I saw was swirling mist. Then I thought of that Chinese, how he had melted into the fog and how he could be a few feet from me right now, his rifle aimed at my head.

I hurried on.

The hotel café doors flew open and empty food tins were booted into the street, the clatter drawing stray pigs that charged around me for the rubbish and rooted gleefully, obscenely pink against the soot streets. There was news here, that much was certain. That group of men roping that boulder last night. That large man, absurdly dressed in white, hands tied behind his back. And that Chinese, that rifle.

Words crammed into my mind. Headlines and subheads. Commentaries and stories. What torture to have the words and not the means because, without a newspaper, none of them would gain the heft of news. I darted around the pigs and turned back up the street to the General Store, where light was now spilling from the window.

Desk lamps with green shades lined the long counters. A thin man, balding, leaned on his elbows, his green visor staining the tip of his pointed nose and chin.

Newcomer, Miss?

Sinclair, I answered. Lila. I approached him with hand held out to shake his. He reached under the counter and dropped a package into my palm.

Tea, the man said. What your uncle used to order.

I nodded and pushed the package onto the polished wood counter. He knew exactly who I was, though my last name was different. Uncle was my mother's brother. But word had spread. No surprise. In such a small place, I was news.

Mister, I began.

Parker, he corrected. Just Parker.

You knew my uncle, I said.

Well enough. A going concern.

Until he met his death, I said.

Until he met his death, he agreed.

There was no sign of sympathy on the man, but it was hard to see anything under that visor. His eyes flashed green, though they were likely pale blue.

It was a shock, I added. He wasn't that old.

His sister was much younger.

My mother, I replied.

Uncle must have told him about her. I waited for this Parker to tell me more. He didn't. I was in a hurry and wanted to ask about the press, but out of politeness found myself filling the silence. I saw a man last night, I said, dressed all in white, which you have to admit—

I waited for him to finish my sentence. Is absurd, he might've said. Foolhardy in a coal town. Again he didn't respond, so I added, His hands were tied behind his back!

Hmmph, he said.

Then I almost fell into a black hole in the middle of the street. There should be signs—

Mind the holes! he said. Exploratory digs, they're everywhere.

Well I suppose.

No supposing. It's a fact. This is a mining town.

I studied the shelves above his head. Tins of peas and corn, of beets, of sardines and corned beef, of peaches and pears. To the side, in the corner, a pickle barrel.

His thin voice dragged my eyes back. You ready to run the newspaper, Miss?

Lila, I repeated. I plucked my notebook from my pocket and gave it a flutter. Ready for news, I replied. I taught grammar once, and history.

That last fact was to make me seem some sort of expert, though I'd actually found the schoolchildren to be worse demons than my little brothers.

Not what I meant, exactly, he said.

You mean because I'm a woman.

Could be, he said, drawing out the words. You a woman who knows how to run the machines?

My arms went loose. He'd found me out. The wasp thumped against my ribs again, desperate for escape.

Didn't think so, he said.

I shook my head, thoughts ranging until they latched onto a point of logic. That's why I'm here, I said, to ask you who my uncle had to run them.

Ran them himself.

In addition to writing all of his articles? And interviewing? Going to meetings—

Then I stopped. How much did I want this Parker knowing about me and my concerns? And the fact that, clearly, I had not expected to operate machinery. Tinker with the parts, certainly, as I had done already, just to see if I could. But I had thought there'd be someone else. At least, I hadn't thought at all about whether there would or wouldn't be someone else. I hadn't thought at all beyond digging up news and writing it down. I knew that would mean running the business, too, and I looked forward to it, just as I had when my brothers went overseas, all four of them, and Father and I were left to run the fruit farm. We did a good job. I did a good job, more and more it was left up to me, to cut the orchard grass and pick the fruit, load it up and drive the truckload to the jam factory in town. When the war ended and the twins and Robbie came back, Father suggested that if I wasn't going to marry I needed to find a way to take care of myself. Had I said I wouldn't marry? I was still sore about the Poznikoff boy at the jam factory, John, whose people were from Russia. Blasted pacifists, our father said. You stay away from that coward. Why should our Will have to sacrifice his life, when a Doukhobor can fold his arms and refuse to fight? I said how else could I meet a boy—the rest had been blown to bits. And more things, many more things said that day, too many to dwell on now, in the General Store. It was enough to recall that Father took over the runs and then the boys returned and I was left with teaching as my future. And now? I just assumed there'd be an assistant, an apprentice, I don't know, someone more familiar with the intricacies of producing the newspaper: setting the type and loading it, if that's even what the process was called, adjusting the pressure, fixing a paper jam and now that I thought of it, inking the press. I hadn't thought I'd be alone with all that.

My thinking had exhausted me. I leaned on the counter for support.

Your uncle tried to hire a man once, Parker said. Just to help out. But he was no mechanic. He was an Australian. There's the Chinese, if you're fool enough to go there.

I saw a Chinese yesterday—I began, but Parker spoke over top of me.

They call it Lousetown, he said, if you see what I mean. Where all them live. Chinese, Hindu, whatnot.

He lifted his visor. Yes, his eyes were pale blue and they bugged clear out of his head. He opened a drawer and began digging around it, done with the conversation. He stopped only to raise both hands as though to indicate that I'd been warned.

Finally, he looked up and asked, Anything else?

I straightened up.

A man on the ship, the navigator, he gave me a headlamp.

It's on your bill.

Peaches, I said, pointing to the shelves. Corned beef. Sardines, too, please. And bread.

I was hungry, and asked for a pickle as well. He handed it to me wrapped in waxed paper, and I ate it as he returned to our previous conversation.

The mine is directly behind your back door and Lousetown is directly behind the mine. You could climb Black Mountain to have a look around and get your bearings.

That great big hill, you mean?

He worked his mouth for a time. Chinese call their paper *The Times*, he said. *The Chinese Times.* That's where you'll find a printer.

I thought of asking him about rifles in Lousetown, but something stopped me. Parker talked about those people the way my father talked about Doukhobors.

It's in English, I gather, the newspaper?

No.

Then why isn't the paper a Chinese name?

Ask them. Here's your bread.

A package of flour landed on the counter, followed by a pound of paper-wrapped lard.

He shook his head at my obvious bewilderment.

Thought so, he said. You could pan fry it instead.

I nodded vigorously, though I knew no more about frying bread than I did baking it.

He slapped open a paper bag and filled it with my purchases.

I swallowed the last of the pickle and crumpled the waxed paper into my pocket. Hungry as I was, I would be glad to dump the bag inside my front door, and set a course for Lousetown.

If I was fool enough to go there, Parker said. I had travelled all the way to Black Mountain by myself. What was one more short trip?

ACCURSED CREATURES

Behind my shop the land sloped into a haze-streaked hollow. Hovering at the three-foot level was thicker fog that stunk of smoke. My building had turned its back on the mine, with all windows aimed toward the street side. It was only by walking down the side of the building and around the corner that I was able to see this back view for the first time. It brought me to a standstill. The outline of the pithead towered in the grey distance like a double-decked outhouse, tall and rambling and leaning, as though it had been tipped by misbehaving boys. All that was missing was a crescent moon carved in the door. Crouched around it was a jumble of tin outbuildings, each as black and filthy as the next, with orange fires crackling over the rubble-strewn blackened grounds, a set of shoulders hunched over each, tending the flames.

The low whine of a motorcycle cut through the thick air and I turned to watch it appear. Headlamp first, glowing like the moon. Beetle-nosed sidecar next. Then the driver, goggled as though he'd risen from the ocean, his leather dripping like second skin. I waved and he pulled the bike up beside me, oily steam leaking from its vents and joints. A leather boot with silver buckles planted itself into the dirt.

Where to? the taxi driver asked, lifting his goggles to expose pink circles around his eyes. Careful, he added. Trout Creek behind you.

I looked back and sprang clear of the creek that steamed where it met a channel of black from the mine, just a few feet from my back door. Some sort of fish bobbed belly-up in the mix, unearthly white.

I pulled my eyes from the sight and told him: Lousetown.

Without a word he slapped the goggles back in place and gunned the engine, leaving me in a greasy cloud with the joined creeks bubbling behind me.

I would walk then, my sole companion the fish that turned in slow circles beside me in the water.

But no. To my right, two lines of miners emerged in the gloom, startling me with their sudden proximity, close enough for me to make out their features. The far line trudged toward the pithead, grim-faced, about to go under, while the near one lurched from it, black-faced, metal helmets studded with lamps. Limp-armed, lunch pails dangling.

These were the sort of men I'd like to interview for the paper, men like my friends' fathers back home who toiled in the smelter and in the nearby mines. This mine seemed to have a ready supply of them. There they staggered beside me, exhausted and filthy, resigned to the prospect of coming back tomorrow. Blackened lips muttering. Scottish brogue, Irish lilt, American drawl. The last one a torrent of Italian, or was it Spanish? The tall one could be a Swede or a Dutchman, his fair hair dusted grey by coal. The short one—a Welshman? All different, but all one in the cold look they gave me, the outsider, the niece who might be just like her newspapering uncle, prying where she wasn't wanted, vulgar in her lavender-grey, a blush of colour in their ashen world.

And then a sound I can't stomach, though I heard it many times from my brothers and their friends, a sound from the back of the throat, a wad of mucus hurtling towards my shoes.

I leapt, but not soon enough, my pleated hem catching the slime.

What animal—

My voice broke and I told myself, Don't cry, don't cry, don't you goddamn-well cry. If you do, they'll think you're afraid. And a part of me was, it really was. Why would they do such a thing?

I stopped, heard the sound of the men wheezing, the dry rasp of their sleeves against their shirts. Each man regarded the blackened ground, toed it with a black boot—shame or plain weariness replacing the rabid moment. They were done with me now, and turned away.

I could've shouted after them, I want to know who spat on me! Was it on purpose, don't deny it.

My thoughts roared with accusations, requests for apologies. In the end, I found that my anger abated, too. I swung around, leaving them and the creek and my floating companion. I had other concerns.

Up the trail that tacked the south side of Black Mountain, the charcoal surface was a scruff of crab grass and creeping yellowish brambles. Round one clump and out of eyeshot I stooped, slopped water from a puddle onto my hem. The water was black, and left a grey streak, but better than what was there, green-black slug of gob.

I marched on, more tired than I liked to admit, the cruelty of the miners heavy on my shoulders.

In my mind I composed a letter of woes to my brothers, then tore it up.

On the summit my throat, squeezed tight since I passed the pit-head, opened to the cool air. I had automatically faced west, a gasp caused as much by delight as from air rushing in. While the town itself was cloaked in grey, the sun shone outside it. Even so, for miles I saw nothing but parched hills of grey. Only in the distance was there green next to a stretch of water like rippling silk, a deep, deep blue, the Pacific, sparkling where it chopped, studded by distant craft, a white bird or two, dipping, screeching. I turned to the south. A second, larger wharf I hadn't known existed until now. I could barely make it out through the bank of grey, but it seemed the coal carts climbed a ramp and tipped their contents into the hold of a coal hulk, because a second line of them came back along the hills, empty.

My shop, scarcely visible, marked the end of Zero Avenue, with Parker's General Store next to it. Behind both of us, as I had just dis-covered and Parker had told me, was the mine. There was Trout Creek, on a course to empty its grey self into the sea. I stopped turning, having completed the circuit.

Further north, on the other side of the pithead, the blurred outlines of one wooden shack after another, twisting paths linking them, boards thrown down across what must be streams. Lousetown. And some-where in there, *The Chinese Times.*

If I could spot the *Times* from here I could shorten the trip. I'd like that. I'd like even better to turn back, send a letter saying that the task was impossible, that I couldn't do it all by myself.

And then what, head back home?

Parker could go ahead and call me a fool, but I needed to go down into those shadows. What would they do—shoot me? All I wanted was to find a printer to run my press: a wise, old Chinese experienced at unlocking mechanical quandaries.

Bald branches stirred and snapped about my knees as I descended, sending up nits and bugs that threatened to bite. I flailed at the air with my hands. I had no need to fear an attack in Lousetown—I was already under siege. A grasshopper landed on my hem, its eyes dull stones that didn't blink, its legs thin as twigs. I smacked it off.

Up ahead, the fish had beached itself on the creek's bank, its white belly gleaming in the grey light, then, closer in, a horned snout, its mouth pulled back into a hideous grin. Sockeye salmon take on ugly shapes before they spawn and die, but their brilliant red compensates. This was not like any fish I'd ever seen. It wasn't just dead, it was dis-eased. You couldn't touch such a thing, let alone put it on the dinner table. I nudged it with my boot, marvelling at its mangled mouth and blistered skin. I pulled out my notebook, flipped the pages. What had caused this?

-->≡⊃

Dark as a winter afternoon.

Lighter than dusk, at least. In Black Mountain I could only see across the street but here I could see all the way down the length of a block. The road narrowed to the width of an alley, shadow upon shadow, winding through lopsided sheds and huts. It was a wonder they survived the wind, or the weight of snow each winter.

The very thought of snowflakes in this place. Ashes, floating from a fire.

The sun still smouldered behind a belly of grey. More strands dropped from my knot of hair and stuck to my neck. I twisted them around my fingers and clipped them back into the knot.

I called out, Hello.

Boardwalks and hitching posts, false fronts and upper balconies, all the wood silvered from exposure, but none of the rippled metal from the other side. A splintered shutter opened a crack. Dark eyes glittered in the slice of black air, until it slammed shut.

Dust heaved up from the ground as I turned to study the cramped and tilted rows of shacks. Some might have been shops and places of establishment previously, but none had been operating recently. These were ancient structures compared to the tin boxes that lined Zero Avenue, raw with their yesterday newness.

It took everything in me not to turn and run.

Paths twisted to either side of the main alley. At least I could see no holes on this side. I heard something heading my way, though. The steady crunch of boot heels on the road, foreign voices rising. Men.

They rounded the corner, emerging two by two in the shadowy air. A funeral march. A body lying on boards shouldered between them.

The voices stopped abruptly and their dark eyes looked straight ahead, as though there were no woman standing before them. If there were they might have to answer any questions she might have. Nothing as formal as a funeral, for the black-haired corpse in white suit was face-down, hands tied behind his back. He was the same man I had seen last night, I was sure of it, with that posse behind him. Who else wore white in a coal town? And with his hands tied? These men showed the same grim determination, but they weren't from the posse. They were Chinese.

This dead man they carried must be one of them. I dug in my pocket for my notebook.

Pardon me, I said, stepping toward them. Who was he?

But they swung away without answering. The corpse slid on the boards, threatening to fall off into the dirt. My hand jerked, wanting to fly to my mouth. I fought the impulse, arms stiff by my sides. The men simply hoisted one side of the boards to right the body. The only sound they made was the crunch of their heels rounding the next corner.

I should have asked them about *The Chinese Times*, instead.

A door that was open a moment ago clicked shut. I strode over and knocked, the rough wood piercing my knuckles.

Please, I shouted at the closed door, where can I find *The Chinese Times?*

A mere two feet away a cement culvert had been dumped in a ditch. Giggles exploded from inside the tunnel. Children.

Hello? Giggles again, then a foot, an arm, and two little wretches squirmed out, grubby-faced, dark bangs falling into bright eyes. Boys or girls? I couldn't tell.

A tiny hand pointed while the taller child chanted, Pretty lady! Pretty eyes!

My father used to say I had eyes like storm clouds. I shot a glance at the gunmetal sky.

Two hands tugged at my sleeves and I followed, down those same alleys I had peered at and avoided. Clomping onto boards balanced over muddy water, tipping and slamming back down with each footfall. As the children dragged me along, old men in black and grey melted into the weathered walls, disappearing before I could make eye contact. Tiny back yards sprouted shirts drying like scarecrows, their arms strung through with sticks. Chickens. More pigs. And at last, a glass-paned door with gold-painted Chinese figures.

The children pushed through the door, running ahead of me.

Inside the shop, the clatter and slap of the machines muffled my entrance. Men in smocks stood at tables, cranking large metal wheels that turned rollers. My lungs tightened at the sight of sheets of paper spurting forth. The presses were in working order, the table tops jiggling from the effort. I squinted, eyelids heavy and damp in the muggy air. Menus, from the look of it. And invitations. One press was larger than the others, though smaller than mine. Rising from it were belts that seemed to go right through the low ceiling. Unlike mine, it had not been given its own second storey. Also unlike mine, its parts had loosened, its joints unfolding, then drawing back, an enormous insect bouncing on bent limbs, ready to strike, ink glistening from its mouth. Fear scuttled up my spine. I crossed my arms to steady myself. It was grotesque, yet there was also something thrilling about the rumbling and shaking, the very size of the thing. It puffed steam like a train engine.

The smallest child leapt up and down at the base of the machine. Both waved their arms, mouths open, their words swallowed by the roar in the room.

Up high, a man stripped to the waist sat astride one section of the shuddering machine. Attack it from above, not below, yes. A white undervest washed so many times his skin glowed through the thin cloth. He swung around, his back to me, bare upper arms bulging with the effort to work a bolt. Between his shoulder blades rested a thick braid of black hair, sleek as the horse tails we plaited for parades, their muscled haunches exposed.

It was him, the one I had seen at the dock holding up that package shaped like a rifle. The others—I scanned the pressroom to be certain— had shorn hair, as had the men carrying the body. I tucked loose strands of my own hair back into the knot, re-folded my arms. Where was that rifle, now? He leaned his weight onto his palms and turned himself around, finally seeing the children, and perhaps me, though he didn't look my way. But the others must have seen me. They stopped cranking the smaller presses. One by one the clatter stopped until there was only the pounding of the one, large machine.

He jumped down and landed before the children. Their filthy faces broke into grins and their shrieks were discernible now as they hung from his arms, one on each side, crying Uncle! as he lifted them up into the air, spun them around and then set them down again. He raised a hand, palm up, and they stood back, hands folded behind their backs, waiting. I did the same. From a pocket he plucked an apple. An apple! Then from the back of his belt, a large knife. He lifted it high and then down in one swoop, the blade singing through the air as it dropped and cut the apple cleanly in half. The children clapped their hands and he handed a half to each. They bit large mouthfuls before running from the shop, cheeks full, juice dribbling across them.

Only then did he turn to acknowledge me. He seemed not such a threat now, though I flinched when he wiped the blade with a rag and slid the knife into the back of his belt again.

I had intended to introduce myself, clean, crisp and formal, then ask if he or anyone else were interested in a job, that is, if indeed he spoke

English. Instead I blurted, Where did you get that apple?

He stood back, head up, chin out, that mouth of his downturned, and said, You think I stole it?

English, all right. And cocky. I tried for humour this time, though I was only half-joking.

No. In fact, I'd buy one from you if you had another.

No reply. He unhooked a smock from a rack, slipped it on and wrapped it tight.

The silence was maddening, and I said, I'm Lila Sinclair.

Bonjour, he said, and bowed slightly. Vincent, he added, and then a second name that sounded like Cruise.

I tilted my head. It didn't sound Chinese, and I felt my eyelids drooping stupidly.

He spelled it out, C-r-u-z. Then he bowed again, stiffly, with a hint of annoyance.

That wasn't Chinese, either. But he spoke French as well as English. So I said to him: It almost sounds Spanish, your name, but of course, that can't be right.

Portuguese, he replied, looking directly at me.

I pressed my lips into a smile. He was making fun of me. I was in too much of a hurry for this, but I tried not to rush my next remark.

I'm looking, I said, to hire a printer for my newspaper. *The Bullet.*

—Bullet?

Bulletin was what my uncle called it. The paper's mine now and I've given it a new name. It has a printing machine something like this one. Are you for hire, Mr. Cruz?

His bottom lip curved further downward.

Follow me, he said.

He swung around and hiked up a narrow flight of wooden steps behind the press, assuming that the unwelcome outsider wouldn't know what else to do but follow. He was right.

The steps led to a door that opened up to the roof. The apparatus that connected to the press did indeed go right through the ceiling, with pulleys to a concave metal dish that was at least ten feet wide, and a stamen like a flower's, aimed upward.

It's run by the sun, he said.

Here on the roof we were directly in the path of the largest of the hills, Black Mountain itself, and the wash of shadow stained everything it touched. My skin must have looked grey. His lips were black.

Sun?

You just missed it. Every morning, for about four hours, right there, through the hills.

He pointed.

That's the east. It's all the light we get, but enough for this.

His hand indicated the dish.

I had noted the difference in light, here. The cloud cover was higher and thinner in Lousetown, allowing for the sensation if not the fact of light, except for those four hours, apparently, when the rising sun slipped both under the bank of grey and between those hills, and blazed down upon this dish.

But, I said. Why not coal to run the press? It's everywhere.

He studied the quilted sky, and I tried to imagine where the sun might be, possibly to the southwest. By the time it moved around the mountain it would have set.

I like to make things, he said at last. I made this.

I walked around the metal dish, impressed. It beamed softly in the grey light, a sign of the future. I pulled out my notebook.

You can't print that, he said. It means we don't need their coal. Company won't like that.

This Vincent Cruz stood in front of the dish, hands on hips, as though blocking it would erase it from my mind. I flipped the notebook shut.

Why d'you think we call this place Lousetown? he asked. To keep them out. Louseville, we say to each other. Our joke, this fancy way of talking about lice.

He pronounced it the French way, Louse-veelle, but his accent was hard to place. Chinese, of course. French. But something else, a clipped, rapid way of speaking.

Why show me, then?

He ran a hand along the curve of the dish.

You don't have one of these, so your machine's going to be different. I can try, but —

I'd pay you for your time.

Would you, now?

Even when he smiled that bottom lip arched downward. It was a cheeky smile.

Keep this a secret, he said, and you might have a deal.

His bold manner astonished me. Did I not put away my notebook? Was I not offering him employment, deserving, therefore, of some re-spect? Would he talk to a man this way?

Of course, I said.

If you want your press to run again—

I stiffened. His comment could be taken two ways. I thought of the knife in the back of his belt, of that rifle. I shouldn't have come up here with him.

He indicated the door and we headed back downstairs. I insisted he go first.

I grabbed a railing to steady myself. I should have eaten more before I left the shop.

I paused on the landing to say, A dollar an hour.

Either a smile or a sneer, a flicker too fast to catch.

This could be a mistake, inviting such a man to work for me. Maybe he wouldn't show up.

I descended the last step, and he stood aside to let me pass. I walked sideways, my back against the railing, keeping my distance.

The clacking of the little machines had resumed. Rows of insects rubbing their wings and legs, devouring leaves of paper, disgorging them spittled with print.

Steam laden with paper dust stung my eyes and I lifted a sleeve to rub my lids, heavy as lead. It was too close in here. I needed air, and looked around for the shop door.

Hey, he asked, you okay?

Yes. Fine.

I wouldn't admit otherwise, not to him. But I wasn't fine. The heat, possibly. The steam. My vision was blurred. Pounding behind my eyes. And my face, burning. I banged a hip against a counter, an elbow on metal.

Doorknob snugged in my palm, at last, I stepped over the sill. Cool air. Fat drops from clouds the colour of coal dust struck my cheeks. I turned to look for the children who brought me here, and saw myself in the polished glass of the shop door.

My eyelids were swelling shut. I'd been stung by those accursed creatures on that mountain.

I felt my throat swell. But I wouldn't cry, not now, not if the miners couldn't make me.

Soon, my eyes would close completely and I'd be left with the vacant stare of that grasshopper. Ugly. Well, so I would be. So what. I'd goddamned if I was going to ask him to help me home. Pay him to run the press, yes, but a favour? No. I burst from the doorway, stumbling, half-blind, determined to find my own way back.

THE FAMOUS MAN

Wheels clicking along a track. Coins rattling in a jar. A set of keys, jangling.

The printing press—running at last?

I jackknifed up and out of bed and the floor swam beneath me. I was blind, too, my eyes stuck shut, a weight bearing down on them. I groped for the bed and sat. The weight fell clumsily from each lid, two damp wads landing one after the other into my lap until I pushed them off. My eyes still strained under heavy lids, the bedding painfully white. Then I recalled: I hadn't unpacked my sheets. I hadn't yet slept in my new bed.

Stupid with sleep I decided I was dreaming and forced myself to look again at the bed, at the two clumps I'd pushed onto it. Dirt.

Startled awake now, I jerked my head around. Dark space and rough boards above, around. A shack. Not my bed not my bedding not my printing press running itself downstairs.

Where was I?

Despite the weight of my eyelids, they lifted high when I spotted the dead man in white laid out on a table beside this bed. Flesh crept along my scalp. Nipples and navel contracted in one wave of nerves as the corpse twitched, then groped with a hand for something on the other side of the table. Not dead at all.

Two odd clumps had been placed on his eyes, too. What strange medicine was this? I'd heard of coins placed on the eyes of the dead but not lumps of dirt on the living.

His hand emerged with a bowl and he planted it onto his big belly. A roasted popping corn smell of what must be rice, and a whiff of chicken broth. Next, a pair of wooden chopsticks that fluttered and clicked against the insides of the ceramic bowl, bringing food to his mouth. The source of the sound.

Sightless, on his back, he snapped his wooden sticks adeptly, like they were extensions of his fingers, the limbs of a grasshopper, clicking closed. A telegraph, tapping. Yes, this unusual man was news.

I clawed at my pocket for a notebook and pencil. I was here to run a newspaper. I should be able to tell false from true. What had made me think the man was dead?

My rustling caused the large head to swivel toward me. The black clumps fell from his eyes, black strips of hair fell forward, his face bloated and bruised, deep purple against pale white, lips swollen and bearing a cut, nose ballooned to twice the normal size of a nose.

Well, well, he said. A woman! I'd kiss you if I wasn't so battered and bruised.

I nodded as I flipped over the cover, thoughts racing: Not Chinese, either.

There's bloody few of you in this place, he said. That's what I get for moving to the Wild West of North America.

That, too? I asked, pointing my pencil at his face.

They gave me quite a thumping, he said. And I'm not some one-gun bum what can be easily surprised.

A growl of a voice, I noted.

He stopped to rub his broad chin and claim, A two-gun bum, that's me.

And he laughed heartily.

I scribbled as I asked, You have guns?

Did. They stole 'em. I was outnumbered is why. Fortunately my friends came to the rescue.

Friends. I wondered. Those men who shouldered him like a cadaver?

He twisted around, his belt straining at the waist of his white trousers, and shouted into the air, Would've appreciated a softer spot, but don't mind now that I see you've given the bed to the lady.

He pronounced it ly-dee, a cowboy twang leavened by a Cockney accent.

Who are you shouting to?

Oh, he must be gone. Doctor. Healer of our wounds. Maker of this fine meal.

His flipped the dark hair back from his forehead, exposing a widow's peak. He was older than I first thought, and larger. Then he eased back, contemplating me and the discarded clumps on my bed.

And who got you? he asked.

I never thought. I must have looked a sight. Well, so did he.

He blurted a possible answer to his own question, *Monsieur* Mosquito? Wasps?

Before I could answer a figure stepped into the room, that cocky printer who had threatened me. Vincent Cruz. I slipped my notebook back into my pocket and dropped my eyes.

I see you've met Morris, he said.

She has, Vincenzo!

Despite myself, I smiled at the new version of his name.

I shifted and pinpricks stitched across my belly. It had been hours since I'd left my shop and its lavatory upstairs. I was ready to burst.

The big man swung his thick legs around to sit on the edge of his wooden table.

But, he added, we haven't been formally introduced.

The printer then told this Morris character who I was, and what I did.

Morris Cohen at your service, he said, rolling his R's. A ly-dee newspaper publisher. I wondered. I saw you writing in that book.

I shot a quick glance at him. His swollen face scanned the room.

Vincenzo, my friend, he said, and then something that sounded like, Chay fang. And you, my dear?

His question had me flummoxed. I spoke no Chinese.

He leaned over to one side to look me in the face, questioningly. No French at all? In Montreal we couldn't buy a loaf of bread without a *s'il vous plait*.

French. I had a smattering of it from my schooling, but none of it had come with a Cockney accent. I understood at last: *J'ai faim*.

Not hungry, I said. Thank you.

Though I was. All I'd had today was that pickle. But my guts were full enough, and I crossed my legs at the ankle to hold back the floodwaters.

One of these little bowls is not sustenance enough for a man my size, he said.

Morris, Vincent said. Why don't I fix you another?

He rattled dishes in the far corner, and brought out a brimming bowl.

I'm a Jew, Morris said, so these are strange enough.

He tapped the sticks together.

I'd been staring at his carrot-thick fingers, and yanked my head up. Then down again as soon as I realized what I'd done. Pain shot across my skull. I wanted to run. Scrub myself clean. Find an outhouse, something.

Eating pork, Morris continued, took a whole other sort of getting used to. The fact is I've developed a fondness for bacon. But my friends here eat pork with a frequency that would stop any Jew in his tracks.

Even me, and I'm not like any other Jew.

And then he did something with his face. I stole another glance and I think he winked at me. For God's sake. With his face in that condition—and my eyes in theirs.

He said to me, I suppose you want to know why I'm here.

I hadn't until he mentioned it.

Ask me anything you like, he said, and began talking without waiting for my reply. Ever since Saskatchewan I've been hearing about the national leader.

Saskatchewan. The name threw me for a moment. I knew others who'd come from that province. John's people.

He's the top item at every tong meeting from here to Moose Jaw, Morris said. I'm here to see him.

Tong? What is that?

Secret society. I've been made a member myself with the explicit understanding that I not reveal the ins and outs and other particulars.

I saw him give a speech, Vincent said. I ever tell you that? Before the revolution.

Still looking down I asked, Revolution?

That would explain the rifle.

It was clear the two had discussed the subject before, but for my benefit they explained.

We dumped the Manchu dynasty to make a modern China, a republic.

Morris' rough voice added, The uprising started in 1911. Everyone was chopping off their pigtails.

Queues, the printer said.

Precisely. To show rejection of the old ways. Even here. Not everyone, of course, my friend.

I did this for my pop. He had to cut his. Too Chinese, the bosses said.

Ahhh, Morris said, politics of another sort.

I lifted my head carefully to study Vincent, but his head was turned. When did the revolution end? I asked.

A revolution, Morris said, does not begin on one day and end on the next. Our leader's struggles continue. The warlords in the north still support the dynasty.

Warlords! I said.

And the foreigners. Those bosses don't want things to change, either.

He has been in exile many times over the years as the balance of power shifts, Vincent said. *He* needs a unified army to fight those warlords.

And a rail system connecting all corners of China, Morris said. I plan to discuss this with him when our leader comes here to raise support.

Here? I blurted. Incredible. Does the famous man have a name?

He is a man of many names, Morris said, as is the Chinese custom. He waved his chopsticks as he recited, Sun Deming. Sun Wen. Rixin. Nakayama Sho. Well, that's what the Japanese call him. Sun Zhong-shan. But to you he would be known as Sun Yat-sen. Last name first, their custom as well.

He paused then, perhaps waiting for me to acknowledge the name. I'd never heard of it. Instead, I told them, I'd like to meet him, too, arrange an interview—

Vincent made a sound like a snort or a curse, cutting me off with a snap of his hand. Then he checked himself and half-smiled, his bottom lip deepening into a frown, adding, He's important. He's our president.

I said that was exactly why I wanted the interview.

My fingers twitched against the pocketed notebook. As soon as I got home I would write all this down.

And if the President of the United States were here you'd ask to interview him, too?

The cheek of the man. Yes, I said, I think I would!

In my heated reply I had forgotten about my swollen eyes and had kept my face lifted. Quickly now, I dropped it.

Morris bellowed appreciatively, My dear! You make a fine newspaperwoman. Doctor! Join us! We are having a fine debate.

The door had opened without my noticing, and a man shuffled over. Shoes, red, the toes coming to a point and curled back, embedded with mirrored sequins stitched in place with bright yellow thread. I thought of Parker's words: Chinese, Hindu, whatnot. Hindu, I decided.

I lifted my chin and forced my eyelids up again. Why not? They've seen me, now.

Jesus. He had spectacles thick as headlamps on a truck, making his eyeballs underneath bulge like a toad's. The lenses flashed with each movement of his head.

Black flies, he said to me, aiming a gnarled fingertip at my own bulging eyes. They blinded you. And with the heat, too, he said, you fainted. Right in the street.

He scooped up the clumps from my bed, then turned to scoop up the other two from the table.

Come, my darlings, he said. You've had your fill, I see.

He dropped the two black creatures into a jar he tucked into a pocket.

Leeches, he said to me, to take the blood from the gentleman's blackened eyes. Then he added in a reassuring tone, Yours are just tea bags, miss. A tiny poultice for each swollen eye.

May I see? I asked, and reached out to take up one saturated silk pouch by its dangling string. I'd never seen tea in bags, not up close. An American invention. I was disappointed all the same that my bug bites didn't warrant more exotic treatment. What a story for a letter to the boys, leeches on eyes. But something for the newspaper, at least. I handed it back.

I don't faint, I assured this doctor.

Well, then, miss, with the swelling from the bites you couldn't see where you were going. I suppose you hit the post. Just two feet from my door, down you went.

That explained the pounding in my head as well as my eyes. I looked down, at my lavender front ground in dirt. I must have staggered and then fallen forward.

Exactly. That's being knocked unconscious, I said, not fainting.

All right, but let me have another look.

He poured water from a jug into a pan. The sound was excruciating. Up, he said. More.

I'd been hugging my knees. I lowered them, squeezed my thighs together and sat up.

He lifted one eyelid, then the other, dabbing with a cloth. His brown hands smelled like soup.

Not a concussion, he said, dropping the cloth into the pan and taking it to the far corner. You'll be fine. You went down like a boxer.

I smiled until I considered the look of my eyes. He had almost reached the door again when I called out, What about my eyelids?

He adjusted his spectacles and smiled. They look normal to me, he said.

Well, they would to him.

Then Morris was on his feet and heading for the door, too.

He said, I need to rustle up something that'll stick to my ribs. My friend here has the appetite of a sparrow.

And he slapped his big stomach with a flat palm.

And I need clean clothes, he added, holding his jacket open.

So did I, though I didn't want to draw further attention to my appearance.

Walk her back, huh Morris? You're safe, now.

I leapt to my feet.

True, my friend. There's nothing more to take. They have my guns. Come with us, Vincenzo. You can lead the way.

First, I said, I need to use—then I faltered, wondering what to call it, convenience, contrivance?

There's the yard right behind you, Vincent's voice said. Or the latrines. Up this alley, then over two more.

I shook my head. I'd never make it, and, with no other choice left me, hurried for the door to the yard.

Outside, I peered into the darkness, wondering who might be watching. Too bad. Too late. The cool air hit me at once and I wrestled out of my leggings. This was a time when a dress would have been better. Just lift the hem. I barely got my linens pulled down. Heard and felt the rush of water. And relief, such incredible relief. Elbows on knees, lavender hem gripped in my fists, I considered where I was, this foreign patch of dirt backed by a shack and surrounded by a leaning fence, on the other side of it more rows of shacks and fences. Kitchen noises. Banging pots. Sizzling of food. Scrape of spoons. Sounds of home. I would have cried but for the plain ridiculousness of my present situation.

Another fight to get the leggings pulled up. Back inside the shack, to the right of the doorway, a jug of water and a bowl on a stand. I washed my face with my hands, dried it on my hem as there was no towel, emptied the bowl out the door, then looked up into a rusted mirror.

Hooded eyes, still. But to a stranger, perhaps normal. I could relax, now. Hold my head up. My shirtfront was filthy, but there was nothing I could do about that.

An abrasion on my forehead as well. I tugged down a lock of hair, poured more water and cupped it into my hands, swished it around in my mouth, then opened the door and spat a stream into the yard. If I were a man I could have just stood in the doorway and relieved myself from here. I recalled that man by the saloon, aiming his spray into the street.

Just one day in this place and look what I'd come to.

We set out, and the skies opened.

You want this? Vincent handed me a folded newspaper.

Night had fallen, and in his other hand he carried a lamp to guide us. No headlamp for him, and I remembered why. No holes.

I walked between them, the newspaper a tent over my head, raindrops tapping. I glanced up to see if I could read the columns but as Parker had said, they were in Chinese print, except for the masthead *The Chinese Times.*

I turned to Morris, curious, newspaper crinkling about my head, and found him to be shorter than I had expected, our eyes almost level.

I saw you earlier, I said. Twice, actually, when your friends were carrying you, and when you were being prodded down the street by what looked like a posse. This must have been after that fight? So, it was about something else?

Yes, it was another matter entirely.

I had fed him that answer, and scolded my careless self.

I swivelled around to the printer, but he was gazing at the sky.

My next comment wasn't aimed at anyone in particular, though the sight of him looking up had prompted it.

Black Mountain is an odd place, I said, always in darkness.

Black Mountain, Morris remarked, is no darker than the streets of New York or the alleys of London. Where we have hills, they have tall buildings. And don't forget their pea soup.

The great mists of Shanghai, Vincent added. It's built on a bog.

However, this is no city, Morris said. Careful, or you'll wind up bushed.

I'm from a small place, I replied.

He nodded. Yes, but that was home, you had distractions. Dinners and parties. A theatre, perhaps?

Now I was nodding. There isn't even a library here, I told him.

And your home, it was where?

Nelson, I said. In the Kootenays.

Doukhobor country!

His response had the effect of a set of truck headlights, turned suddenly onto John and me by the factory doors.

Good God we were never so glad as when they left Saskatchewan for your Kootenays. Prancing around, naked as jaybirds. Shedding their worldly possessions to be closer to God.

The Shanghai Russians were nothing like that.

The printer's voice, incredulous, and I turned to him.

No, no, I said. That was just one sect. The radicals. Freedomites. Most aren't like that.

But what an eyeful those few gave us! Have you seen one of their protests, my dear?

—No, I said.

Because I had and I hadn't.

Count yourself lucky, Morris said. I've never beheld such a spectacle. No wonder the Russians kicked them out.

It was a mutual agreement, I said, because they're pacifists.

Naked as the day they were born.

Only in Canada, not Russia. They didn't begin those protests until Saskatchewan. I don't think so, at least.

Lucky us. It would be one thing if they were young and beautiful. But a group of grannies in the altogether, their ancient husbands, too, stripped bare!

As abruptly as his outburst had begun, Morris switched to a new topic entirely.

Well, I'm off on a mission, he said. Vincenzo will see you the rest of the way.

Wait. I thought you would—

But he turned sharply, nose in the air as he set off, on the hunt for dinner, I presumed, while I was left with the image of flickering flames and nude limbs and a package the length of a rifle.

In my mind I picked through my pockets for something sharp. The tip of a pencil. A jab to the eye, if needed.

We walked in silence until I asked, Morris Cohen, he's a good friend of yours?

We reached the end of the next stretch of shacks before he answered. He's an okay guy. He's got our respect.

Like your national leader?

I could feel a smile in his pause. No, he said, not like him. Us Chinese think of Morris as a good buddy. One of our own. It was a Chinese, a restaurant owner, who was being robbed this time, and Morris came to the rescue. Knocked the guy out with a punch. Not many white guys who'd do that. And he likes to gamble, Morris. So do the Chinese, so we get along.

You, too?

He shifted. I could hear the movement of his arms.

Coming here was a gamble.

He could have been referring to himself, or to me, coming to Lousetown today.

He continued, Morris says he's no hero, and not much of a white man, either. He says, I'm a Jew. To an Englishman, I'm as good as Chinese.

From under my newspaper I could see that Vincent had captured even the mannerisms of his friend, raising his shoulders and lifting his palms as he spoke.

Just look at *them*.

His chin indicated the surrounding shacks and their occupants. Chinese labourers, I gathered.

I figured a printer like me who could read and write in English and French could do better, could get a job anywhere in the west.

How did you learn?

Doesn't matter. Here I am, printing Chinese.

And some English.

He laughed a harsh laugh. Menus!

More than that, if you came to the *Bullet*.

I stepped around a puddle, newspaper held high, before I realized what I'd said. Did I really want him as my printer? Quickly, I asked, What part of China were you from?

His answer wouldn't have mattered. I knew little about the country. Rain spattered onto the newsprint. Beneath the dampening sheets that smelled of ink and something like the ocean, I listened as he continued.

All over. My pop was a baker. Trained with the Portuguese. So did his father, but old pops was the tops. No Chinese could bake bread like he did, European-style. He was a hit with the western bosses. He worked in their kitchens and we followed them as they spread up the coast, from Hong Kong to Swatow, Amoy, Foochow, Ningpo. Finally Shanghai.

He paused and said, It's a great city, full of internationals, French, Russian, German. American and British. Japanese, too.

American. That was it. I could hear it in his manner of speaking, a casualness, and in his vowels, slightly drawn-out, flattened. Another accent in there as well. He said *too* as though it were *teww*. French or Chinese, I wasn't sure.

His arms and hands moved high and wide as he described. The French Concession has houses big as museums. Trees up and down the streets. Our leader lives there, when he's in exile. In other parts of China they want him dead.

I lifted the page to study him. What a complicated man, with his modern thoughts and traditional hair, and now his clear love of the foreigners in Shanghai. Weren't they the very bosses who made his father cut his hair? Weren't they the people his leader wanted out of China? His leader's struggle was the sort of news I was after for *The Bullet*: far-reaching, thought-provoking. There had to be a way to write about him without risking his safety. I'd have to work on that.

Some parts of Shanghai aren't so swell, he said. Some look a lot like this. Shacks. Laundry poles. No streets, just a dirt path on a dirt bank sliding into a stream. Watch that water.

He reached for my wrist, then pulled his hand back just as I recoiled, newspaper crushed at my waist as one hand plunged into my pocket for the pencil.

We stared at each other for a moment, my swollen eyes fully exposed now, but they were the last thing on my mind.

The main creek's farther up, he said. It's clean. This one's a slop bucket. You want to find your own way back—follow its stink.

I didn't reply, wasn't sure he was expecting me to. He kept walking and so did I, dropping the crumpled paper into the dirt. The rain had lightened to a drizzle, anyway.

We heard this place was better, he said, but nope. Just another treaty port. English on that side, us, here. Crazy, isn't it? To go to all that trouble to drag the worst of Shanghai here, to Black Mountain.

His outpouring had left me feeling wrung dry.

We were approaching the pithead now, its shithouse shape spilling dung beetles into the night. I could hear their muttered accents on the wind, see the eerie sight of their headlamps beaming fuzzily in the fog, blotting out the bodies that walked beneath them. I had left my own headlamp at home, not expecting to be out this late, and in strange company, not wanting the ridiculousness of one on my head.

He said nothing more to me than the simple words, Monday, then. In a flash he had darted back into the jumble of shacks.

So, it was decided. I had my printer.

CROOKS, COWBOYS AND IDIOTS

It was still dark when I woke. I had slept fitfully. A swig from the bottle was of some help. I fell into dreams of home, clumps of mist rolling like tumbleweeds up the hill from the lake. White and filmy, not grey like here.

I flipped off the wool coat that had served as my blanket, the mattress vividly striped under my arms, the sheets still not unpacked.

Home was just a train ride away. Board at the coast in time for breakfast, roll through the valleys, sparks flying as the tracks curved around mountain sides, sometimes tunnelling right through them, branching out into spur lines for the mines, copper and coal and silver, slowing past the fields and the squat, two-storey Russian communal houses, finally reaching Nelson after breakfast the next day.

They'd be picking the pears right now, the fruit so heavy they'd prop up the branches with rakes.

I counted on my fingers: six of those harvests since my father seized the fruit runs to stop me from seeing that boy. John. English for Ivan. Six years, yet here I was thinking of him again.

We had met during cherry-picking season. He had hair so blonde it looked white where he stood in the shadows of the wooden delivery doors. Our hands brushed that first time when he helped me lug in the baskets of red fruit. Sometimes I drove, but usually I was the swamper on these runs, dragging crates of fruit off the back of the truck, while Will or Robbie drove. The cherries from our region were noted for their rich colour and size, as big as plums. They were hand-sorted, the best of them laid out like jewels in small wooden boxes, eight to each, to be shipped out by train. The rest were trucked out to the factory to be cooked into jam. On the next run, before one of my brothers backed up the truck to the delivery bay, I took a cherry from the basket beside me and bit into it to redden my lips.

Apricots were next, and the sight of them ripening made me restless. I wanted to pick them two full days before they were ready.

August had barely begun when war was declared and my brothers enlisted, even the twins, considered too young to handle the driving but suddenly old enough to fight. Pete and Pat, always said in that order so that our father could make a joke of saying pitty-pat, but with them gone he said it a lot less. I did feel for him, then. Even so, the absence of all of my brothers meant I could drive the fruit runs. I could also see John alone. During the next weeks, over the steaming kettles of apricots, raspberries and blueberries, we stole glances. And by the time the pears had ripened, we had kissed behind the wooden doors.

We were three-quarters of the way through the apples and plums, a bumper crop, two precious weeks left. We hadn't talked about what would happen once those fourteen days ended. They stretched far off into the implausible month of October, a month that wouldn't exist until I flipped over the page of the calendar.

And then without warning, my father took over the runs.

He had been an admirer of the Doukhobors when they first bought the jam factory. They were clean, industrious, and their jam was delicious.

That was before the war. Suddenly he was saying what others in town said. They were different. They stuck together. They were allowed to buy a jam factory from an Englishman and run it as their own. They didn't have to enlist.

It didn't matter that a couple of their boys had left the fold and enlisted, too. Most of them hadn't. John hadn't, and that was all my father could see.

The cherries were in blossom again when I heard that John had married a Russian girl.

All winter I had written letters to him that had gone unanswered. He'd had as much reading and writing as was needed to work on the communal land or in the jam factory, and I thought perhaps that was the problem, that he couldn't read the letters I sent, care-of the factory. I made them simpler each time, hoping one would eventually prompt a reply. I thought of saddling up old Ruby and heading to town along the wagon road, or finding my way across the arm of the lake and hopping the train into town. But why go to that effort if he hadn't? I would wait him out. So I was ashamed when I heard of his marriage, and then glad to read in the papers that the Doukhobors had sold the jam factory to build a new one over in Brilliant. We'd ship the fruit by train, now. I told myself I might never have to see him again.

But I did. Even now I could see them as clearly as I had that day, it must have been the following year, from a doorway on Baker Street, red-striped awning shielding me from the sun, and them: John and his wife, a white-haired infant in her arms already. She wore a tightly-knotted kerchief and long skirts that swept the ground, like a woman from another century. And it struck me then that while other Douk-hobor boys had broken with tradition and married girls from town, *angliki* like me, he had not, had never intended to, it seemed. Maybe I had known that all along. He had been allowed to drift from the fold for a summer, and then was lured back in with a bride.

When my three brothers returned from the war they assumed the rest of the fruit business. It happened gradually. One crisp day I looked up to see that cutting the grass, picking the last of the fruit, and finally pruning the trees had all been done without me. Well fine. I had been absorbed in my own plans to teach even before my father's comment about finding a way to feed myself. I had decided that I would encourage learning and reading and the broadening of horizons, and embrace the very thing John's people had rejected. There would be satisfaction in that.

I didn't last a year.

I rolled out of bed and poked about the cupboards for food. I must be hungry to be thinking of home. I found the paper bag from Park-er's and rummaged through it for the ingredients to pan fry bread. I couldn't find any large bowls in the cupboard for mixing, just a plate. A cup of flour, dash of salt, a few spoonfuls of lard. Knead well onto the plate. I fired up the pot-bellied stove from the bucket of coal beside it, rubbed a bit of lard into a skillet and set it on top. I dropped a big dollop of batter into the pan and it sizzled nicely, though when I flipped it over I found I'd scorched it. Less time on the other side, then. I had enough for two more dollops, setting each onto the plate when it was done.

I could poach a pear, put up preserves, boil up jars of jam. When you're raised on an orchard you can't help but learn to cook with fruit. I could also bake a fish or roast a leg of lamb. Those uncomplicated dishes simply required you to pull them out of the oven when they looked done, shove them back in if it turns out they weren't. But baking required a precision that escaped me, things full of air that wouldn't rise if you slammed the door too hard, crusts that fell apart with too little handling, or turned to shoe leather with too much. I bit into the first piece of fry bread. It tasted of cinders. The second had the consistency of glue in the middle, the last one, cement.

I should have added water, or milk. I would have to try again some other time.

I emptied the rest of the bag and settled on the corned beef. With my back against the wall I ate it cold from the tin, shovelled it really, great spoonfuls of it, my thoughts racing. I had to get things ready. I had to get me ready.

I dropped the empty tin and squatted beside the tub to drink water from the tap.

Running a bare arm over my mouth I moved to my heavy bags, at last unpacking. The bottle of whisky had already found its way out. Now came the clothing, family photographs, a bedspread of red patchwork and sheets I could have used last night, as well as a cranberry glass vase, cracked, most likely after the bags had been tossed from the ship onto the cargo pile. I turned it around and around, told myself it didn't matter, not when, until now, I hadn't even remembered packing it. But the crack in the glass wounded me, somehow, and I had to force myself to put the vase down. I hung my mother's beaded evening bag over my arm and reached for my greatest indulgence, filling the bottom of the larger of the leather bags, a table globe of the world, with my nightgowns and stockings stuffed around it.

It was only by studying this globe that I realized, with a flip of the stomach, that the place I would be moving to, and have now arrived at, was perched on the very edge of a continent washed by a body of water twice as wide, to my naked eye, as the mighty Atlantic. I gave the globe a spin and marvelled once more at the vast Pacific. I had come to the end of the world.

With the exception of the coveralls downstairs, I bundled up Uncle's things to send back home, and filled the shelves and hangers with my own. I flipped open Will's old watch, then clicked it shut.

Not even six o'clock in the morning.

All right, then. Get washed. Get going.

I plugged the tub, ran the taps, added a squirt of my coconut shampoo, then sat back hard on my heels. The soapy water foamed up grey as smoke. It was bad enough that I had to bathe in it. I had planned to toss in some linens, too, but this would ruin the whites, not something that normally concerned me. It was the unexpectedness of it. Under threat of tears I told myself to smarten up. What would stay white in this town, anyway? My eyes dried in an instant, seeing that Morris in his soiled white suit.

⊷⊨⊐

I found the press as I'd left it. Dusty, rusted, immobile. The wrench lay at the foot of the far wall where it had been sent flying when the bolt gave. Not far from the mirror, the clump of rag I'd used to scrub my knuckles and cheek. The pages of the instruction manual were bent open on the floor and my coveralls were puddled nearby as though I'd just stepped out of them. I grabbed them by the shoulders and gave two sharp snaps, then climbed in and buttoned them up while I walked about the shop, slid the wrench into a lower pocket, put the booklet on the shelf with a tray of metal bits on top to flatten the curling pages, and tossed the filthy rag with others I'd found in a bucket in the back of the shop. Above the sink was a stack of clean rags. I gathered several and headed back to the press where I began rubbing dust from every surface I could reach.

Up the ladder, next, swinging a leg over the machine to straddle the parts, just as Vincent Cruz had. The dust here was a greasy fuzz that mere rubbing could not remove. I tipped a tin of solvent onto a rag and soaked it, then watched my fingertips turn black as I cleaned. Again, I tried to loosen some bolts with the wrench. I felt the pull between my shoulder blades, then up my neck and into my teeth. Nothing, except that I'd managed to scrape a thick layer of sludge from the bolts and the works surrounding them. I climbed down.

The sky was lightening now. As I passed by the wall calendar I took up the pencil and stroked through Sunday, September 3.

A hammering at the door had me dropping the pencil. I stepped back to the metal mirror and called out, Just a minute! Fingers fussing to tuck strands into the knot. At least my eyes had returned to normal. I smoothed my collar and shirt front as I dashed to the door, remembering only as my palms skimmed the rough fabric that I was in my coveralls, not a dress. I wrenched the door open.

There stood a man in a vest and suit, with slicked hair and a trimmed beard. His shoulders were narrower than his chest, a shape I have always found unattractive in a man.

He gave his name but in my surprise I didn't catch it, though I know I introduced myself in return.

From San Francisco, he said, and then something about mining exploration. Only when he asked about advertising rates did I come to my senses and invite him in.

There is no paper just yet, I explained, but I can record your order.

I stood behind the counter and pulled out the ledger. A diamond ring on his baby finger, and, through the window, a man with a walrus mustache rocking on his heels and puffing pipe smoke into the fog.

As I scribbled I asked, Is he waiting for you?

My friend and business associate, he explained. Come all the way from Glasgow. Here to see about opening another vein of coal. We're looking to hire men to stake claims.

Another vein?

I stopped writing, interested in this bit of news.

He said with a wink that there could be more, many more.

Coal likes company, he explained. All ore does. Miners talk about silverleadzinc like it's one thing. And it is, to be certain, often found running in ribbons together. Coal with uranium. Copper next to cadmium. Moly in its own vein or mixed with copper and gold.

Molly?

Yes, Moly. Molybdenum, Miss Sinclair. It's like a layer cake down there. And in the streams above, pink quartz with gold nuggets clinging to it like caramel sauce on a sundae.

You mean there could be gold here?

I mean there's everything here if you dig far enough.

He leaned an elbow on the counter and studied my throat.

What a few gems wouldn't do for that neck, he said.

And dropped his eyes to my coverall-ed chest.

I let the ledger slam shut and he snatched back his baby finger.

I told him I would let him know when our first issue was on its way. I said it cheerfully. After all, his impertinence aside, here was my first advertisement, and another story idea.

The door closed and I took up a sheet of paper and wrote the letter home much as I had already composed it in my mind yesterday, leaving out all mention of Lousetown or Parker or this man just now. I don't know why. Because they might worry. Because they might comment. But as I watched his retreating back from my shop door I could see the headline: Coal likes company.

That afternoon, lavender outfit bundled under my arm, I plodded through the gloom to Parker next door. I sniffed the air for a hint of ocean but coughed on the grit kicked up by the motorcycles and their sidecars. An incessant whine. I wanted to smack them with a fly swatter.

Parker was up a ladder, stocking shelves.

Don't climb down, I called out. Just here to ask a question.

Done anyway, he said, stepping down and rolling the ladder to the corner. He rubbed his hands on his backside as he returned to the counter.

You survived your trip to Lousetown, I see.

I switched the lavender bundle from my right side to my left, wondering what he might have heard.

Yes, but all that walking took its toll on this suit. I need to take it to the laundry, if you can direct me. The post office, too.

Same place. The hotel.

They have a dining room, too, don't they? I might stop in.

They have a menu with a list of meals. Mouth-watering concoctions. Trouble is, they don't have 'em.

Then why list them?

Who'd go to a place that advertised tins of peas and ham? They might as well come here.

For the pleasure of a crowded room, perhaps.

Parker hooked his thumbs under his arms and rocked on his feet.

Nicest person there is the dark fella that runs the kitchen. The rest? Nothing but crooks, cowboys and idiots. There's your competition, if you can call him that. Runs *The Bugle*. Named after the Boston newspaper that fired him. Head in his plate of food, usually. Never could decide if it's food or pomade that puts his hair in stripes. Like this.

He released his thumbs from under his arms and drew a set of bars across his head.

There's another newspaper? I asked.

I didn't like that. I didn't like it that *Bugle* was so close in lettering to *Bullet*, either.

Not much of a newspaper, he said. A sheet of mining figures and facts.

That was a relief, and I said so.

Silver Evans, he continued. What passes for a lawman in this town, hired out of New York City by the largest of the mining interests, The Black Mountain Coal Company. People call him the sheriff and he has taken to the title. Wears a uniform of his own making, postman's trousers and his father's jacket with badges from a bygone war.

Parker held up his thumbs and rubbed them against his fingertips.

Wears his moustaches twirled to points, he said.

His descriptions made me laugh, but Parker remained straight-faced.

One more thing, I asked, do you sell notebooks? This one's filling up.

I held it aloft, the pages between the two covers swollen with scribbling and folded corners.

He smacked one down on the counter.

You find yourself a printer?
I might have, I said. I'll let you know.

⊷▥◑

The fronds of the potted plant were not enough to hide me, but there was only one customer and his face was buried in the crook of his arm, an empty glass by his ear. Good. I had inadvertently entered by way of the bar, instead of via the dining room. Not my fault, when the sign in the window said simply *The Bombay Room*, which could be the name of a café. A happy mistake, though. I could use a drink.

I had never been in a drinking establishment before. Drank behind the barn with my brothers, yes. Still, it was easy to see that the polished, wood counter running the full length of the room was a bar, with a row of bar stools that looked suspiciously like motorcycle seats. I sat on one and was reminded of a saddle. A tiger skin was tacked to the rippled tin wall. A fan turned slowly, its wide blades taken from the snout of an airplane. Ebony elephants at each end of the counter. An oriental rug.

The tiger's head bared its fangs at me. The barman, black-haired, red-faced, was polishing glasses and looked up, then started.

Whisky, I said.

Women aren't allowed.

And he twisted his big head around as though he were about to be arrested over my presence.

I'm here to run the newspaper, I pressed, nodding down at my coveralls. Doesn't that make a difference?

His eyes shot over to the comatose customer, then back to me. Rules, he replied. This is *The Bombay Room*. A private club. No women.

What's your name? I asked.

Ed.

Ed. Lila Sinclair. Tell me: Is that man over there an esteemed member of your *Bombay Room*?

I watched his eyes flicker to something below the counter, then to an upper side shelf with three china teacups that rested sideways in their saucers to reveal their decorated insides, all blue flowers and garden gates.

Will you have a cup of tea? he asked.

No—I began, then realized he was arching an eyebrow. Yes, I added. I meant yes.

That a letter?

I hadn't realized I was still clutching it in my hand.

Yes, it is. I came here for the post office, actually.

That's me, he said. Postmaster. I keep the mail under the bar, too.

Too—how much is the, uh, tea?

Same as two beer. And you have to sit at a table.

Add the stamp to the bill, I said, and I slid the letter onto the counter along with the coins.

I'll take your laundry, too.

My head must have snapped up with surprise. Same place, Parker had told me, but I hadn't expected someone like Ed.

This here's the laundry chute for the hotel, he said.

He slapped a dirty hand onto the boxed wooden trough that ran vertically up the wall behind the bar and was, now that I stood on my toes to see, disgorging crumpled cotton.

Lots of room still in this basket underneath. Town people add to the load and then we roll it out.

He held his grubby hands out for the lavender-grey suit.

I clutched it tighter.

You do the cleaning, too?

Nooo, he said, horrified. We send it out to Lousetown.

I let go then, and received a ticket in return.

I stepped over to a table, lifted the sides of my coveralls like they were skirts, and sat. The cup rattled loudly in its saucer as Ed lowered it beneath the bar's countertop, then carried it to my table. I lifted the chipped bowl.

It was a stingy pour. .

I sipped the raw liquor, then said I'd like to order a meal.

Sure enough, but you'll have to order in the dining room. Sorry ma'am, but that's where the kitchen is.

I stood and smoothed my coveralls. It struck me then that had I worn a dress I might have got my cup of tea a lot sooner. I finished the drink in one small swallow and, head high, swung around and then through the side doors into the dining room, slipping into the first available chair at the first available table. My ears, neck and cheeks grew hot.

They were all looking at me, their rows of eyes glistening, while the walls heaved with a constant hum of their comments and the room itself seemed to tip onto its side, trying to slide me out the doors.

Nerves. I decided right then I would order a meal to take back to the shop. I blinked to right the room.

It hadn't been decorated at all, but its bare-board floors and metal walls made me stand out all the more. A wonder of an iron stairway at the far end, though, curving up to the rooms.

Maybe it was the lack of sunlight or maybe the filth, but the diners—there was an odd colour to their skin. I would say green but maybe it was no colour, a white with no pink. Parker was of a similar hue.

I picked up the paper menu and lost myself in the descriptions. It was just as Parker had described, with all sorts of delectable items. Cornish game hen with gooseberry sauce, trout with almonds, a roast of beef and Yorkshire pudding. I don't doubt there are birds of some sort in the woods beyond the grey hills, deer as well, fish in the streams—well, make that the ocean. I'd seen what fish the stream produced. But no man seemed to have time for hunting and fishing. The only creatures that ran wild around here were the pigs. If I were to propose a viable enterprise for the town, an alternative to mining, it would be fresh game. Everyone seemed too busy with what lay below the ground to wonder what roamed above it.

The waiter swung through the double doors, smiling, a white flash of teeth in a black face. *Mademoiselle*, he said, as though I weren't dressed like a plumber. Marcel, at your service. And then he bowed.

I stared, though Parker had described him already. I was transfixed by the health of his complexion. No green.

I introduced myself, name, first, occupation, second. I won't stay, I told him. I just need a dinner to take to my room.

He gestured around him. We get *beaucoup des* gentlemen, he said, *mais les femmes, les femmes*—and then he clapped a hand over his heart in a gesture worthy of Vincent's friend Morris. So beautiful, he added.

Hardly. I swept a hand across my coveralls. Another time.

He bowed again.

What do you recommend?

Crawfish boil. Escargot, perhaps. The best of the French Quarter.

I laughed. How long have you been here? I asked.

A few weeks.

I nodded with satisfaction. Another year here and his skin would turn dull as the others from lack of light.

Anything? I asked, and held up the tired menu.

He folded his white cotton arms, planted a chin in a palm, ruefully. Tinned chicken. Or tinned sardines. Peas and custard.

From a tin as well? I sighed. Chicken, I said, and then in my best French accent, *merci*, Marcel.

Alone now, I studied the hollow room. High up, the most unusual chandelier, the only adornment in the room. I tilted my head. Made of glass like radio tubes, like upside down canning jars. There was so much to note here, almost nothing that wasn't news to me. But to the town? Maybe not.

A man at a side table caught my eye. San Francisco, again. I nodded and he nodded back. To avoid more eye contact and the possibility, though unlikely, now, of him asking to join me, I fished a notebook from my pocket and busied myself writing my observations.

A tweed suit moved toward San Francisco's table, the dour Scotsman, his walrus mustache pulling his mouth into a frown.

Frisco had the ideas but it would be the Scot who'd finance them. That could be a story, and when it was I'd get their real names. They must be in the ledger.

The bar patron had either roused himself, or Ed had kicked him out after I left. He shuffled into the room and stood reeling by the window. With his head held up, now, I could see the features that Parker had described: greasy bars of hair that had been plastered over his bald head had sprung loose and now dangled over his nose. I wasn't surprised he'd been fired, given what I'd seen of the man. Drunk, on both occasions. It was clear to me now that he was the same man who had sprayed into the street.

Morris strolled into the dining room, bright in his white suit that appeared to have been cleaned already, his gruff voice shouting greetings. I sat up, smiled and waved. He waved back, could see plain enough that I was sitting alone, yet he took his time to join me.

Have you another engagement?

Not at all, just taking in the sights. May I, Miss Sullivan? and at last he pulled out a chair, and sat.

Sinclair, I corrected. Lila.

And I leaned forward, impatient. Tell me, I said, what do you know about this Vincent Cruz?

As soon as I spoke, I realized I had asked much the same of the printer about Morris.

A good printer and a good cook. Learned his way around a kitchen from his father.

I mean the man, himself. Is he dangerous?

Vincent?

I saw him carrying something. Like a rifle. I'm not sure. It was wrapped up in a parcel.

Morris leaned back in his chair, studying me. He doesn't suffer fools gladly, he said.

And this leader, Sun. When do you plan to meet him?

Meet?

He shot forward in his chair.

Oh, yes. As I said, he is one of the reasons I'm here.

Tell me, I said again, is there any way you could arrange, that is to say, see to it, somehow, that I could meet him as well?

My lovely, he said. You'd have to make it worth my while.

I sat back as though he'd slapped me.

My dear, he said. I hope you don't think there was anything untoward in my statement.

Well, I said, I have nothing to give you to make it worth your while, whatever you meant by it.

He spread his fingers into a fan on the table and leaned on them. His blackened eyes had faded to a light green-brown bruising, as though he hadn't had any sleep. I could see, now, that his nose was large of its own accord.

What about your paper? he asked.

My paper?

I don't mean all of it, just a percentage.

How do you mean?

I mean I could invest in it. You get the money and the introduction, and I get partial interest. Trust me, I know finances. I used to work in real estate.

How much money are we talking about and what percentage, exactly?

I knew that by even asking I was letting him know I needed money. I didn't like being in that position but it couldn't be helped. How was I supposed to pay for a printer when there was no paper yet to earn the money to cover his wages? The bank money was intended for the cost of supplies to help produce the paper, but the loan had not factored in the added expense of an employee and machine repairs.

Fifty-fifty, he replied.

·No.

Ah, I should have known you'd have a business head. Sixty-forty, then.

Seventy-thirty. The seventy being my share.

Dear girl. That gives me less than a third while you would have the clear majority. And on top of that you get to meet our leader.

Precisely. It's my paper.

Neither of us had yet said how much. I didn't recall the bank or the lawyer mentioning what the business itself was worth, just what the operating costs were. I didn't want to open my mouth and quote a ridiculous sum. But I didn't want him naming the sum, either.

My aunt sold her house on one acre for eighteen hundred dollars, I said. A business would be twice that.

Thirty-six hundred, he said, with such delight I knew I had hit too low.

But there's the press, I added, which is an expensive piece of equipment. Four thousand, two hundred.

Why don't we say current value four thousand as it is not yet producing a newspaper?

He had me there.

We can renegotiate, he said, once you're up and running. Partner, he added.

All right, thirty percent of four thousand is—wait a minute.

I scribbled in my notebook, crossing out numbers. I have never been good at percentages. I had to go at it in a roundabout way. Ten per cent was 400. Times three.

One thousand, two hundred dollars, I said.

I don't have that sum on me at the moment. But as a show of good faith why don't I give you—he dug into his jacket pocket, then through his billfold, and produced a couple of wrinkled bills. Shall we shake on it? he asked. We can have the papers drawn up later.

We can, I began, when the rest of the money is delivered.

We shook hands.

As long as it's understood, I added, that I get an introduction to the leader. Good. For now, I said, I'll give you a receipt.

I tore a page from my notebook and scribbled:

> *I hereby accept twenty dollars as a down payment from*
> *Mr. Morris Cohen toward a thirty percent interest*
> *totalling one thousand, two hundred dollars in*
> *The Black Mountain Bullet.*

I signed it, dated it and handed it to him. I held my breath as I did so, and hoped that would stop my hand from shaking. It was a bold thing to do, and I was both excited and nervous.

Then he pushed his chair back, stood, tipped his hat, again, and shambled over to greet my reeling competition from *The Bugle*. I watched as Morris leaned his back against the wooden rail that ran the length of the wall, foot perched on the brass bar below, and began chatting with the man. I felt a flame of anger lighting up my face. The competition. And moments after discussing investing in my paper. Unless Morris was there to elicit information. I wouldn't mind that. I could hear his hoarse voice, but not what he said. I'd like to know about his financial situation, and what sort of machine he used.

Bugle Boy raised a hand as Silver Evans stepped into the room. I knew that's who it was by his moustache with the pointed tips. He dressed just as Parker had said he would, with the addition of a helmet that was ant-shaped, bullet smooth, as though he were ready to be loaded into a cannon.

Laughter was teasing my pipes and I had to choke it back when he passed. I assumed he was heading over to join Bugle Boy, but no, he took my head-snap for a nod, an invitation to sit.

Sheriff Silver Evans, he said, and shook my hand. Are you crying? he asked.

I waved my hand sharply to shoo away the suggestion of tears. He put his shiny ant head onto the table and sat in the chair Morris had just left. It was all I could do to control myself.

I glanced over at Morris for the distraction and got more than I counted on. Was I seeing correctly? The Scot had joined him, and Bugle Boy turned his back to say something to the Scot, at which point Morris leaned forward, hand reaching toward the man's jacket.

I sat up as high as I could, eyes bulging. It was a look that said, Are you doing what I think you're doing? Don't you dare. My movement snagged his attention. His expression said, Not what it seems.

What else could it seem—unless he was trying to pluck information from our competitor's pocket? A terrible thing to do, the man had no scruples. Still my spine stiffened with excitement. I wanted to see what was in that pocket, too.

Morris' eyes widened then, seeing who was sitting beside me. His hand dropped, empty. A grateful grin, as though I had been warning him in order to prevent his arrest. The shit. I was doing no such thing. But good, good, so his hand should be empty. He could jeopardize our business arrangement with his antics. He was the friend of the Chinese, too, which meant friend of that contrary printer. I wouldn't want to get on his bad side. No theft was worth risking my business, either, no matter how newsworthy the stolen item might be.

The Scot returned to his table. Bugle Boy sat again, pockets intact, but I kept glaring at Morris until he fluttered his fingertips as though he was about to play the piano, tipped his hat at me again, and left.

It was only then that I noticed the faces around me were turning one by one, aghast, toward the other end of the room, so I turned, too.

An old gentleman was descending the curved staircase into the dining room, elegant cane tapping the iron steps. Except for a bowler hat fitted with a headlamp, and boots, he was as naked as a Freedomite.

The Scot leapt to his feet. Jesus Christ, man!

For a moment I stopped breathing for fear that drawing in air would somehow draw him closer, sack of skin and heft of gristle, like the neck of a turtle, dangling. All of it darker than the rest of him.

I glanced quickly at Evans, who was slowly rising to his feet.

Any respectable woman would have screamed and turned her head. But I breathed at last, free now to laugh loud and long, as the Scotsman turned to the rest of the guffawing men, seeking assistance.

In front of a woman! Have ye no decency?

But the naked man rolled his watery eyes about and in a thin, nasal voice said, Not six o'clock, yet? and slowly climbed back up the steps, each lift of leg revealing a distended rectum like a withered phallus. A two-necked monster.

I was snorting with laughter, now, tears coursing, and I mopped at my eyes with my sleeves.

I heard the shot before I saw that Silver Evans had pulled out a gun. My laughter was sucked back into my lungs. I wanted to puke. My ears rang from the blast.

Marcel stood in the kitchen doorway, stunned, my dinner in a paper bag in his hands.

Silence roared about the room until my voice eventually emerged, stripped of sex, deep, and ragged, What's the matter with you? You're supposed to be the law.

Silver's face was twisted, confused.

Indecent, he said. You heard the man. And he waved his pistol at the Scot. It's my job to defend the town, on moral grounds.

I was on my feet, don't know when I stood. But the old man had slid backwards all the way down the flight of stairs, coming to rest with an iron step wedged into the small of his back, thrusting his pelvis forward, his sex a rumpled starfish, wine-stained against a pink thigh, more vivid now than when he was alive.

How do I put that in a newspaper?

II—THE BULLET

Whoa!

Half the day had gone by when my printer arrived at the back door. I had assumed by now that he'd had second thoughts, and I was both relieved and disappointed. After all, who else could I go to? I kept my back to the wall as I invited him in and showed him around.

He wore the same ink-stained smock, this time bound at the waist with a tool belt. On his head, a painter's cap, his shaved scalp hidden, his queue hanging down the back.

When he saw the machine he let out a long, low whistle.

I told him about the shooting as he strolled around the press, but the machine had his full attention. He ran his hands over the curves, the wheels, the handles of the rollers and said, No easy fix for this one.

He pulled a rag from his pocket and rubbed at the brass plate, then stepped back to admire what the rubbing had revealed, a single, ornate letter engraved on the metal eye.

B for *Bulletin—Bullet*, he added.

I inclined my head to acknowledge his correction. *B* for *Beast* was what I had been thinking.

He took hold of a large wheel, tugged it, and told me that the press ran on steam from a coal-fed boiler in the basement. I hadn't realized that keeping coal dust out of the ink tray and the joints would be our first concern.

The second, he said, just as I thought.

I leaped inside my skin when he turned and levelled his eyes at me. I haven't worked on a machine quite like this before, he said.

Oh, I said. Antiquated. Yes.

But he smiled at that. You got a manual? he asked.

I snatched it from the shelf where the tray of metal bits had been flattening it. Maybe he could make more sense of it than I could.

He flipped through the pages, then looked around the room.

This covers just part. Your uncle must have built it himself. Smart man.

I wouldn't be surprised, I said. He loved this shop, the newspaper. It's all he talked about.

Vincent handed the manual back to me. You read, he said, and I'll follow.

He reversed the cap so that the brim was over the back of his neck, and he tucked the braid down the back of his smock. Then he climbed onto the machine just as he had in his own shop.

Can they spare you? I asked.

You pay twice what they do.

And he pulled two metal tools from his belt.

The ink wasn't cleaned after the last run, he said.

My uncle died unexpectedly, I shouted back, though I was still thinking: Twice!

We'll wash it down with solvent, he called out. Someone used a wrench on this.

He didn't ask who, and I didn't offer.

Read me the section on the rollers.

Page 2, I said, and began reading.

For the rest of the day we worked on the press, him asking, me reading, then both of us busy at tasks. A rag and solvent on the rubber rollers. Scraping scum and ink from the metal bits. Sanding grit. Massaging bolts with clots of grease. We shovelled coal and fired up the boiler. A click of the switch and the press shook like a locomotive.

Whoa! he cried. Back to—what was it, page 14? What does it say?

We broke early for supper, backs against the press, sitting on the floor. There were chairs around, but he sat, so I did, too, but I chose the opposite end of the press, where my eyes could slide to the side, keeping watch. Supper for me was fried bread, this batch only slightly more successful, with canned turkey. I wanted what he had, a small meat pie.

My aunt used to make those, I said. Cornish pasties.

Your uncle's wife?

Father's sister. Uncle never married.

Vincent tipped his head back to look up at the press.

I bet he was something. I got here two months ago, but we were busy on our own machine.

He was gone by then, I said. But you would've liked him. Everyone did. My mother was especially fond of him. Or so I hear. When I was quite young she drowned with a child inside her, boy, girl, they never said which, but I always imagined a sister, to make up for all the boys because I was the only girl—

I was talking out of nervousness, and without the distraction of work, the weight of such words was too much, thick and tangled with images of women and wombs, of death as well, and suffused into each of these, me. I chased a piece of turkey with my fork, and tried again.

My father was terrified that one of us would drown in the lake, too. So he insisted each of us learn to swim. From May to October we'd be down at that beach, no matter what the weather, while he stood with a whistle around his neck, blasting out commands. The twins, Pete and Pat, they hated it, but I learned to like it.

Vincent's head turned slightly toward me, his eyes flicked to the side, and then back. He dug into his pocket and said, Here. You asked about him.

He had to lean all the way over, hand outstretched, while I leaned hard from my side until my fingers closed on the book: *The Vital Problem of China* by Sun Yat-sen.

His leader.

I printed them, he said. Feel that cover. High rag content, gives it weight.

The paper was both rough and smooth under my fingertips, as though the uneven surface had been waxed.

I thanked him and slipped the slim volume into my coverall pocket where it tugged, reminding me of its presence, its significance. This was an unexpected gift. Did dangerous men give presents? I had nothing to give him in return, except for paid employment. Still, it wasn't as though this was a box of sweets tied up in a bow. I had stood in a classroom long enough to recognize a lesson in the works, and he was right. I needed to learn more about his leader and his plans if I wanted to write about him.

Vincent stood at once and so did I. He strolled past the shelves lining the wall, scanning the cases of type, the rows of jars, the stacks of paper, while I stood where I was, my back to the press. He called over his shoulder, I can't remember my mother, either.

She died?

Mmm. Bad lungs, I guess. Pop never said. But always coughing. I remember that.

And then he pointed up.

See that? It's a table-top press. I started on one of those. Your uncle probably used it for test runs, or job-printing. You saw—those small machines in our shop running off menus and business cards.

He began packing up his dinner things from the floor.

I followed, and took up my cup to finish my tea.

Back home I used to take my breaks sitting outside the printing shop, on the docks, he said. Watching the boats, thinking about seeing the world.

He counted off on his fingers, New Orleans, Montreal, Paris…

French-speaking, I offered.

French, yes. I wanted anything French. Not like here. This place is too Chinese.

Was that a wicked grin? I laughed, anyway, tea things rattling in my hands. I headed to the sink and asked, How did you end up here, instead?

My plan, he said, was to work my way across the country to Montreal.

The hair on the back of my neck bristled with the sound of his voice close behind me. Travel down by water to New Orleans, back up to Montreal to sail for Paris. I'm what they call a hobo pressman. I'm supposed to stick around as long as they need me, then move on.

He placed the tea pot next to the sink and my left elbow, leaving my skin charged from the proximity, from the need to flee.

Was, he said. The plan had changed.

I heard him climb the rungs of the press at the far end of the room, and then I turned. From this safe distance the grey light drifted in from the window, touching the gleaming metal, the printing machine a sculpture from this angle, as smooth as his silver dish.

He'd had many opportunities to shoot me or chop me up into pieces had he wanted to. If he was going to squeeze the work he did for me into his other work schedule at *The Times*, I had better make it easier for him to come and go when the time suited him.

I called out to him, saying much of this, minus the shooting and chopping, and left the spare key dangling from the switch on the press. Then I left the room before he could see my hands shaking.

That night as I was getting ready for bed I closed the upstairs door and, to secure it, shoved the chair up against the doorknob.

The next day I sat at the desk and tried to compose an introductory editorial. It took me some time to find the typewriter, indeed it took me some time to find the desk. It was jammed into a corner behind the counter, hidden beneath an assortment of file folders and sheets of paper, the legs of the desk itself composed of stacks of old newspapers. I had come downstairs with the intent of pinning up the opera poster.

I needed something to stand on and swept the debris away to discover a desk top, with an inlaid square and a large handle over the top drawer that, when pulled, opened not the drawer but lifted up the inlaid square which then folded back and revealed, rising up from within the works, the typewriter itself. It clicked neatly into place. Clearly, Uncle had not used it in some time.

After I got the poster up I climbed back down and sat in the chair. I slipped a page into the typewriter and rolled it through. No sooner had I begun typing than I changed my mind, questioned the phrasing, doubted the effect of my sincerity, and took up a pencil to strike out lines and add words as I wrote:

> It is ~~a pleasure~~ my ~~deep~~ honour and
> pleasure to ~~have arrived~~ introduce myself
> to the people of Black Mountain. When I first
> arrived September the 1st I ~~was aghast~~ knew
> right away that here was a town ~~wroth~~
> worth arriving at

Would my printer even be able to read this mess, and do whatever it was he did to put these words into the machine? I sat back in the chair, absent-mindedly tugging at the ruffled paper edges of the desk legs, working out a corner that tore free from the stack.

It appeared to be from a commentary, the scrap allowing just a glimpse of the piece: *benefits of organized labour.* The full piece could have said there were no benefits, but in order to free the entire page I'd have to lift the desk, and it was too heavy. Besides, I had heard Uncle's opinion on the subject many times to know he was arguing in favour of a union. This wouldn't have made him popular with the mine. I tried another leg, ripping out a strip of an ad for women's hats. *The Bluebell.* I was procrastinating. I rolled the chair forward, tore out my mess of an introduction and crumpled it into a ball that I tossed into the box of scrap paper. And tried again.

Twinges rippled across my navel and down. I changed position, ignoring them. Then a pain tore up and through me, bending me double. I rolled the chair backwards and tried to stand. Another wave. Still bent in half, I groped past the machine and toward the stairs. Back in school, Bess used to call these my advanced warning pains, chewing up my insides before spitting them out, and that I should be grateful. She had no such alert, and in the auditorium one day she stood to sing the anthem, head up, then down, dark curls hanging about her ears as she watched it all come pouring out, leaving murderous stains down the back of her skirt. I walked her home, a sweater tied around her waist, and her older sister told us that one day we would marry and have children and then all this cramping and blood would be worth it. Bess did exactly that, got married and had four babies in a row, whereas I had been enduring this for seventeen years to no purpose. I rummaged through my things for an old sheet and began tearing strips as we had that day at Bess's, both of us wondering how would a man feel if every month he had to come up with silly excuses for staying home. Polishing the silver. Washing his hair. I tore the last of the strips. Two days' worth, though I might not need all of the second. In that, Bess said, I was also fortunate, though not as fortunate as a man.

That evening I stood in front of the calendar and crossed through the fourth, yesterday. Labour Day. Back home there would have been union parades and picnics and protests. But I heard nothing in the streets, saw nothing. I crossed through today, the fifth, then drew a large circle around it. My printer had to work at *The Times* today, so it was just as well, though I could have managed had he shown up, made frequent excuses to dash up the staircase. A boiling kettle. A forgotten notebook.

Upstairs while I ran water in the tub, I took up the book he gave me and began to read. China should not involve itself in the war. It had no more problems with Germany than it had with England.

I flipped back to the first pages. 1917. Year of the Russian Revolution. One year remaining of the Great War. If more world leaders had felt as he did from the start there might never have been a war. More boys might be sitting down to dinner with their families, instead of having been blown to bits in France. But Sun lost the argument. China declared war later that year. I remembered because it was August, as it had been three years previously when Britain declared war. Sunny and warm, when a soldier could spend a night in a trench in some comfort, when November and freezing rain were far from anyone's thoughts.

I leaned forward, reading. Yes, how did three isles in the northwest of Europe come to control so much of the world? Ah, India, and all its riches.

It was time. I put the book down and squatted beside the tub and plunged the day's worth of cotton strips below the surface. The water bloomed brilliant between my fingers. I added soap and took up my teacher's yardstick to stir the tubful, then turned off the taps. I left it to soak. Later I'd rinse them and hang the strips over the edge of the tub to dry. I was in a hurry to get back to the book.

I dried my hands on my nightdress, and continued scanning the pages on the colonies. Australia and Canada would be useless to Britain without the wealth of India. Africa and the Mayan Peninsula, less important.

A few pages on, several remarkable lines likening Britain's treatment of other nations to the farmer rearing silkworms. When he's done with them, they are destroyed by fire or thrown to the fish.

Set on fire. I sat back, the words sparking the smoke of a memory and forcing me to sit forward again to push it away. I continued reading, more determined than ever to interview Sun. Eventually, hunger beckoned and I closed the book. It would be easy enough to buy a week's worth of food at Parker's. After all, tinned goods were long-lasting. But these trips were an excuse to have company, a conversation. And after a day of confinement, I needed them as much as food.

Night had fallen, that blackest of black hours here.

Parker stood by his door, arms folded, expectant.

About to lock up, he said. Haven't seen you all day.

I was washing my hair.

Thought I might see you 'cause you weren't in on Sunday, either, or yesterday.

He turned and headed inside.

I followed him to the counter and said, I went to the restaurant on Sunday.

I heard there was a commotion.

There was. And just an old man—

Mr. George, he said. First name Leonard.

I knew his name already, from Silver, but right now my throat swelled so that I couldn't speak. Him crumpled on the stairs, pink as a baby bird. A dark stream flowing from under his shoulder blades.

Parker nodded toward the door. You'll have noticed how crooked the road is in spots.

The shift in subject pulled me from my thoughts. I'd like to believe he was being considerate, but Parker's line of thinking had leapt crazily from the first time we met.

I still couldn't trust my voice and so I dipped my head to indicate he should continue.

The holes, he said. They're going to fill them in and straighten the road at some point. The authorities might give us streetlamps, then.

He was referring to our very first conversation. I felt I could trust my voice, now, and I asked him, Why is it called *Zero* Avenue?

He shook his head as though I were a sorry creature to ask such a question. The holes, he said. They look like zeroes.

It was true. They did.

I wonder, I said, returning to the subject of Mr. George, what the authorities will say was the cause of death.

Whatever they say, he said, they'll take their time about it. Ever know any kind of government, civic or otherwise, to be expedient?

You know, I said, I haven't seen a graveyard.

Isn't one. Not anymore. Used to be right where the pithead sits. They were digging six feet down when this one time they struck coal. That was the end of the graveyard.

They left the coffins there?

Oh, no. Shipped 'em all out. Some to Vancouver, Seattle. Some back to the old country. That's where old Mr. George'll go.

Tension migrated up my spine to my head, and I rubbed it. Uncle had been sent home to us, not at our request, after all, but as a result of their requirement.

I see you've hired your printer, Parker added.

Another shift in subject.

I think so, I replied. Vincent Cruz. You know him?

He Chinese?

I nodded.

Doesn't sound Chinese.

I nodded again.

Nope, he replied, don't know him.

He says it will be some time before we get the press running.

That'll cost you.

He seems perfectly decent—well, I'm probably paying him more than he gets in Lousetown.

I smiled weakly. Probably? I knew I was.

Parker studied me with those pale blue eyes, stained swampish by the visor.

Your uncle struggled to keep himself in ink and paper, he said. He'd shut the business down now and then to save on costs. When things were slow.

In summer, I said. He used to come out to visit us, then. But I can't very well do that. I just got here.

He was a frugal man, that's how he did it.

I gave Parker my list, and waited for him to continue.

As he pulled items from the shelves, he said, Your uncle used a bicycle to get around. No motorcycle for him.

No?

Said they looked evil, had the evil eye.

I thought Parker was Cyclops himself with that one big green shade in the middle of his forehead. But I asked, Doesn't anyone here drive cars?

The holes! he snapped.

I nodded quickly. Of course.

Only motorcycles and bicycles can maneuver around them. In your back shed somewhere, if you know how to ride one.

He opened a bag and began filling it.

I spent my childhood on a bicycle, I told him.

Anything else? He held out the bag, stuffed with a small packet of tea, another of flour, a pound of lard.

Sockeye, I said. Two tins.

I left his shop and crossed the blackened grass to the back shed. My fingers groped the edge of the doorjamb for the switch, and a light bulb dangling by a cord crackled to life. There it was, hanging from the wall. I could use a bicycle to get around, to find more news.

I dropped my bag of goods and lifted it down, rolled it back and forth on the shed floor to test it. My brothers and I had stripped down many a bicycle, cleaned fenders and restrung chains, pumped air into flattened tires. These tires were fine but the chain needed tightening.

I left the bag where it landed, and searched the shed for tools.

A SALOON, A WOMAN
AND AN OUTLAW

This morning I heard my printer's voice downstairs, calling out, Hello!

By the time I had unjammed the doorknob and hammered down the stairs, pausing only long enough to score through September 6 on the calendar, he was in his smock and rolling the sleeves.

I rolled up my sleeves as well and then pinned back my hair. I followed him to the stacks of shelves at the side of the pressroom.

I've been reading your book, I said. He made a good case for staying out of the war.

Vincent kicked open a stepladder and turned his cap backwards before answering.

They didn't listen.

I know.

I hesitated for a moment and then added, I lost a brother in that war. He died fighting for someone else's country. I've never even been there. Neither had he, not since he was an infant.

And yet he joined up, he said.

He shouldn't have. None of them should have. But I was just a girl to them and they ignored me.

Vincent launched himself up the rungs of the ladder, and I called up after him, I liked the part about the silkworms.

His back was still turned to me, but I heard him say, Me, too.

I took a long step forward to see what he was doing up there.

I'll be right back, I said. I've left the kettle boiling.

And I raced up the stairs.

When I came back, he had lowered a small machine onto the top of the ladder. It was the same one he had told me about the other day.

You want to print menus?

He grinned.

Be a while before we get the big press going. We could do newssheets for now.

Newssheets. At once I saw them shooting out one after the other from the press, emblazoned with *The Black Mountain Bullet*. While a newssheet wouldn't be the same as a newspaper of several pages, I was itching to print the stories I encountered every day, anxious to convince the bank that I could do the job, the newssheets first and a newspaper to follow.

Grab that end, he said. We can set it up on the table.

We lifted it down. The machine lay under a thick layer of dust, a flat-bed press about the size of two pillowcases laid end to end, with a wooden handle connected to a large wheel. Vincent said it was a basic, hand-cranked machine that would run with some cleaning.

I set to work, oiling and scraping, pulling hard on the wheel until at last I got the roller gliding back and forth.

He tore a narrow strip of paper, dragged out what looked like a large metal ruler from an upper shelf, and pulled open a wooden drawer of slots, each full of lead bits.

It's type, he told me. See?

I was at his elbow, watching his hands. He dropped the lead pieces into what he called a composing stick, part of it shaped like a ruler, pushing them into place. These lines of type would be fitted into a frame he called a chase, and when it was filled, I'd have enough for one page and that page would be my first newssheet.

The newspaper itself won't be much larger, anyway, he said. Maybe four of these pages, a sheet of two pages double-sided and folded in half.

Four? I had pictured several more.

Vincent swivelled and scanned the room. I don't see a linotype machine, he said.

I asked what that was and he said it was a machine that sets the type automatically. The operator punches the keys much as you might on a typewriter, and the lead pieces fall into place.

It's a big piece of equipment, the size of some presses. No one running a newspaper larger than eight pages would do it without a linotype.

Then we'll do seven.

He pulled off his cap and looked up at the ceiling as he scratched his head with the brim, then tugged it back on.

Six, or eight, he said. Even numbers, only. You'll see. Right now, just a line to show you how it works.

What does it say? I leaned in close.

The line was full of backwards letters, the sentence itself, he explained, running back to front.

He took a bit of ink onto his thumb, ran it over the line, then took my slip of paper and dropped it over the line.

Rub your hand against it, he said. Press hard.

I did as he instructed. Then he peeled the strip from the line of type:

The Bullet's New Publisher Is Lila Sinclair

Every printer must do as he had just done, finger each piece of type for font and placement, mouthing the letters and words for correct order. But this was my name he had thumbed into place, my new occupation he had composed and assembled. I couldn't think straight, and continued to stare at the slip of paper, while he, as though nothing of any significance had just occurred, returned to the press, whistling, *How 'Ya Gonna Keep 'Em Down on the Farm*—

The next morning I made tea while I scrawled onto a card:

September 7ʰ
Dearest Robbie,
I have not heard from you in some time and hope
that you are well in Australia. I miss our fights with
Father! (Not really, but I do miss you.) I have let the boys
know that I am settling in at Uncle's, at last. This
is not the prettiest place but it is full of news. I can
send you a copy of the first newssheet we produce.
We plan to practice on one-sided sheets in
preparation of the first full edition of the newspaper …

I scanned the lines as I stood. As much as I tried not to elaborate it still might have said too much. The place isn't pretty, and I allowed myself the word *we*, twice, though Robbie, of all of them, would be sympathetic to my situation, having moved even farther away. I added a few pleasantries, and signed it.

Parker had wrapped my package of tea in an old copy of *The Bugle*. As the kettle boiled I had a look at my competition. Parker was right. It wasn't much of a newspaper. It was the size of a menu and was full of numbers, mining statistics and mineral prices. I was relieved to know my printing machine could accommodate sheets larger than this. He must use a table-top model, as I would for the smaller newssheets. Anything larger would be a waste of machinery.

Downstairs, I found another envelope on the shelf under the counter, and then, because I was there, I went through the drawers of the desk I had unearthed. Broken pencils, a dried up pot of ink, but in the second drawer a silver cigarette case and matching flask. I shook the flask, unscrewed it, tipped my head back for the one drop that was left. I could empty some of my own bottle into it, though, for carrying around. The silver case held rows of little white cigarettes, and I held them up to my nose and inhaled. I'd always wanted to perfect smoking. The only times I tried, I did nothing but choke. A couple of times behind the barn when we were drinking, and once in town with Bess, who stole her father's cigarettes and could blow smoke rings by age ten. I slid both case and flask into my pockets, addressed the envelope, then left for the post office.

Ed was leaning his elbows on the counter, looking more barman than postmaster.

No tea, I quipped, and handed him the envelope. Any mail for me?

Ed crouched, swung a box onto the counter, and rooted through it.

One was a postcard showing Baker Street back home, all brick and stone and those red-striped awnings. I flipped it over and recognized Pat's hand by the left slant of the writing:

> *We are all right. Hope you*
> *are getting on all right, too.*
> *Your ever-loving brothers.*
> *P&P*

It made me smile. Pat was never much for words.

I watched as Ed continued to sort. Behind him, on the wall, was a telephone box. Instead of another letter to the boys I could arrange a call to them, but they would have to cross two fields over to the neighbour's to take it. Besides, making a call meant answering questions more easily avoided on paper. Such as, Are you lonely? Are you homesick? No, it would have to be a letter, a short one letting them know about the newssheets, too.

The pile of mail continued to grow beside the box until Ed scooped it up and dropped it into my arms. That's it, he said.

⟶⊨⊙

A light was burning in my shop window, so I knew my printer was there. I stepped inside and dumped the letters and packages onto the counter noisily, calling out to him.

At last he came out from the pressroom, wiping his hands on a rag, and joined me at the counter.

I handed him one of the packages, a small but heavy square. Machine parts, I was guessing.

He tore it open. Opera, he said, and spun the package around for me to see.

I leaned over. In the wrappings was a lead plate with strange lettering. I must have been wrinkling up my nose because he reminded me, It's backwards.

From the poster above I got my bearings: the large bold wording, announcing *La Fanciulla del West,* along with a series of names below it, the characters, the actors who played the characters, and Puccini himself, while in the centre the type was broken up with a small picture painted in rich golds, greens and reds. A saloon, a woman and an outlaw. There were no dates on the poster, just the words "Coming Soon."

Inside the package with the lead plate was a letter providing the dates and times. It faced me and was upside down to Vincent, but he read it aloud easily, explaining that since the dates and times changed with each new location, we had to set the type for that part of the ad.

Vincent reversed his cap, then folded his arms.

Not my favourite, this one. A western. Maybe the opera company figures it's enough of a draw for a place like this. Nobody here would know good opera from bad.

He had just described me, and I felt my ears redden. My father listened to opera recordings on the gramophone. I liked the sound of some, but not enough to ask what was playing. I was better with words than music.

I've finished your book. Are there others?

Vincent tucked the plate and letter under his arm while I put the rest of the mail in the top desk drawer and the paper scraps into the box.

Yeah, he's written lots of articles and lectures on the modernization of China. His *Three Principles.* I don't have any copies of those.

Three? What are they? Sorry, behind you. Just pinning this up.

I pushed a thumbtack into a red-striped awning.

Nationalism, democracy and livelihood.

He turned and added, Pretty place. Your hometown? Quite the opposite of here.

For a moment I lost my focus as I considered that.

Nationalism, I said. How is that something to strive for when it exists already?

His eyebrows shot up and he looked truly delighted.

Because it doesn't, not yet. You know, no national spirit, just all these people looking out for clans and families. It's the most important of the three. Everyone in China has to see themselves as part of China, or how can we work together on democracy and livelihood?

And democracy, I said, can't exist until China is free of imperialist and foreign domination.

He pointed at my forehead with the folded letter.

Now you're thinking.

The door rattled open then and Morris in his white suit blazed over the threshold.

My dear! he roared. There you are. Vincenzo, my friend, greetings to you, as well! What a surprise to find you here.

He's the *Bullet*'s printer, I said.

Welcome, then! You're my printer as well. Oh, hasn't she told you? I'm her partner.

Vincent looked directly at me, but said nothing.

Not partners, I said. We discussed a minority interest but I still haven't received the bulk of that sum—

That's why I'm here, he said, and handed me a crumpled, filthy bill. And, he added, to place a notice in our paper. Which one of you do I see about that?

The boss, Vincent said, and turned for the doorway.

The boss, said as an American would say it, short and snappy, and yet the tone of the remark was levelled at me like an accusation. I had done my homework too well not to feel slighted by the label. I had let my guard down, too. My eyes followed him as he headed for the pressroom, the plate and letter still clamped under his arm. Morris brought my attention back by shaking out a folded note and, without any prompting, began to read in that gravelly voice of his:

> *Announcing the arrival*
> *in Black Mountain*
> *of Mr. Morris Cohen*
> *of Montreal*
> *businessman, adventurer, & raconteur*
> *here to plumb the depths*
> *of these rich soils*
> *& who cordially invites*
> *interested investors*

for an evening of cigars & brandy
at The Bombay Room

What do you think? he asked. Here, he added, and he handed the note to me.

You don't say when, I pointed out.

That's to be decided. We could add a line saying notice of further details will be posted at the *Bombay*. That'll bring 'em.

I read over the note again. It was too wordy already but a large advertisement would pay more.

You are paying for this ad?

Should I? he asked. I just paid the deposit.

When you've paid in full we can discuss what privileges come with it. The name of your enterprise? I asked.

Black Diamond—no need to write that . . . well, yes, go ahead.

It's a good name. You'll attract some interest, I'm sure. San Francisco seems to think there's plenty more below, just waiting for discovery.

Who?

Oh, someone who came in to place an ad.

Just himself digging around, or others?

Others I'm sure, all with big plans. Coal likes company, as they say.

A remarkable expression.

I explained it to him, as San Francisco had explained it to me.

Morris fidgeted for a moment, rocking on his heels, jangling the coins in his pockets. I'm thinking, he said at last, of the smaller investors. The big ones have their own bigger fish to fry. Why don't we change that? Pencil?

He put his hands in his vest pockets and recited while I scribbled:

cordially invites
investors like you & me
the humble amongst us
seeking their own small share
of such riches as already found
by my fine neighbours
The Black Mountain Coal Company.

I stopped writing.

You're giving free attention to your competition, I noted.

The length of this note was also threatening to run into the two ads as well as any room I might find on the newssheet for the only news article so far, about the shooting of Mr. George. I had planned a long, splashy piece but was now cutting it before I had even begun to write it. There had been no room for even a small item about those leeches.

Morris, why not call them small investors and other interested folk? You can explain further at the function itself.

You're a treasure, he said. Erase it! Let's start again.

He promised payment in a few days.

The next mail drop included an invitation to the opera, also thick, cream-coloured, but in an envelope sealed with red wax. I picked it up in the morning and tore it open right there on the street, scanned the card from top to bottom, seizing on the most important lines:

> *La Fanciulla del West*
> *... publisher and guest*
> *dinner and dance*
> *... followed by the performance*

I slid the envelope into my pocket, and walked slowly back to the shop, my eyes on the ground and the black holes. I'd been invited as a member of the press. Others would have to buy their tickets. While they dined and danced, I would be busy observing and taking notes and writing it up for the newspaper. I stopped and pulled out the invitation again and studied the date. Friday, September 29. I had missed the significance earlier. What marvellous timing. That would be the day before our month was up and the first edition was due. There would be just enough time to include coverage of the performance. The bank would be impressed.

Even so, I felt my lungs tighten for a moment. Three weeks from now. Today was the eighth. And yet, and yet, so much accomplished already. A printer, plans for newssheets, an investor.

Publisher and guest, it said. Who should I take? Someone newsworthy.

My thoughts roamed about the hotel dining room. Not the dour Scot. Or that fool of a sergeant major. For a moment, they flashed upon that absurd, exposed, man. Mr. George.

Taxis scooted around me, a high-pitched whine that filled my ears and snapped my attention from the shooting to the dance. Such an evening would mean a *dress*, and taking one of these wasps to get there, or else risk fouling the gown walking in the black filth of the street.

A glance down showed my hem already smudged. I'd worn the lavender-grey, just in case. Of what, I wasn't sure, until now, at least.

I pivoted and changed direction, heading through the haze to a place I had planned to visit since my arrival.

⇥

Bells clinked softly when I opened the door, a sound echoed by silver bracelets on the brown wrists of the shopkeeper.

We are having a busy day, she said to me, but if you don't mind waiting a moment you are most welcome.

I was not surprised when she added, *Mademoiselle.* She had the look of Paris, a fitted navy suit with a colourful scarf at her throat, though her accent was not quite French. I studied her while she opened and closed drawers. Her dark hair had a slight wave and was bobbed below the chin. Every so often she looked up at me and smiled apologetically for being busy. She had a thin nose, large dark eyes with lids that drooped luxuriously, a plump mouth. She could be a princess from Persia, or the Punjab.

And the room. It had the same tin walls as everywhere else, but these were draped in sheer silk that barely concealed the room's industrial bones. Had she used solid fabric, a customer could step into this shop and never see the pipes and metal. But glimpsed through the gauzy layers, the rust and bolts and corrugated tin became not only softened, but pleasing because of what they were. I turned my head to take it all in. Along the counter a row of lamp stands formed a flight of bare-bosomed women in chrome. Their upraised hands held globes of light.

She gave one of the drawers a final slam and rounded the counter, smiling brightly and saying, At last. What might I help you with?

I held my arms out and asked, Can you do anything with—me? I need something for the opera dinner.

La Fanciulla del West! She clapped her hands together, bracelets ringing. I will be there, as well, she said. I think everyone in town will be.

I could hear voices behind a curtain, shrieks and coarse laughter.

The dressmaker smiled and said, Yes, everyone, no matter who. Are we not modern thinkers? Are we not *avant-garde?* So them especially. And besides, it's being held in their *Saloon.*

I didn't know who and what she meant.

The Bombay Room?

We have two drinking establishments, Miss. *The Bombay* is part of the hotel. *The Saloon* has rooms upstairs, but they are rented on an hourly basis. Sometimes, less.

She smiled with her eyes until I got her meaning. Of course, I had seen my drunken competition outside the saloon that day, spraying into the street. I just hadn't realized what else went on in there.

There was an attempt to rename it *The Salon*, but no one uses it. My name is Meena, she added.

She grasped my hand when I told her my name. The newspaper publisher, she said.

At that remark the curtain whipped back to more shrieks and I saw bare arms and high-heeled shoes, garters that flashed like fishing lures caught up in fishnet, iridescent corsets edged in black lace, glossy feathers in black and dark green, glittering strings of beads.

They spilled out from the dressing room, one after the other, a crude line of chorus girls pulling at their garters and lace and smoothing their robes in honour of my presence, gathering around me as though I were a news baroness, admiring my hair and congratulating me on my newspaper, even though it didn't exist, yet.

Even without Meena's advanced warning I would have seen who they were at once. Their manner as well as dress gave them away as whores, though the word seemed too harsh for the young things. They had not been in the business long. Their attempt to look provocative fell somewhere short of alluring and closer to helpless. Lipstick that was too red and inexpertly applied. A pair of satin heels two sizes too big that flopped about the feet of one girl, as though she were playing dress-up with her mother's things. A corset yarded up hastily on another, the lace-tied centre of its pleated top ruptured by a cleavage shoved off to one side. And I reached forward, instinctively, momentarily startling the woman who began to pull back, even startling myself with my boldness.

It just needs straightening, I told her, my hands back at my sides and pointing with my chin. It's a habit. I used to do the same with my little brothers' ties.

The woman looked down, her brown hair a tumble of curls, and then up, her brown eyes large and languid.

Thank you, miss, she said, and gave a righteous tug to the other side.

Back inside! Meena called to them. We are not quite done.

They shuffled behind the curtain and Meena observed, They are my best customers. No one goes through clothing like they do.

She must be right. I had seen them through the window just a few days ago, and here they were, back, already.

Meena excused herself, disappearing momentarily behind the curtain. It opened again with a swipe of wooden rings clattering along the wooden rail.

They filed past in their velvet coats and hats, the one with the crooked corset turning a shoulder to call out, So nice to meet you, miss.

They would have stories. I filed them away in my thoughts, and waved.

In the sudden silence I could hear Meena's tiny heels clicking as she walked around me.

You are not at all what I expected, she said.

Me! I wanted to say.

You have a perfect shape and height, she decided. A slender ankle.

I made a sound and Meena pulled a measuring tape from her pocket. You don't believe that?

I told her I used to split the seams of my dresses.

Of course you did, she said. You were becoming a woman and you were wearing little girls' frocks.

I studied my shape in the three-sided looking glass. When I was a child there were no full-length glasses in our home, just tiny shaving mirrors nailed up high for our father and Will. Though I had begun to note how my little brothers' boyish bodies, just before they jumped in the water, would take on the shape of men, legs and backsides muscled up like the haunches of a horse, thin undergarments rucked up into their backsides, twin figs tucked between. Occasionally, at the pond near a twisting mountain trail, no trunks at all. A tumble of ruddy flesh that caught my breath. Nothing like my memories of Pete and Pat in the bath with me, pink darts between their legs. The twins had changed before my eyes. I couldn't pass our Italian neighbour's fig tree, its plump fruit dangling, without staring. Perhaps I had focused so much on them I neglected to observe the changes in myself.

The whole time I was brooding over this, Meena was whipping a measuring tape around my waist and then my hips, stopping to record the numbers in a slender notebook.

I was also a swimmer, I told her. I grew these shoulders. And then these.

As I looked down I was seeing that warm afternoon when I stripped and dived into the pond, swimming well beyond them, showing off. Then I rose, water streaming off me, triumphant.

Pat had pointed at me and shouted, Tits!

I had been rubbing across my itchy chest with the backs of my arms and only at his outburst saw plump nipples like ripening plums, angry red. In that instant my world changed, because I had. I was no longer invited on their hikes. Couldn't climb their trees or sleep in the tent with them. I was alone, now. A female. I hated it.

Your bosom? Meena asked. She dropped her voice, A handful each, that is exactly what a woman should have.

I slapped a palm over a breast and sighed. More than a handful.

Meena smiled with her eyes. A man's hand, is what I meant.

I showed just enough surprise that she must have guessed that no man's hand had ventured there. Another woman might have been proud of that. But not me. I flushed from my throat all the way up to my ears, the shame of it, to have been so poorly loved in my twenty-nine years.

She pulled the tape around my chest. Thirty-four, she announced. And what man will you bring to the opera?

I'm not sure. It would be have to be someone with interests in mining.

And why is that?

Why—because I've been invited as the publisher. It's business.

Business, she repeated, and shook her head.

Do you have someone? I asked.

She turned me around to measure me from nape of neck to ankle.

Yes, she said. Fifty-eight.

My side reflection showed I was only slightly taller than the delicate Meena. Not much thicker, either. I cast a sideways glance at her bosom, but her curves were ensconced in a ruffled blouse beneath the scarf.

The lavender-grey had been cleaned and pressed but was, I could see now, still ill-fitting. Meena tugged at the pleats and tisked.

I could never wear such a skirt, either, she said.

Either.

We need something modern, yes?

She continued measuring, height, hips, waist, neck to waist, and called out the numbers, sixty-six, thirty-six, twenty-three, eighteen and one-quarter. At some point during our talk a shop assistant had appeared and taken over the recording of numbers.

Mr. Bones, she said to him, What do you think of blue?

His head was bent, but I saw the flash of his glasses just then as he turned.

I hissed, Is that Doctor?

Her face went soft for a moment. Mr. Bones, she said, is not really a doctor. Are you, dearest? she called out.

I heard him chuckle. He had shuffled to a table against the wall.

Did someone tell you he was?

I thought back, and said, Morris.

He got his name setting a broken bone is all. He's been patching people up ever since.

Myself included, I said. He put a poultice on my eyes. And Morris Cohen, I called out. You put leeches on his.

Her assistant made not even a chuckle this time. Instead, he rooted amongst bolts of cloth stacked on the table.

She smiled.

He can stitch, that one. He's good with needle and thread. That blue one, Mr. Bones, she said, pointing, and he heaved the bolt onto the counter.

I was thinking navy-blue, sleeves straight, a high collar, like a suit jacket, like hers.

This was darker than navy and yet luminescent. She drew out a length and I saw that it was sheer, like the drapes over the walls.

Sleek, she said, with slits all around so you can dance. She had the pencil again and sketched in the notepad a thin city girl in a shift. She held it under my nose. Yes? And underneath it, something to pick up the colours of your hair.

She pointed to another bolt and it landed with a thump. I twisted away from the mirror to look at it. Almost a burnt orange. Not a colour I would choose. Then she draped the sheer midnight blue over it, and showed the effect of a glimpse of orange through it. I felt my chest tighten.

Some flashes of this paprika shade here and here, she said. With her pencil she indicated slits in the skirts. And here, she added, her palm against her own chest. You will turn heads. You will be most *avant-garde*. Come back here in—she rolled her eyes, counting to herself—one week for a fitting.

On the counter when I arrived home was a bundle of newspapers. Another gift of a lesson. This, it said, is how a newspaper should look. I yanked the string where I stood. Out spilled old copies of *The South China Morning Post* and *North China Daily News*, both weeks old, and I took them upstairs to devour them over dinner. The South China paper was out of Hong Kong, I discovered, and the North, Shanghai. In one was a photograph of a poor area in Shanghai and I saw a place very much as Vincent had described. It could have been taken in Lousetown, then transported across the Pacific and set down onto the page in place of a likeness of a street corner in Shanghai, they were that similar.

Inspired, I headed downstairs first thing in the morning to hammer out my first news story, the shooting of old Mr. George. I typed slowly, rubbing out errors with a round eraser I had found in another desk drawer. It had a hole in the middle, and I strung it through with cord and tied it to the edge of the typewriter for easier access. I reached for it often, smudges blooming where I pressed too hard. The third paragraph gave me trouble. It was easy to describe the shooting but difficult to describe Silver's reasoning. I struggled with the wording so many times I had to resort to striking through again, or leave holes in the page from repeated rubbing with the eraser.

> A man was shot dead
> in the Black Mountain
> Hotel dining room Sunday
> Night.
> Mr. Lloyd George, formerly
> of Wales, was seen descend-
> ing the stairs ~~naked as a~~ wearing
> ~~absolute~~ little more than hat and
> shoes when a shot rang out, leaving
> him dead.
> Sheriff Sylvester (Silver)
> Evans deemed the man's
> appearance indecent and
> his own actions appropriate.
> ~~Citing Insisting on Calling it~~
> ~~Declaring~~ Claiming moral
> defence on behalf of the town ...

In the shop the next night I thanked Vincent for the newspapers, and resolved to set a tiny amount aside from the loan to order my own copies from all over Asia, Europe, and North America, to study their methods of news coverage and headline writing.

The mechanics I had to learn from him. He had arrived unexpectedly, which was the purpose of the keys, the cap crammed into a back pocket, a smock in his hands. I excused myself to go upstairs where I'd left my coveralls. I crossed the floor toward my cupboard, my stride catching for a moment when a beam of yellow shot up the hole. Vincent must have just switched on the lights in the pressroom. I stepped into my coveralls, fastened the buttons, wondering what he was doing right then. I knelt by the hole, palms flat, face turned so that my left eye could scan the room below. All I could see was darkness. He might have switched the lights off again. And then I got the fright of my life when the darkness tipped back and his face looked up, directly at me. I scooted backwards to get clear of the hole, and crawled to the tub where I sat up, knees under chin, eyes closed, blood pounding. What if he saw me? I stood, composed myself, and headed downstairs.

We worked side by side, heads bent, composing sticks in our left hands, thumbing ingots of lead the size of baby's toes. With our right hands we plucked type from the wooden trays, dropping them in place along the stick, left thumb pressing again.

Vincent's fingers flew as he talked, reading my copy and following each line, dropping the type back to front. I was much slower, being new to this line of work—and taking several opportunities to glance up at the hole, relieved to see nothing from any angle, but wondering if that was because there was no one up there to see.

I was given the task of the larger fonts for the headlines. Even so, I misspelled several, unskilled as I was in the art of reading in reverse.

His hand darted out over mine and tapped on the misplaced letters. He took the composing stick from me, pulled out the incorrect type.

Then he showed me how my miscalculations had created a small hole in the page below what would be the centre fold, once it was print-ed and folded.

Not a big deal, he said. Insert one of these.

Vincent had already told me that most shops had images the size of postage stamps at the ready for just such instances: a bell at Christ-mastime, a boat in summer, even a call for advertisements, or an image that represented the newspaper, such as a star or a sun. I had thought at once of a bullet.

Which would you suggest? I asked now.

Surprise me, he said, then slapped the composing stick into my palm and headed for the door and his other job in Lousetown.

I ran a finger along the stick, then my lip. Salt. His. Then I raised the stick and, with the tip of my tongue touching the metal, tasted again.

The next day my fingertips stretched across the calendar from 1 to 11. I took up the pencil and struck through the number, flexed my fingers, turned my hand to my face, next, and practised the grip required for the composing stick.

Better. Each day, better.

The key turned in the lock and I greeted my printer brightly. We set to work.

The first newssheet was ready for printing. The metal frame with rows of lead type, all different sizes, all reversed and running right to left, looked like Chinese.

He leaned over the table-top press to drop the frame in place. With fingers and thumb he squared each corner of a sheet of paper over the frame, then gave me the command, Now.

With both hands on the handle of the large wheel I applied all my weight and cranked, until the slab with plate and paper ran under the roller and then out.

Go ahead, he said.

I peeled back the page and the air left my lungs. I was almost sick with joy.

It's beautiful, I said. It's perfect.

No, he said. A couple of spots where the ink is collecting. We'll fix that.

But he was smiling broadly.

I inspected the headline of my single news article:

Man Shot Dead

Sheriff Claims

Moral Defence

I couldn't tell the whole story, old Mr. George's sex spread out like a starfish, the vulnerability of a man. That would be more truth than the town could stomach. Uncle would agree. But I admired the headline for what it implied, with words like "claims" and "defence." Those words said it all, and for now that was plenty.

The page included a piece introducing me to the community, using the very type that Vincent had assembled:

The Bullet's New Publisher Is Lila Sinclair

The announcement was just a formality, though, as everyone must have known of me by now, but it included a call for ads for upcoming issues. The opera company, hoping for a sellout performance, had already sent us that pre-formed metal plate and it, along with the added date, times and location, took up the entire bottom right corner. Immediately above it, a smaller, plain boxed ad from San Francisco, looking to hire help to stake claims. In the other bottom corner, the notice from Morris, and finally, anchoring the upper left side and down to the centre, my article on the shooting.

To fill the hole below the fold that Vincent had noted, I composed a news bulletin too small to count as an article:

Revolution
Comes to
Black Mtn

It was the first item I had done myself, from writing to setting headline and type, and although it was small with just a few words noting the expected arrival of the famous man, I waited, while Vincent made the adjustments, every part of me electric, for the moment when his attention might move from the flaws on the page to the bulletin. I had written it for him, as a thank you for the book he gave me.

Okay, he said, let's get it rolling.

We took turns cranking the wheel. In less than an hour my newssheets sat in a neat stack.

Most bindery shops use a bone for folding, he said.

He rooted in a drawer and said, Here.

It was long and ivory-coloured, polished from years of use, and looked like it had come from the leg of a deer. He folded a page in half and smacked the bone along the fold, creating a sharp crease. Then he handed it to me and pointed to the stack.

Your turn.

I knew that tomorrow we would take the page form and break up the type, returning each to its slot in the wooden drawer, just as we'd done with the many misspelled and mis-ordered headlines that had comprised my first attempts. There would be more newssheets before the large press was running and we could print the first full-sized newspaper. Keeping the boiler at full steam would be its own problem. The large press had many parts that required constant tinkering until the right tension was reached. The rollers, the ink tray, the type were the few obvious parts that I had become familiar with. The paper was fed from a roll that might break. This would mean the length of paper snapping free from the roll and wrapping around the ink rollers. A web break, Vincent called it. But the intricate inner workings were still a mystery to me. Each stop to reset type for typographical errors or reprint pages for last-minute news, or to clean out breaks or fix mechanical breakdowns, would cost us precious time. Vincent had his other job, or he might have solved all the quirks by now. In the meantime, at least the newssheets would allow me to cover the news.

I was done folding. I took up a small stack and called over my shoulder to him, I'll be right back!

I hurried outside, put the stack down and slipped a copy of our first newssheet inside that wooden frame beside the front door. A crowd began to gather as I tightened the screws on the frame. Some, given the faint rim of charcoal around the pink skin of their eyes, were either taxi drivers or miners, though none that I recognized. A couple of them had plain-dressed women on their arms, their wives. Parker as well. I thought Morris might be there, anxious to see our first product, but he wasn't. My competition was, though, reeling on the steps.

No charge, I told the clutching hands. In celebration of our first!

I saw the slats of the blind flash open, and then shut. Vincent.

I slapped the newssheets into waiting hands, studying the faces above them and delighting in their furrowed concentration. They had been a long time without real news. Some took two copies.

When all the sheets were gone I went inside and called to Vincent. But there was no answer. I found the back door ajar from his abrupt departure. He must have been in a hurry to show copies to his friends in Lousetown.

I was disappointed. I had looked forward to this moment. But I closed the door and headed back out with another bundle so that I could slip copies through mail slots at various points around town, such as the bank and Meena's, but first, the Post Office. On top of this bundle were two envelopes, each containing a single, folded newssheet, in lieu of a letter, one heading for Nelson and the other for Australia. I had no more to say than I had in the last notes, so all I had written on each was the line: Here it is! And then I signed with a flourish.

Ed was there, polishing glasses with a towel. I gave him several copies as well, but he didn't even take a look, just said he'd leave it on the lower shelf for next morning, when the bar turned back into General Delivery and he transformed into postmaster. I supposed I couldn't expect more from him. When he was done here he'd have a few hours to sleep before coming back to sort mail, including my envelopes. And then the laundry to send out. But I felt another slump of disappointment. Uncle had talked about that, the letdown when the rush to get the paper out was all over. There was nothing older than yesterday's news, he advised. Your best work will end up wrapped around a fish. Get busy on the next one. It's the only thing to do.

SHOOT THE BOTH OF THEM

News arrived unexpectedly the next day.

Vincent was already at work when I descended the steps, and had I stayed upstairs I might never have known he was there at all, would never have thought to look through the hole to see him, quietly breaking up the form and returning each piece of type to its slot in the drawer.

I strode across the room.

There you are, I said. I came straight in yesterday after handing out the newssheets, but you'd already left.

I said it quickly because I could see that something was wrong, and I'd sat up late last night puzzled that he hadn't come by.

His fingers flew, dropping pieces of lead into the appropriate slots. Had I not left him enough copies for Lousetown? Had I not thanked him enough for his help?

If it wasn't for you, I said, this newssheet wouldn't exist—

He stopped sorting to shoot me a look that was either contemptuous, or simply astounded.

I had to go warn everyone. Revolution comes to Black Mountain!

The room grew hot. I tried to stammer an explanation: I thought you'd be glad to see your leader mentioned in the *Bullet*, as any visiting dignitary would be.

My throat was swelling and tears were threatening and Jesus Christ I hated it when that happened.

His life is *in danger*, right?

He raised his blackened hands in exasperation, thumbs and fingers pinching tiny pieces of lead.

The foolishness of my actions was only beginning to dawn on me. He had asked me not to mention his sun-powered press and I had respected his wishes. Maybe he thought by that one example that I should know not to write about anything else in Lousetown. But was that fair? He had said nothing about not mentioning his leader's arrival, just that I couldn't interview him, and I would have pointed this out had he not beat me to it.

Announcing his arrival? Same as interviewing him! Either one is risky.

He continued sorting, and then he said something I wasn't expecting. Look. It's not your fault. It's mine. You couldn't have known. Like you said, if it wasn't for me—

That made me feel worse, and I apologized.

The front door burst open then to the sounds of shouted demands for my presence, but what could be more important than this?

Go, he said. It's fine.

I promised to return as soon as I could get away.

Silver Evans was at the front counter, helmet under one arm, shaking the newssheet at me with his free hand. Two of his deputies stood on either side of the open door. A third watched the street.

What do you mean I *claimed* moral defence?

That's what you said.

What did I care what Silver thought of my coverage? If I hadn't had to watch my words over his story I could have filled that hole and never have offended Vincent. I wasn't sure how true that was, but it felt good to shift the blame.

That's right, Silver replied, I said it. But I didn't *claim* it. See? There's a difference. It was moral defence, no claiming needed. The inference is all wrong. Does anyone here blame me for shooting that naked old buzzard?

He left the newssheet on the counter, his helmet a paperweight over it. He turned, arms open as he approached his deputies, as though he were asking one of them to dance instead of seeking their support.

Does any one of you think I did wrong? he asked.

One of them shambled around him and over to me, so close I could smell the wet burlap stink of dirty hair, see his bloodshot eyes.

He lowered his voice and said to me, What's this about some famous China Man coming here?

I tried to hold his stare. The man's reaction was exactly what Vincent had been worried about.

Chinese, I replied tartly. A doctor.

Doctor, he snarled. Coolie. Same fishy stink on every one of them.

I laughed rudely. The man needed to get a good whiff of himself.

He stabbed my top button with a filthy finger. I hear you hired a China Man, too. A printer. That right?

I staggered back, skin stinging where the button pinched.

It was the same sort of question Parker had asked, but with a different tone entirely.

Chinese, I repeated.

Where'd you hear about this revolution, anyway? he asked. From him?

My guts lifted and then plunged, sweat beaded my upper lip. Danger. For me, for my printer. He was right. I shouldn't have run the notice. I should have waited until after the event to write about it, instead of ringing alarm bells with it. I was trying to fill space and I was showing off, yes, showing that I knew more about what was going on than anyone else did.

My silence seemed answer enough.

Thought I smelled fish in here, he said. That's what you want?

And then he pressed himself against the counter in a lewd gesture, his tongue playing with his bottom lip.

I couldn't bear any more of the foul man and I called out to Silver, who moved back to the counter, forcing the dirty-haired deputy aside. Even as I talked to Silver I could still see the deputy, in quick glances, how he returned to stand by the door, how he continued to taunt me, opening and closing his lips like a gaping fish, moving his hands in his pockets as though he were digging for change.

Mr. Evans, I said, I reported accurately what I saw and heard. If you still think there was falseness in my words you could write a letter to the editor complaining.

I should have complained about the deputy, but that would have meant describing his gestures. He would have enjoyed that.

You would print it? Silver asked.

He looked genuinely charmed.

I would, I said.

I could say this because I knew that the minute he sat down to write out a complaint he would become ensnarled in an explanation of the subtle difference between the words *claim* and *said*. And I would most certainly publish it if he managed to finish the tangled piece.

I'll think about it, he said. I have to get the rescue drill going.

Rescue drill?

It was hard to hide the excitement in my voice.

He gave me a wounded look, then sighed. C'mon then.

He slid his helmet off the counter and jammed it onto his head.

It was a curt invitation, but I was after a story for the next issue, and I wanted them out of my shop before they discovered my printer in the next room. I had to hope that he had overheard us, and that maybe he had already left.

I took them out the front door, just in case, and made an elaborate, noisy show of locking up.

The dirty-haired deputy led the way around the building to the pit-head behind my shop, past dark figures clumped around a fire, their orange faces upraised. I fought the repeated memory of flickering flames and smoke to seize control of the moment. Silver had stopped to speak a few words to the men, leaving me alone with the deputy, his evil eyes on me. I felt like I had the printing press pounding in my chest, and pretended to study the threatening sky.

Silver returned with the group and we proceeded together. I was relieved to be in the company of so many.

On Silver's order, I climbed into a cart just inside the entrance, one that seemed to be set aside for visitors. He climbed in with me. Uglier carts filled with dark brown coal had rolled down the rails and waited on a side track to be emptied. Our cart, motored by the pumping arms of a man pushing a metal pole up and down, scooted past and clicked along the tracks, down a slope, iron wheels grinding around corners.

It was warm inside the tunnels, some of them not high enough for a man to stand up. The green-yellow light of lanterns glowed weakly against the rough walls of dirt and the dull metal of their helmets. Another cart rolled behind us, filled with several men, though the dirty deputy was not among them.

Silver said that not so long ago this tunnel was where coal was extracted. With each foot of coal removed, the production line moved another foot inward, the miners, deeper.

We're an up-to-date facility, Silver said. The Black Mountain Coal Company uses the latest equipment. No horses or mules in here. All machines. No stooping over like in the mines back in England.

I swivelled to point behind me at the low ceiling.

No one uses those old tunnels, he said. Not much, anyway.

I suppose the union makes sure of it.

This your first mine? he asked. I've been in a few and every union I seen comes to the table with two demands, work conditions and wages, and every time without fail the conditions are dropped in favour of wages. Why? Numbers. They're easier to argue about than safety. I ask you, we give the miners five cents more or five dollars more and does it make their work any easier? Any safer?

I could tell him about back home and the smelter two towns over, how people like my father had objected to work stoppages for hampering weapons production and the war effort, but how I had friends whose fathers and brothers worked in dreadful conditions there, Bess's for one, so I sided with the union. Arguments at the dinner table. Fists on the tabletop rattling the dishes long after both strike and war had ended. He was fighting for Will, of course, who never returned. When Uncle was there Father had one more against him. But to bring all that up now would take away from the news at hand.

I suppose money dulls the pain a little, I said. But there should be a union. Are you saying there isn't?

His reply was a snort. Then he added, With so many Chinese around? They lost that battle.

And then he looked at me, puzzled that I didn't know better, as he put it.

It was a brief ride, and then I was handed a mask with a corrugated rubber tube dangling like a snake from the metal mouth.

In real emergencies, he said, it'll be attached to a respirator box. These are broken sets, but serve the purpose for a rescue drill. Inside is a mouthpiece you put between your teeth, and a pincer over your nose.

Someone used this before?

Inside the mask I saw the bit like the snorkels my brothers and I wore when exploring the lake, hoping to sight fish or sunken treasure. The twins never cared whose snorkel was whose but I was revolted by the thought of the mouthpiece covered in their spit. I could imagine the taste and smell of it, and felt my gorge rise, as I felt it now.

Silver smiled at me. No doubt he enjoyed such flashes of revulsion in me, brief though they were. Encouraging proof that I was, indeed, female, even inside those bulky coveralls.

For now, he said, you can just push it aside. It's not connected, like I said.

Two of the men from the other cart joined us. Each of us had a mask. We slipped them on, straps tightened around the backs of our heads, then descended by rope and pulley on a wooden platform with metal sides that dropped us into a subterranean room.

Although the hose on my apparatus coiled about freely, unattached to any respirator, the mask itself comforted me with its ability to separate me from my surroundings.

Clustered together in the metal box, we looked like sea demons from those books of my brothers, all bulging glass eyes, with tentacles dangling from a round, metal disk like an astonished mouth. A couple of them had headlamps strapped over their foreheads, but there wasn't much room for them above the goggles. Silver carried a lantern.

He told me as much about himself as the drill, how he was both drägerman and sheriff, serving the people underground and above. His rescue crew from the cart behind us, he added, were his deputies above.

The posse, I was thinking. And among them, somewhere, the dirty deputy.

We landed on the bottom with a jerk, and stumbled out.

In all my years of living in a valley ringed by mines, I had never ventured below ground. I saw the pitheads from a distance, from the roads that led to our house on the lake surrounded by orchard trees. I could only imagine what it was like inside a mine. I had pictured a big cave, like one big room inside a rock. Not this.

Fanning out from the bottom were several narrow rooms or tunnels. I could barely see down any, the filthy fog that spilled out tossed back the beams of our lantern light. Running from one was a conveyor belt with streams of coal, rows of sharp eyes staring at me. The rattle and shriek of the belt was deafening. Silver touched my elbow, then motioned with a hand and I followed him through another narrow room, perhaps an old tunnel as it was quieter.

I would get lost without a guide. Every space diverged into more, some so cramped, we squeezed through, and I was thankful to have kept on my coveralls. Others had ceilings so high and walls so wide I wanted to hold out my arms and spin. Such relief. Had the tunnels looped back on themselves? At one point there were tracks below our feet again and we pressed to the walls as carts of black boulders rumbled past. Sometimes I saw men, half-dressed in the stifling heat, their bare chests blackened and shiny with sweat.

One dug a finger against his mouth to lift a corner of his mask, causing the hose to slither out to the side. Careful missy, he hissed.

I stumbled anyway, and wondered if the rubble at my feet had been purposely thrown there just now, the pick that swung into the air aimed not close enough to hurt me, but close enough to stir the hair on my forehead. Now I understood why they hated me. What hell this place was, and yet they were afraid of losing it, of me with my notebook and pencil doing something to cause it.

I couldn't recognize any from the group that had spat on me, not with masks hiding their faces, though any miners outside the range of our tour likely didn't wear them. This was just for show.

In another large room I tapped Silver's arm and called through my mask, What if there's an explosion? How would you get them out?

We're on the edge of the ocean, he shouted. If there's an explosion, this whole space would flood.

My spine stiffened to attention. I might be able to swim my way out of a disaster, but doubted that most of these land-bound men could do more than dog-paddle, and I said, Tell me about that.

I began scribbling but soon stopped. I was quickly filling this second notebook, and for what? His words disappointed. No one would try rescuing the miners. The drägerman's job, at least this drägerman's job, would become one of fishing out bodies.

Then why this drill?

He said, What else would you have us do?

Where is the owner, then? I'd like to talk to him.

Drummond? Not here. Seldom here. Lives down the coast. Only comes here for special occasions.

Such as a mining disaster. I slapped the pages closed and moved to the side to watch the crew and the lowering of ladders and ropes and other false shows of rescue.

I noticed movement, then, down a side room. A rat? A man, hiding? I pocketed my book and unhooked a lantern. I would investigate while Silver continued conducting his drill.

Several steps into the side room I spied a girl or woman, greasy blonde tresses below the snorkel, in a baggy dress meant for a much larger woman, the cloth coarse as burlap and stained with coal dust, bent over a bench of earth. Retching? Surely not—not in that mask. I stepped forward, all the way around the bend of the side tunnel, and saw too late the girl's bare flank and a chain that looped around her waist and between her legs, slapping rhythmically.

The girl's skirts had been hiked to her hips and a man was clamped onto the back of her, forcing the chain to the side, his trousers at his ankles. His grubby hand gripped an exposed, white breast, squeezing in time as he pumped into her. The girl made an ugly sound in her mask. I squawked into mine and yanked it off. Startled, the man pulled away from the girl, his rubber hose swinging out into the air, twin to the monstrous one below, a circus elephant's trunk, descending on command of my squawk. He bent to his ankles, exposing another hideous view, and hauled up his pants.

The girl curled her lip at me and said, What ya lookin' at? Want more?

Then she leaned back against the bench of dirt, grabbed her hem in both fists and lifted her dress to her neck.

Silver rushed up behind me, mask dangling around his neck, bawling threats that he'd shoot the both of them if he had his gun. I thought he would, too, and I wouldn't have minded so much this time. He pulled the leather belt from his own soldier's trousers and bound the wrists of the offender. The dirty deputy appeared out of the gloom to assist.

Where have you been? Silver asked him.

His reply was a grunt. Then he leered at me.

Silver led me away by the elbow.

All the way back along the tunnels I was seeing the girl's pink nipple fouled by those black fingers, the animal sounds, not a stitch under the baggy garment, as though she expected to be clamped onto like that, as though she were ready and willing. Yet the sight of her flesh when she hiked up that sack was hardly attractive or provocative. Grimed and shapeless, it had hung like a filthy slip inside that dress.

The problem with women in the mine, Silver explained.

I thought there weren't any. That they were bad luck.

We're more modern than that, he said.

I laughed a harsh, rude laugh. But he didn't seem to notice.

Every time we turn around, he said, it's the same thing. We put those chains around their middles to lower them down the narrow shafts, but even in them they find a way. Dressing in leggings makes no difference. I saw one with the flap up so she could do her business and some old bastard found his way in there, 'scuse my language.

She was attacked?

Not that one. Not this one, either.

They work so hard, I said. I'm surprised anyone has—

Time for it? he answered. There's always dodgers. Look at those two—during a safety drill! I wouldn't be surprised if money changed hands, but they'd deny it.

She's with child, I said. She looked it, anyway.

Yes. Well. You can see why.

The man stumbled past, the deputy prodding him along with a billy club. The girl shuffled a step behind him. The back of her dress was wet and smelled vile.

I had come here to tour the mine and study its operations. What I had seen just now was a dark bit of business, but how to write it up for a newspaper? It would require careful wording.

These thoughts consumed me as I returned home, crossing the black dirt between the pithead and it, climbing the two steps to my back door, and I only half-saw what looked to be another bundle of newspapers on my doormat. I bent to pick it up and smelled it and saw it at once, a fish, its snout warped, its skin blistered, draped across my door mat like a putrid offering from an alley cat. I reeled back, spun around to see who was watching. Not a soul, though the grey land curled brown about the edges under my hot glare.

That dirty goddamned deputy—who else? That's what he was doing when he disappeared from the tour. I grabbed the only thing I could find, a broken wooden broom handle that had been tossed beside the step. With it, I stabbed the fish and lifted it from my door mat, then flung it as far as I could, back toward the pithead.

BLUEBOTTLES

At the first hint of day I crept downstairs and opened the back door partway, then all the way. No fish. I squinted into the grey. Maybe the pigs had found it. I hoped my printer hadn't come by again, and seen it. At least my insistence on joining the rescue drill had taken the sheriff and deputies out of the shop. I wondered if Vincent knew I had done that for him, so that he could escape in safety. Was there any other way to compensate for my lapse in judgment? I had spent a sleepless night contemplating other apologies, a raise in his pay, a retraction in the next issue, a promise to do better next time. All insufficient.

Word was out, and the town would be watching.

The calendar over the sink taunted me as I edged past. Every other morning I had greeted the advancing dates excitedly, or nervously, but today I had to realize that I was nearing the halfway point of the month, and while I had produced a newssheet, none of it had gone as I had hoped.

I gripped the sides of the sink and bent my knees until I was squatting on my haunches, forehead pressed against the cool, stone lip, genuflecting to the awesome weight of my own misery. I was tired, just plain worn out from trying. A shipment of paper and ink was about to arrive and I had no money to pay for it. I couldn't afford to give Vincent what I already owed him in wages, let alone a raise to compensate for my blunder.

I lifted my head, staring at the number 13 and the seventeen days left in the month. I needed more money. Morris and his crumpled bills had not been much help. I needed to go to the bank to ask for more. I had not met the banker in person. The deal had been made by letter with no inkling as to the condition of the press. Any reasonable banker would understand if I put it to him the right way. I pushed myself to my feet and made my way to the stairs. I would have to leave my coveralls aside to put on a dress. I had just the wretched thing in my closet from Uncle's funeral.

Upstairs I washed, and then I stepped into its black folds. The only mirror was inside the closet door. It was three-quarter length, cutting me off from the knees down, and mottled and rusted at that. I dragged a chair over and climbed up to get a patchy view of my ankles. Just as I thought, no ankles. The thing dragged about my heels like something John's wife might wear. I needed to look modern, capable, a business-woman deserving of a loan. I got down and dug through my sewing kit for pins as well as needle and thread. I don't know what I did with the scissors. I pulled out a good length of thread and bit it off. On the chair again, balancing, I folded up the hem, pinned it in place, and basted sections around me, yarding the skirt up to my chin to do so. Later, I'd have Meena do a proper hemming. For now, I left the needle and thread where it was, woven into a thick part of the hem, for emergency repairs should the whole works come tumbling down.

As I pinned up my hair I drank my tea and practised what I would say to the bank manager: Good day, Mr. Mooney. How are you? If you would be so kind, because of unforeseen costs, unforeseen by both of us, I would like to arrange an extension of the deadline, or a further advance of funds, perhaps both. I took a large bite from a chunk of pan-fried bread, swallowed more tea, thought again, and rearranged the words.

I dragged out my bicycle from the back shed, wrenched my skirts aside and climbed onto the seat. Hot with the effort, I rode past the pigs, and entered the bank just a minute past ten o'clock, ready to state my case.

Not entirely sure this is proper, Mr. Mooney said to me.

His name must have drawn the man into this line of work, though it was pronounced moo, like the sound a cow makes. When he was a little boy the other boys must have teased him about that.

I settled into a chair across from the expanse of his polished oak desk.

Approving an extension or an increase without your father's ap-proval, he added. Hmmm.

He adjusted his glasses the whole while, smiling at me with his pointed teeth.

I bristled, reminding him that neither title nor will mentioned my father's name as part-owner or even co-signer. He was the executor of the will, the distributor of the estate, nothing more.

He likely delighted in the task, too, his chance at last to see me gone. I recalled a time not long ago when Uncle was visiting and I came into the front room. He was wearing a grey suit that matched his grey hair, a plump, pleasant man seated in a chair by the window, my father standing next to him, sharp-faced, pipe plucked from his mouth. Here she is, Father said, my unmarried daughter. I marched out and Uncle came after me, but not before I heard him say to my father, Was that necessary? And when he joined me on the veranda, the sun fading from the sky, he put an arm around me and said, It isn't easy, loving someone from another world. That took courage. Takes even more courage to say you'd rather be alone than marry someone you don't love. What a pair we are. You and your courage. Me, married to the business. I'd said, At least a business can't marry someone else. He'd laughed and put his fist to my chin and gave a light push, his way of saying I was a fighter.

The seeds of my inheritance must have been sown just then.

Now I leaned across the oak desk and, as planned, pointed out to Mooney that surely the production of newssheets was evidence that a full newspaper would soon follow.

Yes, he said, but you're spending the money on them that could have gone toward your first edition. No wonder you have run out.

The machine, I countered, and explained its neglected condition.

Perhaps I drew out the oo sound in his name for a beat or two longer than was polite. And I smiled thinly.

Eventually, he relented, and I got my funds. Why not? It meant more money for the bank. There would be no extension, though. Two more weeks, he reminded me, as if I needed reminding. Two weeks and three days, to be exact.

I slammed the bank door as I left and huffed down the steps, turned sharply toward the grey shrubs in the back where I'd stashed the bicycle. I was certain he didn't want me to succeed, wanted to stick to the impossible deadline of one month so that he could sell the paper to the first taker and still get more money out of me. I was marching in a halo, all a-glow with fury.

I should have been wearing the lavender-grey. This was the wrong sort of skirt for riding, but I hiked the hem to my knees and launched myself onto the bike, again, silently daring anyone to comment. I had a need to bolt, away from the bank, the avenue, the dark skies, the whining motorcycles, the curious people. I rode past them all.

From the corner of my eye I saw a figure dart. A flap of a long riding coat. I braked and wobbled to a stop, turned half around on the seat, the bike handles awkward in my twisted grip. No one, after all. Maybe I was seeing things, but I didn't think so. It was almost as though the figure was trying to avoid me. Morris, whose inability to come through with the funds had forced me into that unsavory trip to the bank. But no, Morris dressed in white. I swung the bike around and pedalled in the same direction the figure had moved, out of town.

Soon, the corrugated tin buildings were behind me. The outer road that would take me to the other side of the mountain rippled and curled like the ruffles on Meena's blouses. I saw no creature whatsoever, human or animal, just a brightness ahead, as though I were heading into a golden sand storm. I braked as I rounded a curve.

The sun burst like a red ball over the lip of land, flooding the path before me, the grass, the hills with molten light. A forest fire sunset. Blood-red sky shot with the streaks of charcoal. Was there news in that? I closed my eyes, felt its heat.

And then I burst into tears. Jesus.

It was just as well the figure had disappeared and I was alone. I didn't want anyone to see me like this. I wiped at my eyes with a sleeve and set the bicycle against a gnarled tree. Not a leaf on the branches, not a blade of green grass on the ground despite the benefit of sunlight. A parched flatland sprawling to the horizon, the one I had viewed from the top of Black Mountain. I groped around inside the basket until my hand closed around my silver cigarette case and then the matching flask. I pulled them out, one after the other. Then I sat on the ground, dress and all.

Lying back, smoking my cigarette, inhaling, exhaling, clouds rose to meet clouds. In no time a tickle teased my throat and I was bent double, coughing, again. I flicked the half-spent butt into the grey ground, unscrewed the flask. One sip. That helped. And another. I wiped my mouth with my tacked hem, dropped the flask and case into the basket, climbed back onto the bicycle and began pedalling in the direction of my shop.

A smell worse than fish wafted up and over the road. I couldn't place it, and pumped away from it, hurrying home, and then, intrigued, I braked slowly and swung the bike around. The wind had shifted. I stopped and let the handle bars nudge my hips while I scanned the horizon.

Right there.

A clump of something between two hills, obscured by a blot of dead trees. I righted the bike and rolled forward, small stones popping up around the tires. Up an incline and around a bend. Now it was crushed tin cans under the tires. The dump. I slowed and dropped the bike against an abandoned Dodge, perhaps as cantankerous as Will's Ford because it had been stripped of anything valuable. No wheels, no doors or engine hood, either, though what value the latter could provide eluded me.

The foul smell grew worse. With the tip of my black collar wrapped over my nose I toed at the garbage as I walked. Leavings from dinners at the hotel, piles too large to be booted out the door. Mostly tins but table scraps, too. No one was going to toss them onto a compost heap. It would be hard to grow anything with all that grey dust and grit landing on it.

There were old lamps, too, broken tables and chairs, mattresses with sprung springs and tufts of stuffing, but also furniture that must have been dropped off whole from residents in a rush to leave, now stained from sitting out in the weather, dusted grey, amongst the trash. Sofas, wing-backed chairs, china cabinets, some with a coffee table anchoring the conversation corner, a mad party set amongst the piles of moldering kitchen scraps. Photographs, too, and I found that puzzling. Even those departing in a hurry had the time and room for photographs. I crouched and clawed through them with my free hand. Family portraits, a cameo shot of a woman, the sort of likenesses you expect to see on a mantle or a dressing table, not tossed in a pile at the dump. Where were these people now? I could write a story about them for the paper. And then I dropped my collar. In one frame grinned the likeness of poor old Mr. George, only not so old here, and next to him the woman from the cameo shot, smiling as well. I didn't want to leave him in the dump. I slid the print out from the frame, slipped it into the back of my notebook.

That's when I heard a snuffling. Pigs. Not the little pink ones I've seen in town, but, as I reeled around to look, enormous black-splotched ones, red-eyed and putrid-smelling, with shreds of rotting food and paper hanging from their hairy chins and ears.

I straightened and took a step backward. Shoo, I called out.

Their mottled ears stood up. A snort or two.

Go. I slapped a hand at the air.

Mistake.

One lifted a foot, put it down again as if reconsidering, then lifted it again and stepped forward, two little trots. That was it. The others charged, snorting and barking.

I ran for my bicycle and slid on something wet, jerking myself upright to avoid falling. A leg and half-face of a pig under my feet. One of their own. An earlier meal, too, by the look of the bites. I lurched forward, feet flying under me.

In my pocket was one of my pieces of petrified pan-fried bread. I threw it behind me and it landed in a cloud of dust. The herd was momentarily distracted. But no, even the pigs wouldn't eat my bread.

I would have jumped into the Dodge except that the doors were gone. They'd get me in there.

So I grabbed the handlebars and dragged the bike onto a flat patch, tried to leap onto the seat, only the tight skirt bound my knees together. I let go of the bike, clutched the hem in both hands and pulled—pulled until I ripped it up the side seam—took the handlebars again, swung a leg over and began pedalling, the herd hot on my wheels, snorting and squealing as they slammed into each other in their rush to get at me, as though I was better than any meal they'd found in the dump today, old pig included. My thoughts raced. Flashes of their weight bearing down on me, the bristles of their snouts, their teeth, biting and tearing in a frenzy. Me, pulling free, swinging the bicycle at them, bashing their heads in with it. But then I'd lose my only means of escape.

I pumped until my thigh muscles burned. Even so, my horrific imaginings were replaced by headlines: Marauding hogs. Wild pigs. Cannibals. What a story, what a story. I pumped and pumped until I couldn't hear the pack anymore, and then I risked a look back. Gone. They'd gone back to the dump. Better pickings there than on the open road.

Before I could return my focus to the road, the front wheel caught the edge of a hole and sent me flying. I stifled a scream. Only the pigs would hear me and please oh god please let them not hear anything right now or sense my panic or smell my sweat on the wind. Mid-air, falling, I told myself, Get up as soon as you land. Get back on and keep pedalling.

But I landed tangled in the bike, the sharp edge of the fender deep in my calf. I saw the blood before I felt the pain and then I bent forward, trying to stop the blood with my hands. Jesus Goddamn Christ. They'll smell this. It pooled in my palms and leaked between my fingers.

I pulled myself up onto my knees, and the waves of pain brought waves of nausea. I crawled in my ruined funeral clothes to the basket and seized the flask. I sat and tipped the flask over the deep gash. The pain sang right into my eyeballs. But it would cleanse the wound and mask the smell of blood. Then I took a long swig for courage.

At the edge of the path, alone, I hauled up my skirts, plucked the needle from the hem, bit the thread once more, knotted it, then stabbed the sharp point into my skin and through to the other side of the gash.

Quickly. The pain was up my legs and inside me, like waves of monthly cramps. I made wordless, animal sounds. I cried so hard I couldn't see and had to wipe my eyes and nose with my sleeves, though I allowed myself these tears. I deserved these ones. Pulled the thread through again, and felt it tug all the way through my womb, then another stab, then another upward pull. Just three stitches to close the wound, but equally as many swigs on the flask to do it. At least the bleeding had slowed.

A shadow appeared then and I snatched up the flask to throw it, my best weapon.

On a dead branch above, a crow spread its wings and tilted its head at me.

I tossed the flask back into the basket, grabbed onto the tree trunk, then a low-hanging branch, and pulled myself up on one leg, the other bent, like a balancing crane's. Below in the dirt, a dark, wet patch. Already, flies had gathered, a carpet of bluebottles.

On both sides of the ripped side seam my hem was dangling. I tore a strip and bound it around my stitches, lifted my bad leg over the seat and let it dangle on the other side, throbbing, while with my good leg I pushed along the dirt, and wobbled my way home.

Behind me I heard the crow land, cawing and pecking at the flies and the soaked dirt.

I arrived at the shop, dripping blood, the wound in my leg pounding.

Vincent saw me through the side window and met me at the back door, an arm around me to help me over the sill.

I bubbled an apology into his smock about my news blunder, about why I didn't return. I hadn't seen him since the day of the rescue drill, since he'd told me what I'd done. I don't know what I expected him to say. Maybe: It's all right. You've suffered enough. He'd already said it was his fault, not mine. Having endured such pain, now, perhaps I had redeemed myself and could truly be forgiven.

But he sat me down in the chair with less tenderness than I had hoped, and flew out the door. My gaze dragged itself to the gaping door. I saw him leap onto my bicycle.

I had dozed off but awakened when I heard voices and saw, once again, Vincent on the bicycle, this time with Mr. Bones balanced on the handlebars.

Behind them, emerging one by one in the fog, the two children, who pushed themselves along on scooters made from roller skate wheels and a metal platform, salvaged grillwork, perhaps, I couldn't quite see, but the handles were scrap metal, including cogs and wheels that flashed even in the gloom. Vincent must have built them. Children liked such gadgets, brought them to school when they weren't supposed to, the regular children, that is, not the ones who were never allowed such things, the ones for whom education alone was a luxury that could be withdrawn, they were the real concerns, though it wasn't them, just the problems around them, the adults, John's people, letters to the government that found their way into the newspapers, the board of education, threatening fires and nude protests if their children were forced to go to school. Ridiculous, we all agreed.

The door burst open and Mr. Bones stood on the sill for a moment, surveying me bleeding there before him, half-conscious, delirious. Behind him was Vincent.

Not a doctor, I said, rolling my head to direct my concern to Vincent.

Mr. Bones simply made a clicking sound against his teeth. Accident-prone, he said at last. Aren't we?

They must have carried me upstairs. Whatever concoction Doctor had given me knocked me out for the rest of the day. When I awoke I ate a simple meal, then stripped off the ruined black dress, washed, pulled on a thin shift, and climbed back to bed under a single sheet.

Fall weather would be welcomed, now, but the sun had smouldered for days behind the banks of grey. Heat from it and from the boiler had built all day and night, collected upstairs and pressed down on me like a damp palm. I had the windows open, too, but I soon kicked off the sheet, bare legs and arms welcoming the air. It was still warm. Hot. My stitches burned and itched. I tossed and turned until the twisted sheet bound around me like a rope. I kicked free, first one leg, then the other, the stitched one throbbing, then arms, too, swimming for freedom as they did in the lake, only the achingly cold water had turned unbearably hot.

I grabbed my pillow and limped down the stairs to the shop where the air was cooler, and slept on the spartan boards next to the press.

Sometime later, the shop door slammed and my eyes opened.

Vincent rounded the corner, stopped abruptly, and his arm shot out, palm up.

Sorry, he said. Please, don't get up.

I gathered myself up anyway, but he backed out of the shop, hitting his elbows and knees on jutting pieces of machinery, blackening his shins in his hurry to leave, much as I had that first time in his shop.

A cool tongue of air slid over my shoulder and I tugged up the strap that had fallen.

As I limped past the metal mirror I saw a strange, young woman in a shift, an ordinary cotton garment every other morning until this one, when its thin fabric revealed shadow and shape, and, out of range of the mirror but visible all the same, everything between neck and knees, giving rise to the musk of my own thoughts as I climbed the stairs.

Did I love the Poznikoff boy? Bess asked me that once, though I'm not sure I answered. I described how he looked. He had hair like the sun, I said, on a white-hot day. Or something like that. We were interrupted. One of the babies, probably.

For the rest of the morning and then the afternoon I sat in the window, stitched leg propped up, looking down on the greyness of Black Mountain, notebook in hand but unable to focus on the notes written there, unable to focus on writing more. I was agitated by the morning's events, and my thoughts drifted back to a simpler time, one I could examine from the safety of now, as though I were finally having the talk with Bess that we never did have.

I loved having a boy to think about. There were others besides him who hadn't joined up, some too old, true, and some infirm, but some who were all right and had stayed behind to run family businesses. None of my brothers had stayed, trusting instead that father and I could manage on our own. I drove the fruit runs, and those runs took me back to the jam factory where John worked. It was as simple as that.

I loved the flash of sunlight through the trees along the wagon road and the perfumed steam rising from the kettles of boiling fruit, the colours inside the factory walls, reds, golds and purples, the feel of a blackberry on my tongue, fuzzy and dry until it burst, bittersweet. He'd popped the berry into my mouth, then grabbed me around the waist and kissed me. Who wouldn't fall in love with a moment like that, one that promised so much more?

I suppose I loved his pacifism, too, although it came from his upbringing and not from his own thinking. Politics didn't interest him. He didn't read books or newspapers. He was an infant when he arrived in this country, and yet he spoke with a Russian accent. He was hard-working, practical, would never build something for the joy of invention. And

I couldn't imagine him striking out to see the world. He wouldn't stray far from his community, not for more than a summer. I must have known that from the start. Maybe that was all I had wanted too.

My father's disapproval heightened the attraction. I can see that now. The rift between us had begun years before I met John, and now it gaped even wider. Had swimming really been the start of it?

I was inspired from an early age by famous women swimmers. They competed in races against men. One of them won a twenty-two mile race down the Danube, and tried three times to cross the English Channel, a similar distance. The west arm of Kootenay Lake was almost the same distance, but because I was still a girl, I figured I could practise first by jumping in further down the arm. Robbie was all for it, and said he could row the boat next to me. That touched me because the boys, the twins especially, didn't do much with me anymore. But this was not mere play. This was an event, a challenge, and each practice would not only strengthen me for the full length, but build public interest. He had a friend at the newspaper who could wait on the beach with a camera. I'd be famous, too.

Ever since the twins had shrieked over my bare chest, I had been swimming by myself, and in those neck-to-knee, wool-skirted costumes that were heavy as a sack of rocks when wet. For a swim of that duration I needed something with less drag. One of my brother's old striped leggings and undervest would be lighter.

Don't tell father, we agreed.

There is a wonderfully awful sensation when you submerge yourself into a lake. Weeds stroke your arms. Fish nudge at your calves, your inner thighs, and when you put your face under, the whole world turns green.

I felt fast as lightning, my arms slicing the surface. So cold, at first, but then the heat of what you are trying to do takes hold, you have energy, and just a bit of cheek as you picture yourself rising from the waters, triumphant. But as the hours slid past, you got tired. I got tired. At one point my arms felt dead.

I can't do it, I told Robbie. Water up my nose, down my throat. Coughing, choking.

He pulled me up into the boat and I sat in the bow, blanket around my shoulders, shivering, defeated. I pictured the teasing twins, my doubting neighbours and school chums, the newspaper photographer walking away, disappointed. I threw down the blanket and swung a leg over the side.

That's my girl, Robbie said, and I slipped back into the dark waters.

We brought no food. That would bring on cramps and our father had lectured long about the dangers of that.

As we neared the beach and the promenade I could see a crowd gathering. I pulled myself out of the water, rubber-limbed, forcing myself to smile in preparation of camera bulbs flashing. Then I heard them, shrieks of laughter, gasps.

My father was there, red-faced. We can see what you had for breakfast! he bellowed, and threw a blanket over me. Robert, into the truck with her right now!

There was no photographer. Father had chased him away. I felt my face crumple and mouth turn down, and wrapped the blanket tight as I ran after Robbie. This was to be my victory, and my father had ruined it.

For several days after he berated us for our lack of concern about safety, about scandalous attire, Robbie increasingly sullen in his presence, me, venomous in my defence. Robbie was right there beside me, not standing on the shore with that whistle! You try swimming in a bloody wool bathing suit with yards of skirt and see how quickly you sink! You don't care about my safety. You're just worried what others will say!

We were never the same after that. Fraternizing with a pacifist was one more way to get back at him. Women got the right to vote a year before the war ended, and my father lost no time pointing out that I got it only because my brothers had enlisted. I lost it when they returned, and wouldn't get it back for another year, until the law was changed for good. The hurt of that was relieved by the sheer joy of seeing them again, though they were not their old selves. Robbie came back empty-eyed and grieving for Will, more so than the twins, who had each other, and me, who hadn't seen what they had seen. Once more, we argued with our father. Robbie wondered aloud how our father wasn't a pacifist himself given what had happened to poor Will. And on it went. It's one more reason Robbie eventually moved to Australia, and me, here. I breathed in raggedly at the view from this window, grey upon grey. He was glad to be rid of us both, our father.

My leg still throbbed the next day, and to take pressure off it I sat behind the counter to read, my foot resting on a shelf. My call for ads had produced a swift and unexpected response from an outfit down the coast in San Francisco. I was delighted, even when I eventually realized it was addressed to Uncle, which meant the company couldn't have seen my call or my announcement that I was the new publisher. But an ad meant money. It proposed flights up the coast, with stops at various ports of call including here. The date of the inaugural flight: September 27. Incredible. Twelve days from now and two days before the opera. Again, I felt green and tense as well as excited, thinking about the end of the month. I would have no trouble finding news for our first edition. Though why the craft would stop here, I couldn't imagine, not at first.

Gradually, I saw the appeal. Even miners took holidays, and a few hours up in the air, especially away from all this grey, would draw those who sweated below ground. The flight company must have figured that larger stops along the route—Portland, Seattle, Victoria, Vancouver— would make this one worthwhile.

The letter and ad had come in a package that included plates, much as the opera company's had, this one a relief of the airship itself, a Zeppelin. In the palm of my hand it looked more like the impression of a bullet, and I was dazzled at once with the idea of a design for my own masthead one day, its snout firing us into the future.

I gathered up the package and its contents and carried it straight to the pressroom to leave for Vincent. I knew my foolish announcement was still in his thoughts. This would brighten them. He had never mentioned seeing that stinking thing on my doormat. Good. It couldn't possibly help my situation for him to know that it was a result of that story.

I had already limped to the post office and back, though I was supposed to keep my leg elevated. Now I had an appointment with Meena for my fitting. I walked quickly, excited. This ad from San Francisco meant money, yes. It also meant progress, bringing us modern transportation, sleek and silver and flying high above the filthy fog. The airship might be a common sight on the east coast and in Europe, but not here. It would ignite the imagination. And the fact that both money and progress had arrived in one bundle charged me with an energy that took the pain from my wounded leg. First the opera, now this.

Meena shrieked when she saw the stitches. It looks like a tarantula crawling up your leg!

It's all right, I told her. I just have to keep it dry.

Your beautiful dress, she said.

Until she saw the butchery, as she called it, Meena had been pinning and clucking. Your slender waist. Your strong shoulders. The material drapes beautifully from them.

I twisted around in the three-way mirror and only now saw how truly ugly it was. The back of my calf blighted not only with three stitches to seal the wound but a knot on either end.

Black? Meena cried. A pale peach is all that was needed.

It was all I had with me.

Why didn't he at least re-do the stitches?

Doctor said I did a good job.

Doctor again, is it?

It doesn't hurt anymore, I lied.

The possibility of pain didn't seem to concern her. I hadn't realized I'd been limping, but she told me she had seen there was something wrong the minute I walked through the door.

You dragged your leg behind you like a wounded soldier, she said. I thought perhaps you had pulled a muscle getting off your bicycle.

I hadn't brought the black dress. Even Meena couldn't fix it—split up one side, hem ripped right off. And I could imagine her shrieks if I had. What is that? An old rug?

I turned back to face the mirror. The gown was everything that she had described, the burnt-orange silk flashing through the slits in the deep blue.

With your limp, she said, it will flash like Morse code. S.O.S. Woman injured. The stitches will show with each step. We have to lengthen it. We have no choice. Oh, that will ruin the flow.

She shook her head. Which means, she added, we might have to widen the skirt, too.

I tried to picture the wide skirt, and saw John's wife, again. I shook my head.

Can we try something else?

She crouched to measure and then sat back. And have you an escort, yet? No? There's not much time.

She pinned and unpinned, measured and re-measured, muttering the whole time.

I have it, she said. Same blue, but we'll have to get rid of the paprika altogether. Yes, well, my dear, there's no helping that, now, is there? Taking it to mid-calf length, ghastly. Not a flash of orange but a full assault.

She re-sketched the shift and, just around the knee, her pencil flying, added a froth of material that would cascade at varying lengths about the legs.

You see? Pale, to contrast with a midnight blue sheath. That way it can be longer and wider below the knee without looking it.

White? I suggested. I want to look business-like, remember.

Too stark, she said. A blush.

I smiled but I wasn't happy. I'd gone from bold to delicate.

The bells above the door sounded, then. It was one of Meena's best customers, the one with the crooked corset.

Miss, she said.

On her arm was Morris, and his eyebrows shot up when he saw me.

Mr. Cohen—I said.

My dears, he rasped. Morning to you all, and you especially my lovely Miss Sinclair. I really must be on my way. Business, you know!

But—

I had wanted to ask about his investment, such as how soon? Bills were piling up. He was gone though, before I could get the next word out. Had he not noticed the very blight on my leg that had caused Meena to shriek? Perhaps not, or he would be concerned, if nothing else, about how my injury might affect the business.

Lila, Meena said, would you mind? Just a hem check.

I limped aside to let her customer past. She climbed on top of a stool.

Meena held a sheet up before her, and when she lowered it her customer had dropped her street skirt and was wrapped in a vivid green silk that barely covered her bottom.

I've been reading your newspaper, she told me as she balanced on her perch. Terrible, that shooting in the hotel. I heard nothing but jokes till I read your accounting.

At last a compliment, and in gratitude I shared a summary of the next issue.

I didn't know girls worked in the tunnels, she replied.

Worked! I said it with a funny laugh that caused Meena to stop pinning and her customer to look up. Both faces, expectant.

I told them they were going to be privy to things I could never print in the paper, and then I described my discovery of the girl and that man, of what appeared to be going on, at first, what was really going on, and how I wondered was there a child on the way.

The woman pushed Meena's hand away and leapt down from the stool, demanding, Is she charging for it?

It was the sort of reaction I was hoping for, only I hadn't expected her hot concern an inch from my nose. I stepped back.

It was a problem, no matter what the answer. If the girl charged, then she was taking work from these painted women. If she didn't, then she was doing for free what they charged money for. Either way, she was interfering with their business.

With a shimmy to remove the green silk, then two snaps of her garters and another shimmy to pull her street skirt back on, she was gone.

Meena sat back on her heels and looked up at me for a moment or two longer than made me comfortable. She made no comment, other than to sweep the air with a hand to indicate I should climb up on the stool. Still, there was a clear censure behind her request to have me stand immediately where that customer had stood. I did as she instructed, toes twitching from the proximity. And rightly so. After all, who was I the other morning, on the floor like that, taking longer than necessary to pull up my strap? My sheer chemise had been as vivid as any green silk.

As Meena measured and scribbled we heard the throaty rumble of a vessel, most likely a tug boat towing a coal hulk to or from the upper wharf.

At last she stood and said, Now my dear, let's see those fingers.

She lifted both of my hands.

Will the ink come out?

Most of it, I said.

Most of it—my dear, dear Lila. Gloves, long elegant ones past the elbow. That's the only solution.

Voices shouting in the street stopped her scribbling. It was a lustful sound we weren't used to hearing in this town.

Her heels clicked to the window where she cried, The opera troupe! Lila come see. They must have hired their own boat.

That was the sound we'd heard. I lurched after her, my nasty stitch work throbbing again from all that standing.

A short stretch of street was visible in the misty daylight. It had filled with a lively procession in all the colours from the poster, made more brilliant by the blue-grey backdrop of the town. There was a diva in a crimson dress with a tool belt slung bandolier-style across her juddering bosom. A man in jade green followed, pulling a cart of luggage, another in gold carrying boards across his shoulders. Then three musicians in tuxedos, gone in the knees, I noted as they passed, one pushing a red wheelbarrow filled with a case that must hold a cello, certainly a cello with its womanly curves, the other, lumpy cases in each hand that might contain a violin and a trumpet, and a third with a flute glittering from his jacket pocket and a leather box that might contain a drum or tambourine. Bringing up the rear was a man who seemed neither player nor musician, in a brown pin-striped suit and matching vest festooned with coils of rope over each shoulder and a bundle of tarps strapped to his back.

They stopped to unload before the iron skeleton and dome across the street. The diva bent forward, massive cleavage like a slice of the Fraser Canyon, to drive tent pegs into the ground with a hammer from her tool belt. The yellow and green men took the tarps from the brown man and began hoisting canvas over rope and across the top of the skeleton, erecting walls where a moment ago the gloomy view was the rambling mountainside through the iron framework.

Now, players and musicians ducked through the tent flaps, carrying their luggage and instruments inside.

What do you think, Meena asked me. Have they come from an afternoon performance somewhere down the coast? They're still in their costumes.

It is strange, I said. The show doesn't start for two weeks.

I struggled out of the pinned fabric, until Meena rescued me. I agreed to return to have my hem properly lengthened and, in my own clothes at last, limped out the door and into the street, elbowing through the gathering crowd, movement easing the swelling around my stitches.

I slowed as I passed the tent, craning my neck, but pushed forward to inspect their vessel. I lurched along the wharf where the water churned in oily bubbles around a wooden tramp steamer, hull peeling, trim missing, and listing to one side. I backed up when the crew lashed several trunks and suitcases together and let them tumble down a ramp and onto the ground.

A voice shouted from the deck, Clear a path! and a group of men on the ground shoved cargo to either side of the walkway from the dock to the street. Then, a sight that sucked the air out of the crowd—a horse, shiny and black.

Several ropes jerked steadily as the shrieking beast was swung over the railings. It grew deadly silent as it was lowered to what must have seemed its death. As soon as it touched ground it was kicking and rearing up. The same group of men that had been tossing cargo converged to calm the animal, and loosen its belly harness. It snorted fiercely, its eyes rolled, its haunches gleamed.

A handler led the dancing hooves away from a black hole and down the street, disappearing into the mist, calling as he walked, his words garbling into the distance, Toooooogaw. . . Misssscon.

I had no idea what the words meant, but I hesitated. A horse, here.

The opera troupe back up the street. Which one should I follow?

While I longed to touch that horse, run my palms over its flank, tug at its mane and rub its muzzle, I recognized that I was longing for the familiar, for the horses I had cared for on our orchard, Ruby especially, but also Star and English Bay. I knew exactly what it would feel like to grab that mane and launch myself up and onto its back, feel its ribs between my knees, how to nudge and steer with them, propel a thousand pounds of muscle thundering across a field or down a road. So I chose the unfamiliar, instead, the actors and the world of theatre, the dome with its edges tied down and the entrance flap constantly snapping with performers coming and going.

I bent my head and stepped through the canvas. Inside the tent that was propped up with the arching iron girders, was the closest thing to light I'd seen in this town. Buttery light, and the blaze of colourful silks.

No stink of coal and oil in here. Not yet. Old makeup cracked on their necks and cheeks and I breathed deeply, its perfume the smell of roadside dust on wild roses. They stripped with abandon as though I weren't walking among them, notebook open. The one in jade green sang deeply as he sat, grabbed the toes of his tights in each hand, head of thinning hair bobbing at his knees, and gave a yank, brandishing them high and exposing a tumble of flesh. The one who once wore yellow bent over, bare-cheeked, his sex dangling darkly between his legs as he dug in a trunk for his blasted pair of trousers. The woman sang as she powdered her bare breasts and underarms, tool belt tossed to the ground.

I'm from *The Black Mountain Bullet*, I called out. Who has a minute to talk to me about your opera?

My pencil hovered over my notebook. Preferably someone fully clothed, and there he was, leaning against a trunk, the one in the brown pin-striped suit. It was worn, I could see now, and the same brown as the fringe of hair below the brim of his bowler hat, framing a light brown face. He was reading a novel. I couldn't quite make out the cover, just splashes of browns and reds, but it was either about a ranch or a murder. I'd seen enough of them in Pete and Pat's hands.

You, I suggested brightly. Care to comment?

Here, he said, and tossed the wad of pages to the balding man seated to the right of where I stood, the one who had yanked off his tights.

Cover yourself, he said. Then he tipped his brown bowler at me. Don't mind my old friend, he said.

How can I? It's me who has invaded your dressing room.

The man in the bowler hat grinned and said, That's the spirit.

That book's not enough to provide coverage anyway, I began.

The old friend boomed his appreciation at my unintended compliment.

I wouldn't call that a book, the young man continued. I found it lying on a train station bench. Someone paid ten cents for it, then tossed it aside.

A train station. Then you travel a lot with the troupe.

Always moving.

The metal plates I had just received in the mail returned to my thoughts and I asked, Ever travel by air?

No.

But would you want to?

It would scare the daylights out of me. Would you?

For the newspaper, I said. And maybe I would, anyway.

Really? Nothing between you and death but a thin sheet of silver held up by wooden ribs, same sort of ribs that must have braced the walls of galleons in the days of pirates? Only you're in a flimsy tube sailing in the clouds. No thanks, darling. We all know the principles of flight but can anyone really tell me how it is that thing stays afloat instead of splattering its contents over the mountain tops? I heard that the sides aren't even metal, but canvas painted silver and that the upper hull is filled with gas bags made of cow guts. No, I get all the action I need here on the ground.

Trains go off the rails and down cliff sides, I said. The ocean is no safer. Ships sink.

Then thank the gods our little boat hugs the coast. I can swim for shore. As for adventure, I shall seek it vicariously. That, and he nodded at his old friend and the opened book splayed across his lap, is about a man in buckskin creeping up on an army. All by himself! He'll take them single-handed. But as I was saying, I wouldn't call it a book.

My consternation showed all over my face, I knew.

That shouldn't upset you any more than seeing your newspaper at day's end, he said, torn in half and wrapped around a fish.

My uncle's words. But I flinched, seeing another sort of fish. And then another.

I moved in closer to the young man, careful to hide my limp, hoping to move the conversation as well.

Why two tents? What's in the other?

It's where we sleep. The performers and musicians. And myself, of course.

You're not one of the cast?

I'm a writer of sorts, he said. A behind the scenes man. Benjamin Gill.

Mr. Gill—

Ben.

Ben. So what are your duties, precisely?

He smiled, clearly delighted to be the subject of an interview for once.

Let's walk outside, he said, and raised the tent flap for me.

I adapt the script for each production, he said, stepping out beside me. Each new town requires a new set-up and new stage directions. Sometimes we have to cut entire songs, the arias. It's a costly business but we make do. No hotel rooms for us. We'll be performing our opera in your saloon. That's good because some of the scenes are set in a saloon. You know the story? I won't spoil it then.

I didn't say what Vincent had said about it. But I did tell him what Meena had told me about *The Saloon* renting its rooms by the hour.

Or less.

Ladies of the evening, Ben said. Where would civilization be without them? Then they'll be there to see our production?

I said I understood so, and he seemed pleased.

It ends with a nice example of dramatic irony, he said.

The audience knows what's going on, but the characters don't.

Very good, he said. Theatre background?

Teacher. Was.

Well, you are right of course. The audience is included in the performance. They get the joke while the poor character stands perplexed, scratching himself. But as I promised, I won't say more about this production. You'll see it for yourself.

In two weeks, I noted, remembering my initial question. You're here early.

Preparation, he said. We know the tunes all right but we need to go over the entrances and exits, where to stand. There are no curtains or stage in your saloon, and I hear the metal walls reverberate. It's a challenge for the musicians. The stage directions have to change. Everything has to shift in this place.

He looked around as he spoke, taxis roaring past us.

Also, he added, the little boat we hired needs repairs. We got a reduced rate if we didn't mind an extended stopover.

He paused for a moment, wrinkling the tip of his nose. An odd place, this, isn't it? The very sound of those blasted scooters. *Vespula vulgaris*. Wasps.

His comment startled me, because it had been my very own. I knew the sound of wasps well. In our orchard they covered the fallen pears like a carpet of nettles, and then lifted at once, should you have walked over them without looking, filling your ears with the piercing buzz. You could run and run and even if you outran them, slamming the screen door behind you, still, you could hear them nosing and buzzing at the metal mesh, hear it in your ears even if you clapped a hand over each. Horrible things.

I smiled deeply. I liked this Ben fellow.

NEXT TO NOTHING

Dinner. Wooden bread with butter and jam, washed down with a mug of strong tea. Even the contents of Parker's shelves were more appealing.

I stopped by the calendar and scored across the date: September 16. Past the mid-point. I left quickly so I wouldn't have to think about that, grabbed the doorknob and yanked the door open.

What a stink in the air.

I slammed the door behind me and turned to lock it and there, nailed to the heavy wood, was a fish. The impact caused the slimy thing to come loose, the foul air growing fouler as it pulled apart. I watched, aghast, as it dangled by its twisted grin and then ripped free, sliding its blistered scales down the door and onto the boards. The same one I'd tossed toward the pithead? It couldn't be. The other would have rotted away by now. As rank as this one smelled, it wasn't that old.

I didn't hesitate. Full of fury and disgust I pulled back my leg and booted the mess into the street. The kick ignited each one of my stitches and I cursed my bleeding thoughtlessness twice over as I bent to ease the toe of my boot against the boards, and scrape it free of scales. Then I limped back inside and closed the door behind me.

For the longest time I sat at my desk, forehead pressed against the oak, unsettled, sickened. Of course the dirty deputy was behind the fish, but he might have convinced others to do it for him. That way he could remain guilt-free. I might have several people aiming to hurt me. Who in this town would do the bidding of that man? One of the other deputies? One of the miners?

I reached into the lower drawer for the bottle, put my feet up on the desk to ease the stitches, and leaned back for a slug.

⊷⇒●

The low moan of the approaching midnight ship roused me. I dropped my legs and stood, the pain in my neck far worse than in my leg.

Two rolls of my head to ease the kinks, a quick wash upstairs and then out the door, the headlamp dangling from my wrist as I limped.

The grey town was quiet. Even the opera players had turned in, their tents in darkness. But toward the docks the night sky was pierced by beams of light. There were shouts, too, and crates bouncing as they were flung from the ship onto the boards below. In minutes, before I had even reached the dock, the delivery was complete and the vessel had pushed off from the wharf. The beams clustered together around the cargo pile, creating a luminescent glow in the centre that, at first, I thought was Morris. I hadn't seen him since that brief moment at Meena's.

In my ear a thin voice that I knew right away to belong to Parker.

Got you a limp, there.

That I do, I said, and turned to him. Bicycle mishap.

He stared at me greenishly and for a long time from under his visor, lit up from above by his headlamp. At last he said, Mind the holes!

I nodded, and told him about the pigs in the dump, how wild they seemed, how they gave chase.

Pigs! He spat something into the dirt, and added, Shoot 'em and be done with it. Ed! Can you get this here crate to me in the morning? I'll be heading back, now.

Miss, Ed greeted. I can have this sent at the same time.

His headlamp beamed onto a package bound in rope and brown paper: massive and round and breathtaking.

What is it? I asked.

A roll of paper, looks like. Ordered by—he lifted the shipping receipt—a Mr. Cruz, V.

Of course, I said.

I had been expecting sheets of paper, but this roll would be for the large printing machine.

You can pay for it now, or later.

Later, I said.

This, too, he said, and his boot nudged a small bundle of newspapers.

I had ordered that one, papers from all over North America, and Hong Kong, too. There should have been more than this, but more must be on their way.

More money required, too, and I felt myself sigh with the realization.

I can take that now, I said, and to free my hands, I swung the strap from the lamp onto my head and jammed it down. Then I turned to him, still thinking about that disgusting creature nailed to my door this afternoon. I must have been banging things around in the pressroom not to hear the hammering.

Ed, I said. Have you noticed any strange-looking fish in the stream?
I suppose.
Do you know why they look like that?
He pulled his head back, suspicious, until his neck was full of chins.
Should I?
No, no, but I plan to write about it for the paper. What do you think
about that?
Fish is there in plain view to be writ about.
Good. I will be sure to say that. And thank you for the delivery
tomorrow.
I grabbed the bundle by the rope and dragged it along the dirt road
to my shop, not realizing until I saw myself in the reflection of the win-
dow that I was headlamped, just like the rest of them back there.

This time, Vincent knocked before unlocking the door, and I made sure
to prepare for his arrival, fully clothed in my ink-stained coveralls. My
thoughts were still in a turmoil from the other morning, but at least I
knew that nothing I did or felt in this town would have anything to do
with getting back at my father. He wasn't here to comment. I was acting
by and for myself.
Still, I was thankful for the distraction of work. We said brief hellos,
and after a fumbled attempt to step in the same direction, requiring us
to shuffle around each other, we got to work.
The type was set, the page locked and ready to be printed:

Opera
Comes
To Town

Strange
Fish

Wild Hogs
A Menace

Modern
Mine
Allows
Women

My story about the opera was little more than an advertisement, and a free one. I kept it short. Ed's answer about the fish was good enough to paraphrase, and became another short item. Parker's response to the pigs was too good to paraphrase and I quoted him directly, Shoot 'em and be done with it.

The rescue drill was less straightforward. I had told Meena and her customer about the girl and in doing so was making assumptions about her. But to put it in a newspaper? I had to be careful and stick to the facts.

Silver provided the solution and the headline with his remark, We're more modern than that. It allowed me to allude to the presence of the girl. All who were present could fill in the blanks. That feathered woman knew the details and if she wanted to share them with her friends, who was I to object? Perhaps they would write a letter to the editor, too. That would be ideal.

There was just enough room under *Commentary* for a suggestion that the holes in the streets be filled. In my next issue I planned on more room for an editorial on mine safety.

Given the missteps on my first issue, I was careful to read and re-type each article several times over. That meant it had taken six days to get this second newssheet out. I had suggested to Mooney there could be four of them before the first edition, which meant that between the 18th and the 29th I had to get out two more, and then a full newspaper the day after.

As we worked I told Vincent about meeting Ben and the others in the opera troupe.

At one point he swivelled around in amazement, blackened hands wringing a grey rag.

Green and yellow—huh. Gunslingers or clowns?

And then, laughing, he added, Like I said. Not my favourite opera to begin with.

Twice he has said my name. Introductions, both times. Once to Morris and once to the town. Ever since he dropped the lead type into place I have been waiting for him to say it again, so many obvious opportunities to do so, such as just now, as though we were old friends, good friends: *Green and yellow, Lila!*

And why not? We worked together.

Distracted, I missed his next request and he had to shout it.

Wrench, he said, right behind you.

You.

I handed out the newssheets that evening and by morning was at the typewriter, working on my next editorial, one that had been on my mind for some time:

> ~~There is a need for p~~ Public
> facilities ~~in this town~~
> ~~Black Mountain~~ are necessary
> ~~If~~ if Black Mountain is to ever
> become a modern

A commotion of loud voices and clanging music outside yanked me from my desk, and then out the back door toward the pithead.

There stood Meena's best customers, a ragged line of them. They had dressed in the corsets I'd seen at her shop, the ones that needed constant tugging to contain the mounds of flesh, with little skirts of green and blue, brilliant in the gloom, and that revealed long legs of netted black stockings hitched by garters, the feathers, and the beads. They strutted before a wagon that had been pulled by a motorcycle. It had come to rest on the ground just below the outbuildings. Once the taxi driver anchored the wagon wheels with boulders, he unhitched the apparatus and got back on his bike and roared off.

In the wagon were three men in tuxedos who blew into brass instruments and pounded a drum to create a saucy tune. The feathered agitators moved to the music, their heels clattering on stones scattered over the hard-packed dirt. Each move involved lifting a placard to expose specific areas, breasts that sprang free with hints of nipples rouged a violent red, backsides bulging beneath lace trim, and little satin skirts at the front that barely covered the area between their garters.

The placards were emblazoned with the words *On Strike*, punctuated by red lips on one side, dollar signs on the other.

I strode around the strikers, notebook in hand, scribbling and observing. Morris was among the crowd of onlookers, distinct in his white suit. I angled over to him, but before I reached him he was shouting out to me, A calamity! And a top news item, my dear. They are essential to this community, the very backbone!

I lifted my notebook and waved it at him to indicate I was right on it. And then I laughed out loud at the image of the women on their backbones holding up the community's men. If not for the strike I would turn around and grill Morris about the money, but I pushed ahead to find a protestor to interview.

Just ahead was the one I'd seen at Meena's the other day, the one who had been on Morris' arm, the one of the crooked corset previously.

Hello, again, I said, and pointed up to the musicians, Are they from the opera?

We hired them fair and square, Miss.

But with all of you on strike, I asked, where will you get the money to pay them?

She gave me a look of wonder, and I realized too late how the instrument players would likely be paid. It must have shown on my face because she smiled deeply at my belated understanding.

I tried to recover, and asked, Care to comment on the protest, itself?

I was hoping for mention of the girl, so I could fully report it this time.

It's all in there, thanks to you.

She handed me a pamphlet, and the line shimmied past as I stopped to read:

> The women of Black Mountain's Saloon have ceased work to protest the presence of similar work being conducted within the premises of the mine, whether with or without financial remuneration, that have taken prospective clients and work from said women at the saloon, and rendered the offenders the same objectionable status as any scab labour.

Women of the Saloon. Good. Better than stating it outright. I read quickly to the bottom, which went on to say that because of the expertise gained by years of said occupation at the saloon and of special skills passed down within the trade, the professional workers should not only be given exclusive rights of such occupation, but be paid in a manner befitting of their special skills. A private meeting was requested between the women and the mine authorities, and until then all favours, services and other duties to the town would be withdrawn. It was signed Miss Deirdre (Dee-Dee) Klein, and was the complete opposite in tone of the protest, stating their requests in crisp, formal English, as in a legal document.

I had been moving my lips as I read, and my next thought stopped me mid-sentence. She had followed the dancing line, so I hurried after her and called out, Where did you have this printed?

Lousetown, of course.

My scalp bristled from forehead to back of neck. There were several printers at *The Times*, perhaps several customers, but only one capable of such writing.

It reads, I said, almost like a legal document.

She turned her head toward me and smiled. We have friends in high places, she said. Very high.

I closed my eyes for a moment, relishing that moment. Yes, the wording had the distinct precision of a lawyer or a banker about it, maybe even Mr. Mooney.

The wagon and the music and the shimmying had the desired effect. If allowed to remain, they would be in the path of the lines of workers heading to and from during the shift change. There would be trouble then. Already a couple of the wives had gathered. I heard one whisper coarsely, Next to nothing! Shame on them.

The band continued its saucy tune and the women continued to move their bodies to match. Dee handed out her pamphlets to the gathering crowd that included some of the evening shift of miners, who'd shown up long before the shift change. She bowed deeply to show her rouged parts to full effect. One wife snatched the proffered pamphlet and tore it in half.

Silver arrived then, and sent his deputies running to circle the commotion and shove the workers and wives aside, away from the protesters. There was much pushing and shouting and releasing of pamphlets into the grey air. Then the noise subsided as a messenger ran out from one of the buildings and delivered a note to Silver, who trotted to a set of steps to confer with someone, the dirty deputy not far behind him.

Silver returned, loudly shouting to this Deirdre that she and her girls would have their meeting right then and right there in the mine office.

I moved closer as she called to her girls to cease and desist, at the musicians to kindly stop their tune.

Miss—I whispered, pulling her aside. Deirdre, I said.

Dee, she replied.

Dee. Let me cover this meeting for the paper. It is exactly what—

I stopped because she had wrapped her fingers around the wrist of my writing hand, gently squeezed, and looked deep into my eyes, again.

Not that kind of meeting, she said.

Oh, I said. Well.

And I tried to laugh again to cover my embarrassment, but it vexed me, too. Not just because this was a wrong-headed notion of negotiation, giving, it seemed to me, exactly what the women of *The Saloon* had purported to be withholding, first to the musicians and maybe the banker and now the mining authorities, but also because of the sort of man who would be at the getting end.

I looked around for Morris. He might help me dissuade her. But he had vanished.

That filthy toad over there, I said, indicating the loathsome deputy. He is dangerous. You should be careful.

We know all about him, she said. We offer him two for the price of one so that one of us can keep watch. We know what we're doing.

She turned to the deputies and called out, Just one thing, first. That girl is gone. Right now. Or no deal.

I hadn't expected this. Everything up until now was exactly as I had imagined, a few surprises, the band and the costumes, but all in all the sort of story I was looking to feature in my paper. A good story. An offence committed, action taken, resolution reached. I had brought the perceived offence to their attention, true, but from there, events had unfolded without intervention from me, and unfolded in a most newsworthy way. That was supposed to be the end of it.

And I hadn't considered what might happen to the girl. Perhaps that a group of women would have a talk with her—and what group would that be? The wives? The women of *The Saloon*? Well, maybe that her boss might pull her aside, or Silver, that she would be warned to cease such questionable conduct, that if she wanted to keep her job in the mine her work should be limited to the harvesting of coal, and furthermore, furthermore—I hadn't considered any further, any more than that. Hadn't seen events out to their ugly conclusion, unfolding before me now as the girl emerged from the mine, dragged out by two deputies, her heels kicking up a cloud of black.

She didn't look at all frightened, lifting her chin and pulling her arms from their grip.

Dee and the other women saw her and began to shout horrible things, that she was a humping scab, a filthy tart. They threw hunks of dirt at her.

She replied with rocks, dropping a shoulder to snatch them up, her baggy dress exposing her limp breasts.

When the deputies grabbed her arms again and yanked her up, she shrieked at the whores and what she called their slimy sluice boxes.

I can smell your stink from here! she cried, and pulled free again from the deputies.

The women began tearing and pulling at her and although the girl was outnumbered she fought hard. They slapped and kicked and punched each other for the right to have worse done to them. Was I the only one who realized this? Their screams ceased to contain words, just sounds, low and guttural and odious.

One of the deputies blew a whistle and then several more appeared, wielding sticks to break up the fight.

Then it was all over.

My notebook swelled with filled pages. I shoved it into my pocket and it banged against my leg as I walked away. I had brought them to this. I was the one who told Dee all about it, hoping for a reaction. I got one. I could still hear their voices, shrieking, could still see the girl dragged out in that gaping dress, could imagine those women of *The Saloon* and their sordid notions of negotiation, occurring at this very moment, a few feet from my back door.

ALL NIGHT

I woke up vowing to never tamper with the news again. Today would be a new start. The sounds of metal clanging told me Vincent was already at work. I washed and dressed and hurried downstairs, struck through the 20 on the calendar as I passed it, and added the flourish of an asterisk to remind me of this new day.

No fish was draped across the door mat out back. I strode down the hall. Or nailed to the front door. I stepped into the pressroom, at last.

We said our good mornings and I included his name in my greeting, hoping that the more I said it the more he would be inclined to respond in kind.

Not today, though, and so we set to work.

The old machine rattled to life, clicking along at a relaxed pace that allowed me to lift sections of the newsprint, scanning for splotches of ink. The run was only halfway through when a roar like an avalanche or an earthquake sounded and rocked the walls of the shop, lifting the iron legs of the press from its platform even as it spat out test impressions for the upcoming first edition, loosening the bolts and threatening to ruin the machine. I raced to the back of the press to find Vincent already scrambling up the ladder. We had reacted as one, the security of the machine our first thought, even over our own safety. In a flash my mind had rejected the idea of natural causes. The tunnels ran right below us, extending out to the sea. The upheaval, I knew, had to come from the mine. Only briefly did I consider running out to see what had happened. My livelihood was at stake, here.

Help me, he called, balling up his smock and then his shirt and tossing them onto the floor. He coiled his braid and pushed his cap down tight over it.

The giant paper roll snapped loose then, bouncing across the floor and unravelling in a tangle of crushed and smudged paper in a far corner of the room. Several metal bolts, sprung free by the release of the heavy roll, clattered to the cement floor. A ragged remnant of paper slithered and snapped through the pounding machine, jamming the works until they shrieked. Ink sprayed and pipes steamed as I yanked and rolled my sleeves to my shoulders and climbed up after Vincent.

Grab that, he shouted, pointing.

I seized the knobbed lever and shifted forward, lifting the rollers from the ink. Pistons still pounded and he reached past me, arms snaking through mine, to snap off the switch. Clouds of steam filled the room as the machine shuddered to a stop.

There, he said, and released me.

At the front of the machine, not far from where I had stood, checking pages, the blade of the paper-cutter had risen up with the impact of the blast and bitten down onto itself, much as a child would, biting its own lip when it falls, breaking a tooth. I jumped down for a closer look. The blade's cutting edge was now warped and chipped. It was ruined.

Vincent had crouched beside me to inspect it, then stood.

We'll have to cut the pages by hand, he said. I'll bring a knife.

He held his hands wide, indicating a mighty blade.

I had seen it cut an apple, and only now realized his hands could also be indicating a parcel the length of a rifle.

It's a good thing the old press is so slow, he said, otherwise we couldn't do it. We'll have to fold by hand, too.

A siren began wailing, rising and falling with, I imagined, the fatigue of the man cranking the handle. It was a familiar sound to anyone raised near mines, and a dreaded one. Wives would be rushing to the pithead, anxious to know if their husbands were among the survivors.

Behind us, the stopped machine sighed like a wounded beast.

Vincent turned around and climbed back onto the machine, and I followed. The broken web had wrapped itself around the ink rollers. He reached into the press and began pulling out strips of blackened paper, passing them down to me to toss into a metal pail below. Once that was done, he shouted further instructions over his shoulder.

I climbed down, lifted the floor hatch and backed my way down the wooden ladder to the dirt floor of the basement. There, I threw water on the coals to dampen the fire and cool down the boiler. I unbuttoned my coveralls, tying the sleeves around the waist of my blouse. I fanned the sides of the thin cotton to let in more air, then climbed the steps upstairs.

I opened windows, scrambled on hands and knees for the scattered bolts and screws, returning them to Vincent's hands.

This needs both of us, he said.

We bent our knees and tugged at the giant roll of paper. It was strung through with a rusted shaft of iron that fit into two indentations at the rear of the press, like a spindle that turns as the paper unrolls. Vincent had wedged a wooden ramp under it. We wore gloves to stop the metal pole from tearing the palms of our hands.

The bolt of paper finally budged, rolling across the cement unevenly, paper catching and tearing as we tugged and grappled and steered it up the ramp toward its metal berth. We would lose yards of it to this rough journey. With each tug and tear I was seeing money spilling over the concrete floor. My money. Yet I was glad of this chance to work beside him. Every awkward moment between us, every blunder on my part, vanished with our joint efforts to fix the press.

Put your left shoulder under, he said, and indicated the pole.

He put his right shoulder under the pole on his side.

Use your legs, he said. Slowly.

I lifted until sweat burst from my brow and down my cheeks.

Now forward, he said, just a bit.

I did and the weight of the thing took over, tumbling itself into its berth with a thud. I lost my balance in the process, and might have slid down with it, but he caught me by the knotted sleeves around my waist and righted me.

We climbed around the press, a giant wrench between us. He took the end for better torque and I grabbed the middle, adding my weight to help tug or shove and therefore tighten the loosened screws and bolts.

In the grey glow of the pressroom turned mustard by the burning lights, we grappled all night with the machine. I grew filthier by the hour, I knew, because I could see myself reflected in his own slick skin and smudged cheeks, in the strip of wet running down the back of his undervest. We drank water to quench our thirst, and as we neared the end of the night, whisky. We clinked glasses to toast our success at bringing the machine under control, then our success at starting it up again. The room shook to signal its rebirth and I felt the vibrations all the way up my legs, buzzing around inside me like a hungry insect. I wanted it to stop. I wanted it to buzz even harder. I was breathless by the time Vincent pulled out his watch and declared it four in the morning. Time to go.

Now I could go see what had happened at the mine. I shoved the jars and putty knives aside and washed my face in the work sink, drank straight from the tap, then undid the knot of sleeves and buttoned up the coveralls, smoothing my hair as I stepped out the door.

A crowd, veiled and indistinct in the mist, had gathered between the pithead and my back porch. Coarse laughter, hoots.

All night with her, China Man?

It was the voice of the dirty deputy, ugly, and low.

I couldn't see Vincent. I pushed my way past shoulders and elbows, shouting into the thick air, Silver! Are you out there?

The sheriff had to be close by, and sure enough his helmet emerged, gleaming weakly in the fog.

Now, now, now, he said, drawing closer. What seems to be the problem?

He's harassing my printer! I shouted.

At the sound of Silver's voice the crowd drew back, and at last I saw Vincent, rolling a shoulder, getting ready.

Gonna' fight me? the deputy said. Gonna' lose, China Man. He lifted his head and spat on the ground between them.

Enough, Silver said. Will someone explain?

We were working on the press, I said. That's all. The explosion damaged it.

That's all. Such words reduced us to merely employee and employer, or perhaps mechanic and helper, and surely neither was adequate, though necessary, given the mood of the moment.

Silver stepped between the deputy and Vincent, waving his stick, insisting that both move on their way.

Just then, a second tremor shook the ground beneath us.

That's Number 5 going! Silver cried. Clear out. Everybody out!

Concerns about what might have happened in my shop vanished under the threat of another explosion. Boots thudded and heads bobbed, decapitated in the mist. I saw the goggled faces of taxi drivers, blackened boots of miners, grimed skirts of miners' wives. I had lost sight of Vincent and found myself alongside one of the women from *The Saloon*. I supposed the whole town had come out to gawk, at the explosion, first, and then at Vincent.

That was my printer, I said.

The only one of them I wanted to talk to was Dee, given what she had said so recently about the deputy, and I asked where she was.

Taken sick, miss, she said.

Tell her that I asked after her.

I stopped and turned at the sound of shouts and thuds. Miners had emerged in the mist, carrying out the dead. The bodies were loaded into coal carts and sent hurtling to the docks.

Coal. Men. Whatever the mine had given up that day. What was news to me didn't seem to strike anyone else as remarkable. They simply nodded sadly as each body made its noisy descent.

At my back porch at last, I turned one more time and peered through the grey, wondering if my printer would return, today, or ever. And I felt a shift, then, as though we had climbed that mountain of a press together, working as one, only to have me slip short of the peak somehow, and be left dangling, inches from his grasp, the late hour and the accusations about it making any such further contact impossible, and that no amount of scrambling was ever going to put me back up there, again.

MEET TWO-GUN COHEN

One week to go. One more hand-cranked newssheet after yesterday's, then finally, the first edition from the big press. I stared at the calendar, the 23 scored though, now, and let the pencil drop by its string to clatter against the wall.

When Vincent appeared in the pressroom doorway yesterday I had looked up from the table and held his gaze.

Thank you, I said at last, for coming back.

And I asked if he was hurt.

Nah, he said.

He stayed only long enough to help set type, and to test-run this third sheet, then he was out the door the instant the light began to fade, to avoid any possibility of him working with me at night, though in this dreary place, really, what was the difference between night and day, though of course there was, there was, and he of all people knew that, leaving me to crank the wheel myself and run off the copies. I did so with a full chest. It was lonely work. How different from the first newssheet, when excitement surged through both of us—briefly.

This one had included the ad for the airship as well as the opera, and just two news items:

Mine
Kills
Ten

Next To
Nothing
— A New
Kind Of
Protest

My column, however, ran the entire length of the page and included two commentaries set apart by headlines:

The Need
For Safety
In The Mine

and

Let Us
Oppose
Violent
Ends

Finally, there was Silver's letter. For simplicity's sake I slugged it:

Letter to the Editor

Since handing it out last evening I had heard no reaction to my coverage of the explosion, or to my editorial on safety. There was no denying that it had happened, that men had died, and that safety was an issue. In my second editorial I addressed the rights of workers to protest a threat to their livelihood, if done without violence, verbal or physical, as well as to stay at one's task all night if the job demanded it, without fear of false accusations. I didn't go into details. The town knew very well to which two incidents I referred.

Perhaps the lack of detail was the reason I had received no complaints. I hoped Vincent would read it. He who can read upside down and backwards should not take long to see that the first letters in each line of the four-decked headline about violence spelled a message to him.

Silver's letter was such a tangled attempt it drew not a single comment except from the man himself, who was pleased to see his name in print and asked for ten copies to send to family members back home. It was a relief, not to be confronted by shouts or by foul fish nailed to the door. Though I wondered if that meant I was not doing my job.

It had been raining all morning, then stopped and the air upstairs grew warm. I turned off the radiator and slid the window up, hoping for a cool breeze. The room grew dark and a cloud of creatures with little black wings poured into the window and filled my room, vibrating in front of my eyes and stirring the air around my ears, not a buzz but a constant hum. I flailed at the air and sent little bodies into the walls, but they circled crazily and then flew crookedly back into their cloud formation, around and around the room, landing on the ceiling and walking over the plaster, into the lampshade where they crackled and went up in smoke, sizzling onto the still-warm radiator like a coat of dripping, black paint.

The press—

I pounded down the stairs and flung open both front and back doors. The cloud was there before me, whirling around the machine, offspring to the hive. I snatched up a broom and batted them out the doors, protecting the machine as he would have, slammed the doors shut, dashed up the stairs to close the window and stood in the empty room. Breathless.

Back downstairs, I climbed as I had done before and peered into the rollers, the ink tray. I rubbed bodies from the rollers with a rag, lifted them from the ink tray with a putty knife. The press itself would have to be stripped of ink once Vincent arrived. I didn't know how, but he could show me. I smiled, hesitantly, thinking of that. I cleaned my hands on a rag, wrote him a note, and left it by the press.

I was too restless and excited to return upstairs. I headed over to Parker's to see if the cloud had entered his store.

Black moths, he told me. An infestation shaken out of some tree or shed by a disturbance of nature. Barometric pressure. That's my guess. A sign that autumn is coming. That's storm season on the coast. November is the height of it, but October is the start.

A week from now?

Maybe. You'll know it when it hits. It's not just a blast of a wind that shakes the walls. It blows away all the fog, too. People get pretty excited about it around here. Sometimes just for an hour, or for as long as an afternoon, we see light. Not always sunlight, either, but a brightness. Think of a long winter coming to an end, like in January when you get that hint of spring. Not because it's warm or even sunny or has stopped snowing or raining, but because the days are getting longer. It's that return of light that we long for, and here it's cause for jubilation.

Back home, I said, we watched for birds returning. Have you ever seen a bird, here?

He lifted his shoulders like someone behind him was helping him out of his jacket.

In Black Mountain? No, can't say I have.

I've seen a crow, I said, on the other side of the mountain. But I mean songbirds, small birds.

There aren't any trees here, he said. They'd need branches to land on.

One more thing, I said, and held up my notebook and shook its well-worn pages. I need another. This one's filling up, too.

Parker pulled open a drawer and dug around for a minute, dumping envelopes onto the counter, followed by loose sheets bound with ribbon. At last he produced a small booklet about the size of Meena's notepad, but thicker.

Nothing larger?

Your uncle ordered those special, he replied, dipping his nose at my notebook. I can get an order in for you.

That order would take a week, at least, he told me, and I needed something sooner. I took the small notepad, noted how neatly it fit into my palm. It would be perfect for the opera.

I was calm after talking to Parker, reassured that the moths flew into his place, too, and that the experience was shared and not mine alone to endure. I stood on the veranda outside his door, trying to imagine the haze suddenly lifting, the sky brightening, turning clear and blue. My efforts, instead, brought me the unmistakable visage of Morris, large and white. He was no more than a few yards ahead and I called his name, but he deliberately and abruptly turned the corner. What was he up to?

I hurried down the steps and across the street, my leg hampering my usual long strides. Was he avoiding me? I hadn't seen him for days, and the last two times were brief encounters. I cut down the side streets, watching for him, keeping to this side of the mountain, away from any threat of wild hogs, wading through tall grass that flanked the roads. Here there were signs of an overgrown orchard. From a time before coal was discovered? Not even shrivelled fruit on these branches, but still, places for birds to land. I'd have to mention that to Parker, though I could have imagined him sizing up these little trees and proclaiming them too short for roosting.

Beneath my feet were the tunnels that ran outward from the pithead to the ocean, and black holes. I was careful to step around them.

Again, the snap of cloth like a flag in the wind, and a figure darting between corrugated metal shacks. Thoughts shot across my mind, a volley of them. Not Morris this time. Someone half his girth, like a woman or a child. I couldn't be sure, but in dark clothes. The same figure I saw once before? Perhaps Morris was following him, and in such a hurry he couldn't answer my call.

I stared up and down the rows of miners' quarters. Parker had pointed them out to me but I hadn't looked at them up close. A shabby collection not unlike the shacks in Lousetown, only metal, and the lines straighter. But I saw no sign of any figure, large or small.

I returned to the tall grass, stopping outside an abandoned house, mostly wood, uncommon in this part of town. Winding up through the uncut grass, a growth of unusual roses bloomed, shrivelled and stunted from lack of sun, yes, but also blue. Parker said the owners moved away when their child fell ill, but I think someone on their behalf should contact a horticultural society. Blue roses are rare. This may be the only place in the world where they grow successfully, though several rose clubs have tried. I read that somewhere.

The door was off its hinges and I walked in. There was no one around to challenge me.

Tiles below my feet, rose and cream ribbons coiling up through the dust, in the corner a tea trolley and tea set with gilt edges glowing through the layer of black powder. A radiator in the hallway, a finger smear showing bronze through the black. Someone had been here before me, looking around. The sofas, the drapes, the plaster cornices on the ceiling, the glass knobs on doors and cupboards, all coated in the dark dust. The parlour was missing its radiator, just a hole and scrapes in the blackened floor where one had been disconnected, then dragged away. An opera window above, in greys and greens that were probably blue, red and yellow.

In a grimy mirror I saw myself in ink-stained coveralls, as though I, too, were a presence from the past struggling up through the grey film.

Back out through the overgrown garden and onto the path. Even a little sunlight would bring the blooms back, though I admired the stubborn rose and turned for one more look. It would be spectacular, given a little pruning and care. And sun. How lush it could grow with a few hours of sunlight in Lousetown.

I no sooner twisted back around than a head popped up from one of the black holes in the road.

Jesus Christ, man!

It was Morris. He climbed out in a cloud of black dust, face florid, white suit filthy.

You scared the living hell out of me, I said.

My dear, he said, you're jumpy. Bushed! Just as I warned. It happens to the best of us. Strange town, isolation.

Strange, I said, yes. You ignored me when I called your name just now.

Apologies, my dear, I must have been preoccupied.

I saw someone else, too.

Oh?

I craned my neck, still hoping to spot the figure.

Maybe a child, I said. But there aren't many around here. And it was someone sneaking about. Down there, where the miners live.

The white miners, he said, turning. The rest live in Lousetown.

He slapped the dust from his arms.

Let's hope it was a child, he said. One of the miners' progeny.

And where on earth have you been? What have you been up to?

Oh, here and there, this and that.

I had hoped you might come along after the explosion to see if the shop was damaged.

I knew you'd send word if it was.

To where? I didn't know where you were and if you're going to be a partner I should know, and besides that Vincent was surrounded by the crowd, with that filthy deputy shouting accusations, all because we had worked on the press all night, and I felt wretched about that—

Not your fault, dear girl.

Yes, it was. Because of that article I wrote about his leader.

You were doing your job.

I was, I said, nodding and gobbling up his willingness to find me faultless.

Morris hooked his thumbs under his arms and expanded, his voice loud and ragged: It was nothing new to our Vincent. When he was a child he learned French by sitting in on the lessons given to the bosses' children. Yanks, I believe. He was quick at languages, so he was welcomed to join the children on outings, as long as they spoke French. This one time in the park the nanny charged over to them, seeing that he and the girl were holding hands as they ran about. All very innocent, they were children, but children who were growing up quickly. His father lost his job because of it.

I saw with new eyes the moment Vincent extended his hand to me in Lousetown, then pulled it back. I had pulled back, too.

That's when he decided to grow his hair, I said, for his father.

I suppose.

The significance silenced us both for a moment. Then I pointed at the hole.

What were you doing down there?

Studying for signs, he said.

Signs of what? You dropped something. There, behind you.

He bent to retrieve it, presenting a trousered bottom ridiculously white and streaked in grey.

Of treasures the earth gives up from time to time, he said.

He straightened, took my arm and turned me around.

They drill these holes, he continued, and sometimes don't go deep enough. They give up and move on to another find.

Exploratory digs. I know.

His eyes darted toward my other hand as it pulled the notebook from my pocket. It was a relief to be back to the familiar.

I wouldn't want everyone to know about this. Because everyone is reading your fine newssheets. Our fine newssheets, he added. It's what everyone's talking about.

Do you read *The Bugle*? I asked.

I had looked at one more copy and the only piece that qualified as news, about the explosion, contained several spelling mistakes. I supposed the article was included because the disaster affected numbers, and *The Bugle* was all about numbers.

Yes, he said, but our *Bullet* is better. And when you listed the dead you listed the Chinese, too. How did you get their names?

Vincent, I said.

Yes, yes, Vincent, Morris said.

I had no idea what he meant by that until he added, He was not happy that *The Bugle* made no mention of the Chinese. He said it was tempting to refuse to print it.

He runs their machine, too?

I just know he prints the paper. Their machine. His machine. Does it matter?

I stared off into the grey distance, seeing the giant paper roll snap free, a ragged strip of it slithering through the machine that pounded and shrieked until we brought it to a hammering stop, and then the two of us grappling with its parts all night in the steam and oil and ink.

Morris then asked a question that jerked my attention back to the present. Have you heard of the coal mines of Africa? Let me explain. Wherever you have coal deposits and running streams, he said, you have this too.

I peered into his open palm at something that sparkled.

Just a sample diamond. Thank you for spotting it just now. I must have dropped it. Well, go ahead and write that down. It's not as though I found any here. But if they're in Africa, then you can bet they're in other places, too. Just be so kind as to not give away the exact location.

Of what?

The stream. Listen.

And I heard it gurgling, close by, in the grass. I made a mental note of the foot trail toward it, how it curved to the left, ending in a hole.

Coal and water, he continued. Perhaps diamonds. As your source said, coal likes company.

This is what your brandy and cigars meeting was about.

Yes. May I escort you back to town?

I've only just set out for a walk.

Walk with me, then! He grabbed my elbow and turned me, again. You've got me thinking of Lousetown. There is, he said, a small cantina where they serve a delicious hoisin duck with vegetables.

Lousetown. He had my interest, now.

Duck? I asked.

Pigeon for all I know. Some sort of bird.

And let me guess. Canned peas.

Oh, no. Crisp greens.

Here?

We had some back at the doctor's. Oh—that's right, you weren't hungry then. Are you, now? Come, he said. Be my guest. I hate to dine alone.

I should change my clothes.

Yes, there you are in camouflage again, my dear girl. An army term. A bit of visual deception—you blend right into the grey town in that grey fabric. The better for prowling about, unnoticed, while you gather news. And look at my suit. It has seen brighter days. No, your outfit will be just fine where we are going. And your beauty will shine above it. Please, join me.

He didn't need to ask again. I was limping alongside him, quickly. Fresh greens, yes, but no choice in the matter, either. He had my elbow in his big paw, still, and although I told him of my stitches he did not slow his pace, nor did his response have any bearing on my injury.

Excellent, he said. Now, let's put away your notebook. We are done with work for the day.

I already had put it away but he was distracted, looking up and down the narrow lane as he talked. For the curious child, he added at last.

⊶⊨⊙

Morris led me along a jumble of shacks crouched at the stream's edge and connected by a crooked boardwalk. The sun was setting, I was certain. To the west there was a faint glimmer you would never see on the other side of the pithead, and it gave the water a molten sheen.

This time not a single door slammed. Neither had they when the three of us walked back from the doctor's, but there had been silence. It had been late, so we were simply left to ourselves. Or maybe they hadn't recognized the friend of the Chinese with his face black and blue, maybe I hadn't seen them, my head shielded under a newspaper much of the time.

But I didn't need to see them this night. I heard them, the high-low pitch of their language, the excitement in their voices as they called out, Morris! Mister Kow-hen!

He put his arm through mine and patted my hand with the plump pads of his fingers.

The gathering residents breathed *ah-h-h-h*, and added something that sounded like, Missy Kow-hen.

I suppose I responded predictably, pulled my arm away, twisting my head back and forth like an ostrich's, that bird-beak of a smile my brothers claim I wear when tense. I'm not your missy, I hissed. Tell them.

Enjoy the spectacle, he said, tightening his grip. How often in this life are we welcomed so warmly? This, he said, could be your future.

His free hand waved at the crowd.

Mine?

Yours, mine, ours. This is the new world, new times, with all types mingling together.

Well, if they had accepted me, perhaps it was because of him. Again I was seeing that open face of the solar dish, the stamen toward the sky or, given the angle of our approach, toward me. I was someone important. The newspaper publisher. Another friend of the Chinese, the one who listed their deaths as I would anyone's. The fact that I was walking with Morris must have put me in particularly good light.

The new world. I repeated it to myself, rolling the words over my tongue. The newly arrived metal plate embossed with the airship, that had since inked itself into a paying advertisement in my paper, hovered in my thoughts.

Morris, I asked. Have you ever travelled by air?

I have, indeed. From Paris to London.

Morris described the finest crystal, a private smoking room, luxurious furnishings, until I grew impatient.

But what is it like to *fly* in one?

You barely know you're up in the air.

But what's the point of that? I want to feel the wind in my hair.

You want to be sailing on the open seas, my dear.

I mentioned the ad for the Zeppelin, and he said he had seen it.

The advertisement itself, excellent, my dear. It's money for our newspaper. But for the town? Landing will be difficult. It would have to attach itself to something. I've seen pictures where they tie up to the mast of a ship that's docked.

Our ship arrives at midnight, I said, and then I sighed deeply.

The advertisement didn't state a time. They must figure we'll know it when we see it. That would be a waste, to arrive and depart in the middle of the night. It could hitch itself to the coal hulk. But who'd want that?

His grip loosened and he patted my hand, again. You and I could travel the world, my dear, and never have a dull moment together. We are ideally suited. Opposites in every way but our thirst for something new. We have identical curiosities. We are explorers.

I flashed a smile, despite myself.

We had reached our destination, an old lopsided boardwalk, and reeled over the slats that dipped and groaned beneath the weight of each step.

The cantina shack was made from graying driftwood and other scavenged pieces. A window from a house, a wooden door from a boat that forced us to duck our heads. Over the door hung a lopsided sign: *The Lonesome Café*. Inside, two oil lamps glowered, one by a coal stove, the other over a long, wide board that spanned the width of the shack and served as a counter.

Several Chinese sat at the board, miners, perhaps. Some of the opera troupe were at the counter, too: Ben, once again, his old friend, the big-chested singer, and two of the men. The musicians, I presumed. They had discovered in mere days what it had taken me weeks to find. An establishment that served fresh food.

A large, brown-skinned man in knitted cap and sleeveless white undervest stood at the stove, spooning breaded oysters into a buttered pan. For an apron he wore a striped tea towel tucked into his trousers. The oysters sizzled as they landed and a smell of ocean filled the small room.

Sit, he said.

I did as Morris showed me, dragged a stump forward and sat at the board like we were at a café counter.

Our cook poured us each a mug of tea, then slammed a bowl of sugar and tin of condensed milk onto the board. The holes in the tin had congealed with old milk the colour of glue. He leaned over and aimed a yellowed fingernail at each hole, jabbing once to break the seal.

Wolf, Morris said, my lovely acquaintance here didn't know you serve delicious greens, or how you come by them. Go ahead and show her. I can see to the drinks myself.

I sat up, curious, imagining a giant warehouse of greens.

The aproned Wolf scooped fried oysters onto a plate, added a slice of buttered bread, a brilliant clump of green, like spinach, speared by a single blade of asparagus, and sent it sliding down the counter to someone who had just entered by way of a back door.

Marcel! I called out.

Mademoiselle! he called back, doffing his cap.

I would ask why he cooked at the hotel instead of here, but we were shouting as it was, and I imagined his answer would be similar to Vincent's, that they paid twice what anyone in Lousetown would.

I bent my head in greeting to Ben and his old friend. Ben lifted his chin and smiled. The old one lifted his stem of asparagus and waggled it at me.

I turned back to Wolf. He finished smoking a stub of a cigarette till it was a pinch between his fingers, then dropped it and ground it into the boards with his boot.

You're the one who runs the newspaper? He leaned forward, his fishy tobacco breath and dark eyes roaming over my face. Thought so, he said. None of this goes in it. Agreed?

I sighed. Agreed.

He looked at Morris, and then raised his eyes to the shelves above the stove with rows of bottles of every amber-coloured liquid I could name, bourbon, rye, rum, tequila, brandy, and some clear ones as well, gin, vodka, schnapps. There was no attempt to hide spirits here. I knew what he was thinking, though, and soon he pointed a brown-stained finger at Morris.

I'm staying right here, he said, to watch my stock. You take her. You know the way. Take a basket while you're at it.

Morris rose, and I got up to follow him. Why were the best news stories unprintable?

The boat jerked with each dip of the oars, darting forward like a water bug.

We crossed what Morris described as cranberry flats. Beads of brilliant red bobbed in the cloudy water and tumbled against my fingertips as we glided over. The prow ground into gravel and Morris clambered out, lifted the basket and set it on the ground, then dragged the boat up onto the beach of an island of sorts, a mound of earth in the middle of the stream, hidden by the pithead, or I would've seen it from the top of the mountain. The wicker handle over his arm, he led me straight ahead to a gate of woven vines and branches within a wall of green growth. It swung open as though on oiled hinges.

We found ourselves in a fog thicker than any I had seen in Black Mountain, obscuring my sight until we shut the gate behind us and stepped through it. Directly before us, a fountain bubbled and steamed vigorously from a white bathroom basin on a gleaming white pedestal. A row of office fans on tall stilts spun their blades and aimed their silver snouts in a variety of directions, scattering the steam.

The coal dust dries out the air, Morris explained, so some plants need misting. Others don't like it damp. They need it redirected. The gardeners have thought of everything.

Tomato plants were trellised over two car doors and an engine hood that leaned against the green wall. The gardeners had obviously visited the dump.

For added warmth, Morris said. The metal heats up and gives them a boost.

Heats up? How?

We get the morning sun, he said.

I nodded to myself, thinking of Vincent's rooftop dish. *The Times* must be close by.

A coal cart brimming with leafy greens and onions rolled past on a track.

Gents, Morris greeted as we walked. Two Chinese men pedalled furiously on stationary bicycles.

They give us a power boost, Morris said, along with that up there.

His fingertips indicated another solar dish like Vincent's, nestled amongst the green growth but pointed upward. Running out from below dish and bicycles were cables and wires that connected to black boxes, and from there more cords that appeared to stretch from one end of the garden to the other.

We could have light all night long if we wanted, he said. We could build a crystal garden for the winter. But either would give us away. You'd be able to see us glowing and twinkling all the way to Black Mountain, even through the fog.

So what will they do in winter? Close the garden?

Vincent's working on it. Radiators, he said. Over there.

Two cast iron radiators leaned against the green wall, waiting, as he explained it, to be hooked up to the existing pipe work that fed the fountain. I knew where they got at least one of those radiators. I'd just been there, looking around the abandoned house.

He's a goddamned genius, Morris said.

Yes, I said. He told me he likes to make things.

That chandelier at the hotel made of radio tubes? Most of what you've seen so far? All his.

Glorious heads of roses glowed in the evening air. I bent to breathe in their perfume.

These are lovely, I said.

Miners' helmets with headlamps nestled in the dirt of the rose bed, and lit up the blooms, turning the petals sheer as silk.

Like the tomato, Morris said, roses like a good drink of water, but need well-drained soil. Even tomatoes can't touch those heated metal doors, or they'll blister, but roses are even more delicate. We're experimenting with these lamps. I've also suggested a stone wall to retain the heat without hurting the blooms. An upcoming project.

And then he added, These roses remind Vincent of home. Shanghai.

These are his, too? I asked. I've never seen—

And then I stopped. Because why would I?

He sells them. Always doing something to make money. That's a secret, remember. He shot a dark look toward my pocket and the notebook it held. I nodded my understanding. Mostly, he continued, the girls at *The Saloon* buy them. Says it gives a boudoir smell to the place.

The word *boudoir* rumbled in his throat.

He says that?

I couldn't contain the venom behind my question. My mouth filled with a bitter taste. I had literally spat the question at Morris.

No, he said. The girls do.

This is a secret? None of their customers demand to know where the flowers come from? They might want to buy some for their wives, too!

My temper scorched the very words that left my lips. I said the word *customers* as though it were a cuss word, and then stepped to the side to let a coal cart of rutabagas trundle past. My chest heaved and I could feel my cheeks flame.

Morris turned slowly, his eyebrows arched above the rolling mound of yellow roots. Perhaps my outburst was the last thing he expected from a newspaper publisher.

My dear, he said, anyone going there has other things to think about.

Up ahead, the bent backs of workers emerged, their straw hats bobbing like pinwheels in the grey air, illuminated here and there by embedded miner's lights. The sight soothed me and I felt my pulse slow. Rotten tomatoes had been thrown to the ground, a clotted carpet that stuck to the passing feet of the pickers, of each of us. I paused to wipe a heel against a rock, the pungent smell of tomato as rich as its colour, especially so, wrapped as it was in the damp, metallic grey of the air.

Morris knew his way around, stopping to comment on the positive effects of mounding the soil, and on which herbs kept what bugs away. He surprised me with his knowledge and I said so.

Gardening became my *raison d'être* in the wilds of Saskatchewan.

You worked on a farm?

I did. And because I had a talent for it I was assigned the task of keeping a garden to feed the hordes.

He was being obviously evasive.

You fed a village? I asked.

I had a growing suspicion about what he would say next.

My fellow-sufferers in Prince Albert's least hospitable establishment.

You were in jail!

Falsely accused, along with my Chinese compatriot. I stood by him and he taught me to grow vegetables. My favourite was the eggplant, *aubergine,* such magnificent colour—

What were you accused of?

Ill-gotten gains.

Ill-gotten how?

What does it matter? I was innocent and yet I was thrown behind bars for a year.

Gambling, I suspected. Not so innocent. Picking pockets, maybe. I hadn't forgotten the sight of his probing fingers in the hotel restaurant.

He added, The only fresh air I got was when I worked in that garden.

The pickers in this garden must have seen us, certainly they heard us, but they didn't look up as we approached. At the end of the path we stepped over an irrigation ditch, and he handed me the basket. He lowered his hands to the ground and tugged, once, twice, and laid a bouquet of carrots against the wicker bottom, next, green onions.

Here, he said. And he leaned over the vegetables to clip a rose, the bud still closed tight. I could see from the others that it would be a blush-coloured bloom so pale it could be almost white, ghostly against the night, illuminated, as he held it aloft, by the miner's lamp below. He placed it in my free hand and I thanked him, though I wished it had come from another. A book and newspapers had been offering enough until I saw these blooms.

Aloud I remarked, I wonder why they didn't build the town here. Black Mountain, I mean.

We had stopped at a corner collection of old hip waders, an umbrella stand, and women's bloomers, knotted at the knees. They had been filled with soil and the tops of each sprouted green spears. Morris bent over them with his clippers.

My dear girl, he said, remarking as Parker might. The coal's over there! Why would they build here?

And he dropped a bunch of asparagus beside the onions.

These have long roots and like deep soil, he explained. Most asparagus have packed it in for the year, but the lamps have convinced these it's still spring.

The basket was heavy on my arm when he stopped and raised a hand and said, Ah, my blushing beauty.

An apple. He plucked it from the tree and was about to lay it on top of the mound of vegetables. I had seen an apple neatly sliced in two and now at last I had found where it had come from.

I put the basket down.

May I have it? I asked.

Why, of course. Would you like two? Ten?

I laughed. No. One is enough.

And I slipped it in my pocket before picking up the basket again. We were back at the garden gate, now. The fountain did double duty as a wash-up station, and as we passed it we stopped, as the pickers before us had, to clean our nails and knuckles in the hot water. Two headlamps glowed from the pedestal base, and when I crouched to look closer I noticed a brush stroke of blue on the porcelain base. It was the same blue that trimmed the hole in my floor. It was my sink.

Morris!

But he had pushed ahead to the rowboat, and I had to run to catch up.

I turned back to look one more time, but the sink was cloaked by the green hedge and woven gate as though it were exactly where it should be. And really, how could I demand that they return it when the sink could never foam and steam in my room above the shop as it did so gloriously right there?

The gardeners had filed out and around us, their route marked by bobbing globes of light from lanterns held discretely low, to conceal them from view of the distant town.

It was a short walk to the water. Surrounding this entire mound of an island, and the stream that forked around it, was Lousetown. It was well-hidden.

I knew I was right about the glimmer of light from a setting sun, because now it was completely dark.

Morris slung a lantern over the prow as he warned me again, No one in town knows of this place. They must think Lousetowners live on nothing but the sacks of rice that arrive by boat. They aren't allowed to shop at Parker's.

They are somewhat fortunate, then, I said.

He inclined his head and smiled as he rowed. From here, the green walls as well as the garden within had melted into the dark air, though I could still see the glowing image of my sink.

And what about you? I asked him.

Sometimes I'm one of them, sometimes not. It keeps me on my toes, trying to determine where and when I'm welcome.

I told Morris I'd tie up the boat while he carried the vegetables in. I stood on the wharf and turned in circles. I had hoped to be able to spot *The Times* from here, but it was too dark. I could see nothing except the dim lights from *The Lonesome Café*.

In the five minutes I was away Morris had gathered a crowd. I returned to find him sitting with his back against the counter, thumbs under his suspenders, talking thickly. The diva had departed with one of the men, leaving me the only woman.

I was in Saskatchewan, Morris was telling the gathering, sipping whisky in the kitchen of the local bordello. Madame Zed, she called herself, short for Zelda. An old-timer for that business, but a magnificent head of dark hair on the woman. As seasoned as her newest was not, but they both spoke the same lingo.

We have a new girl, she says to me, and she calls out, Get your can in here and meet our favourite guest!

The girl makes her appearance. A pretty thing with a head of blonde curls. As we say in Montreal, she has *un grand balcon*, gentlemen, *un grand balcon*.

And he held his hands out as though he were holding up an armload of firewood.

Yes, eh? *Oui?* I can see that she'll be popular with the customers. Madame Zed turns to me. Cold-Ass Marie, she says, meet Two-Gun Cohen.

Well, I tip my hat and she curtsies and then Madame Zed says, Cold-Ass, get this gentleman another shot. Which she does, and when she pours my drink I ask her, Why do they call you Cold-Ass?

Feel, she says.

The men guffawed and then Morris saw me and jackknifed to his feet.

There you are, we were just talking about mining claims. Here now, have a seat, my dear.

Wolf was still at the stove, tea towel at his waist, dishing up dinner.

Three fingers, Morris asked him, raising his mug. And for my lady friend as well.

They were the same mugs that had held our tea.

Wolf took up a bottle and slammed it down. Help yourself, he said. But don't forget. I know exactly how much is in it.

Morris dipped his head in acknowledgment. Every customer I could see had a metal mug, perhaps because glass was breakable. Certainly they were not an attempt to disguise illicit contents. The shelf with its glittering bottles made that plain enough.

Two fingers, I told him.

Over a platter of hoisin bird with crisp greens, and mugs of whisky, I asked him, You just made that up, didn't you? About being called Two-Gun Cohen.

Made it up? I'm wounded. I'm certain I told you when we first met.

You referred to yourself as a two-gun something. You didn't introduce yourself by that name. It's the first I've heard of it.

Like a Chinese, I have many names. Here, let me pour you another. In my previous life I was Morris from Montreal. I loved that city. The red brick and the cafés and the Saint Lawrence. It was almost like London and the Thames. But one big difference. In Montreal, you don't have to be an Englishman. Some would even say it's preferable if you aren't. In London, it seemed to me, no matter where I walked, a hollow sound followed me, like a low, howling wind.

He puffed up his cheeks and said, Joo-oo-oo.

Outrageous, I said.

We clinked mugs.

I don't hear it so much anymore, not unless I try to lunch in the clubs, or step onto a golf course. Well, who in blazes wants to golf anyway? What woman would want me, working up a sweat like that in those ugly checkered pantaloons? Jesus Christ I haven't dressed like that since I was twelve. And checkers. I'd look like a table cloth. You go ahead and laugh, Lila. I would, too. God almighty. No, you'd better not be Jewish, not on a golf course.

More? he asked.

I held up my metal mug.

See, in Montreal, he explained, I was like everyone else. I wasn't Morris the Jew. I was Morris from Montreal, *Maurice de Montréal.*

The drink was making him even more talkative than usual, and me, less so.

I was in the dry goods business for a while, he continued. That's where I developed a passion for suits. The cut of the fabric, the weave that determines the drape of a cloth. The suit makes the man, I believe that. Makes the woman, too. Take your camouflage. Your preferred look and colour—

I wear more than this.

Indeed you do. But of the same hue. The outfit you wore the other day. Charcoal.

Black, I corrected.

Though the town would have coated it in dust, lightening it. He had me there.

And the very first time I saw you, he said.

My lavender-grey travel suit.

You see? Lavender-*grey.*

Almost a light plum, I said, forcing myself to speak in order to slow him down.

No, plum is a mix of red and blue, darkened with black. It has little of the white needed to grey up the black. Plum is more like burgundy. Which is redder. Wine, redder still. I made fabric and colour my business. Now, wine or puce, the difference is a matter of personal preference.

The apple nudged against my thigh, reminding me of its redness, and of my printer.

Does Vincent ever come here? I asked.

Sometimes he works here.

As well as the garden?

That's his recipe, he said, pointing at our platter with his chopsticks. I told you he could cook. How else do you think a Cowichan like Wolf got to cooking hoisin crow? He's industrious, our dear Vincent. Always looking for ways to make money. He'd make a good Jew.

And Morris laughed at his own joke.

Their paper used to have some incomprehensible Chinese name until he came along. The Bing Bang Boom or some damn thing. He said *The Chinese Times* would be both English and Chinese at the same time, and sell more copies because of it. He was right.

In a moment of self-pity—I blame the whisky—I told him about my run-in with the deputy with the greasy hair.

He calls the Chinese fish. He says they smell like fish.

I've never heard such rubbish.

Someone left a dead fish by my back door, and then my front door, too. I think it's that filthy deputy. It's a message to me. He doesn't like it that I include Chinese concerns in my news.

Such as the leader coming here, he said. And because you hired Vincent.

I nodded, his understanding forcing me to consider again how much of it I had brought on myself with that one little news announcement. Even so, I had thought that this man, famous for throwing another out the door for trying to rob a Chinese, might muster up a few more words of sympathy, especially for someone like me who was being tormented for similar alliances. But he offered nothing more.

It was hard to focus on what Morris said after that. It seemed he had returned to our previous topic, but each time the door opened I expected to see Vincent.

I know my colours, Morris was saying, just as I know my fabrics. I would have stayed there, I would have. But –

Stayed where? I asked.

My girl, I don't believe you've heard a word I've said. I must be tiring you.

Not at all, I lied. It's the drink.

My head was swimming, my thoughts fuzzy, so that much was true.

He raised the bottle. Another?

I shook my head.

Now where was I? It was Montreal, he continued. One day I was looking at a bolt of white linen and I said, I want to get me a few suits of this. I want to see the tropics.

He stopped to drain his mug.

I doubted he had more than two white suits but in this town even ten wouldn't be enough. This was the first meal I'd eaten that hadn't come out of a can, and after a while I didn't mind how much he talked, I was enjoying myself. I alternated between fork and chopsticks, the latter to simply slow me down. The sticks slid through my fingers, allowing half of each mouthful to drop back onto my plate. I moved my grip further down, pinching the sticks near their tips.

Why not black for the road? I asked.

He leaned forward, took my left hand in his as though he had something to confess. I pulled it free.

I'm getting to that, he said. But my, oh my, you have an appetite, one to match my own. I might just have to marry you, Lila Sinclair.

I put utensils and mug beside my plate and sat back.

He sat back in his chair, too, and roared. My dear, don't you worry! I'd have to rob banks to feed the two of us. Another drink? Still no? Had enough? Well, to get to the tropics I had to travel west. Westward ho. I felt like a cowboy. That was my turning point, he said. I could be a tailor. Or I could be me. And so, I got me some boots.

He stuck his foot out and I noticed for the first time a pair of well-tooled, leather cowboy boots.

And I got myself a hat, he said. A pair of Levi's, Jewish name, Lee-vi, a branch of our family from Chicago pronounced it Lee-vee, but they weren't in the dungaree business. What was I saying? Boots? Shirts, that was it. Then I set out, sending the white suits ahead in a trunk.

You went by horse?

I recalled the black beast that arrived kicking and squealing. Why had I forgotten it? And something else—but Morris had roared ahead with his story and I scrambled to catch up.

By train. It was in Manitoba that I bought my belt and holster and my guns. I bought myself a dark grey suit, too, for sitting in the dining car. But when I was out on the land, it was the dungarees I wore. A little bandana here.

He touched his neck where a white collar, unbuttoned, revealed a roll of flesh.

I bought a hat, too. Not just any city hat, but a real cowboy hat. Turns out I love being out on the land. But I love the cities even more. Not so lonely. I was gambling in Moose Jaw when I lost my shirt.

He laughed, looking around him to see who else was listening.

And my denims and my hat, he added, his voice louder. Almost lost my boots, too, but I won them back.

My eyes shot to the side, away from the vision of him in nothing but his underwear and boots.

That was in my friend Al's place, in Moose Jaw. A bigger shyster than me. Smart man, he tunnelled under the border so he could run booze across. But he wasn't smart enough to win my boots. I was going to have to shoot my way out, but he acquiesced, the fucker. 'Scuse my anglais.

Acquiesced. There are some words that beg to be recorded. They are beautiful, full or round or long, their sounds shaping their meaning, this one, a stream fizzing over rocks.

I gave my head a shake. I was drunk. And what about your grey suit? I asked. It would be ideal, here.

His face twitched and he said, Well that's a detail I'll have to expand upon later.

I drew circles in the sauce with the tip of a chopstick, considering. This isn't at all the story that Vincent told me.

Morris from Montreal, I remarked.

Maurice de Montréal, he growled.

As well as Two-Gun.

Another flicker of memory, then. The horse again.

But once more he seized the conversation and in a lowered voice, leaning forward, said, I can't show you here, but. Outside. He stood, then, and after much jerking and twisting of his head to indicate that I should stand as well, he said, in a loud voice, A fine meal, *mon ami*. We are off now for our evening constitutional.

I whispered to Morris that we should pay, but he said it was taken care of.

I was reminded then that he had not yet come up with the money to seal our partnership, or to pay the remainder owing for his advertisement in my paper. Another time. I didn't trust my tongue to pronounce the many and complicated syllables required for such a query.

We left the cantina and Lousetown behind us, walking the path that I had cycled the day of my accident, through the tall grass and around the other side of Black Mountain. Ahead, a black tree branch clawing its way out of a lead sky, the moon, burning a silver rim through shreds of black cloud, a barely perceptible outline of itself.

I took Morris' arm, which he purposely misunderstood.

My darling, he began.

Wild pigs, I explained. We could be in danger.

He let go of my arm and turned to me. Clutching the hem of his jacket on both sides, as though he were about to curtsy, he lifted it to reveal a leather belt and two pistols, their pearl handles glowing whitely above the holsters. I should have noticed the pair sooner, but I could forgive myself, given that they were hidden beneath a jacket the size of Saskatchewan.

You got them back.

—yes.

Damnit, I'd fed him the answer, again. Quickly, I asked, How?

But he ignored my question and said, They call me Two-Gun because of these.

He grabbed the handles and drew: one, two.

Are those loaded? You'll need them if we go much further. The pigs, remember.

He had frightened my tongue into sobriety.

We're stopping right here, he said.

A row of bottles had been set up earlier and winked at me from a ledge of stone. Behind them, shattered glass. Maybe someone else had been practising, because he fired, and missed.

I folded my arms. Shit almighty, he couldn't hit a pig if it was sitting in front of him.

The darkness, he offered. Hard to see straight let alone shoot straight.

Besides, you can't go off firing guns at night. It isn't safe.

In truth I was worried he'd use up all the bullets, and maybe awaken the pigs. And then what?

Perhaps you're right, he said. I'll wait until daylight. He waved one pistol carelessly above his head, indicating the sky.

Stop that.

He grinned and slid both pistols into their holsters.

Some lady friends, he elaborated, were calling me Two-Gun when I had just the one gun.

I had to press my lips into a tight line to stop from laughing. However, it was good to have company, even his.

At last I said to him, You could have simply shown me that get-up back there.

A cantina calls for a different approach. Any of them back there get a glimpse of these matching pistols and they'd be challenging me.

The opera crew? Marcel?

But Morris wasn't listening. He said, I save these for important matters. I can be doubly effective as a bodyguard.

For who? I asked.

Our leader. He's coming here, don't forget.

I haven't. You said you'd introduce me, remember?

I've been hearing about him since Moose Jaw.

So you said. That's why we came up with that deal, correct? Your thirty per cent share of the *Bullet* in exchange for an introduction.

Morris hadn't paid it yet, so I left out the fact that the thirty per cent was to give me money I badly needed for operating costs. Instead, I'd had to go to the bank. And how long until those funds ran out?

I haven't forgotten, he said. You will be impressed. He has a presence that a good leader should have, he is all things to all people. He's not unlike me. Yes, you laugh my dear, but he is as fond of the gentle sex as I am. Married twice. He is a great man, but flesh and blood like the rest of us. Not much of a drinker and I am hoping he is not a total abstainer, or he and I will never get along. But with a leader like him we can take our rightful place in this world. I know what you're thinking. I'm not one of them. Not really. But you are wrong. I am. He will change the lives of people in China and abroad, people that the English look down upon. I have arranged to set up an appointment with him as soon as he arrives.

And with me, as well.

What? Oh, yes. You'll be the first one I tell him about. I will make the proper introductions and, rest assured, he will be delighted to meet you, and he will want my shooting expertise as well.

Not as easy as it looks, he added. And he extended a pistol. Why wait until tomorrow?

Every time I'm ready to discount the man as a fool he does something wise. I'm not the only woman around who'd want to try, but he is one of the few men I know who would indulge me. Well, why not? I needed to know if I could hit pork hide with one of these.

It was heavier than I expected. I needed two hands to hold the pistol upright. He stood behind me, arms circling my elbows, ready to help, as I squeezed the trigger.

A bottle exploded. I lowered the gun and smiled, imagining the surprise on his face. But in his enthusiasm Cohen had allowed a hand to wander from my elbow to my ribs, thumb just below a breast in danger of being measured for a handful. I might have been poorly loved in my twenty-nine years, but this Two-Gun was no remedy.

I whirled around and pointed the pistol right at him.

His hands flew upward and roosted in his vest pockets. You're a good shot, he said.

I've used a rifle. We shot game back home.

I should have guessed that about a woman like you.

He was smiling at me as though I was the most beautiful creature in the world and not someone aiming a gun barrel between his eyes.

I lowered it then, thinking of that blasted opera. I was perfectly fine going by myself and sitting with Meena and her beau. But then I considered the advantage I had right now. I needed someone familiar with the hosts—mining interests, exploration—and here he was. Well, Jewish, which was a concern, among many others. Unwelcomed in such gatherings as a single woman normally was, but wasn't this night the exception? And wouldn't that make a statement, two souls normally banned, showing up together, united? We were going to be partners, after all.

He'd be the perfect guest. As long as he didn't get any ideas. I'd have to put him straight on that immediately.

I described the situation.

Pure business, I explained.

I'd be honoured, he said, and smiled with his eyes.

That's exactly what I mean, I said. Stop that.

A regular firecracker, he said.

THE SMALL MAN

I ate the apple for breakfast. It was a small, delicate fruit, white-fleshed with veins of pink, and it was all I could manage. My head pounded, but that was my penalty from indulging in too much whisky. By mid-morning I had consumed two pots of coffee, and that helped somewhat. That was yesterday. I spent all of the day recording key events in this notebook, and writing and setting copy. I didn't mind the quiet Sunday after such a busy night.

It was tempting to save the best news for this first edition, but it would be old news by then. So I decided to run this item now, in the fourth and final newssheet:

The coal leavings of
South Africa:
One traveller's story

And then I added an item I had almost forgotten until Morris repeated it last night:

Coal likes company
—what lies beneath

Finally, a slender item:

Black
moths
signal
storms

This was the last of the newssheets, bringing me closer to my ultimate goal, the first edition. Five days. My hand trembled just a little as I took up the pencil and struck a crooked line through today's date:

Monday, September 25. I would miss these single sheets. I had done with them what I set out to do from the start, dispense news quickly, like a bullet straight into the minds of the readers. That one newsletter was an unfortunate blunder. Maybe that was to be expected of first attempts.

Did Vincent feel the same fondness for these newssheets? I checked his face: furrowed brow, lowered eyes.

If I asked, though, I might resurrect the topic of my botched news announcement, or of the deputy's crude insinuations. I was glad enough that this time he would stay to run off the copies, instead of leaving me to finish them alone, glad enough that he had returned at all after that incident, though working without comment, as though the only unusual event the other night had been the explosion. It was day, now. No danger of working into the night. He was all business, checking the test run for high and low spots on the page, adjusting the metal bits to lower or raise these spots that would, otherwise, gather too much ink, or none at all.

Meena had placed a long, slender advertisement in the newssheet. We used another engraving that Vincent borrowed from *The Times:* a tall woman in a fancy dress and hat. The setting could be Shanghai or Paris, and with her face turned away, she could be anyone, Meena herself, beneath the wide brim. The opera company placed another ad for a Saturday matinee for those unable to attend the Friday evening performance. Again, Ben brought over their own plates. We used the same type and plate for the airship tour to run another ad.

We were right on schedule for the upcoming first edition. News items that were not pressing, such as an exclusive interview with Mr. Benjamin Gill, would go on the inside pages. We had already composed those and, once these newssheets were done, would start to prepare the big press to run them. That was why Vincent had stayed, of course, for the preparatory work for the first edition, for the money. Strange, to have seen and done so much together, and yet to now behave like unfamiliars, polite to the point of rudeness.

I had worked hard to line up more ads, including one from the hotel laundry offering a special for cleaning gowns, to make sure I could pay Vincent's wages. In time, I hoped to be able to stop borrowing on the business and run it entirely from the earnings from ads. So far, my partnership with Morris had been in name, only.

We were finishing up from the run and had said very little to each other. If I was going to get a conversation going I had better say something soon. I had thought out a number of possible ways to begin, and knew that whichever I chose, what I was about to attempt was provocative. Well, why not. So it should be, given what has been said about us.

The food at Wolf's cantina, I began, is far better than the hotel's.

The remark came out of nowhere, and I scrambled to connect it to something relevant to our task. Though I suppose, I said, that if either of them places ads in the paper, it will be the hotel.

Wolf's. When were you there?

Saturday evening. Morris took me there.

He began to scrub particularly hard at the borrowed engraving, complaining about old ink left to dry by some second-rate printer.

Then slowly, as though he were weighing each word, he asked, Busy that night?

I seized the moment. *The Lonesome* was hopping, I said. A number of the opera crew were there. Did you know that Morris calls himself Two-Gun? No? And he told me that you print *The Bugle*.

Vincent lifted his head.

My competition, I added.

He wiped his hands on his thighs, took off his cap and adjusted the brim, then jammed it back on again.

Others were there, as well, at the café. Miners, I think. Chinese miners. And Marcel. Morris took me outside for a little tour around the place. Oh, I added, smiling, just a minute.

I went to my front desk and brought back the red vase that I'd carried downstairs earlier, for just such an opportunity.

Look what Morris gave me, I said.

I'd filled it with water to just below the crack, and it held the cutting from one of the rose bushes, just beginning to open its pale petals.

Vincent had stopped scrubbing and now looked directly at me, then at the vase.

Then you saw it, he said, where they get their food?

The garden, I said, Yes. But with strict orders not to put anything in the paper.

He smiled tightly, and I didn't need to wonder what he was thinking. I wouldn't make that mistake again.

You told me Lousetown got some sun, I said, but I didn't know there was enough for growing vegetables. And roses.

I waited for him to tell me that they were his, and why. He went back to scrubbing.

Morris gave me an apple, too, and it was delicious.

Though now I wished I hadn't eaten it, had brought it out instead with the rose, as a reminder of that first apple I had wanted. He'd been holding out on me.

I had no inkling, I said, all those people out there, weeding and picking.

He looked up, though at a point somewhere beyond me.

When the moon's out, we all meet on the shop roof. Full moon, crescent moon. Whatever shape the moon is in, if we can see it, it's time to celebrate.

It was the most he had spoken to me all day.

A party? I asked. With the gardeners?

And everyone from Wolf's.

When?

Last Saturday, for one.

I thought you weren't there. I didn't see you.

I was here first, stripping ink from the press.

The moths, I said, remembering.

It took me most of the evening. Then I headed back.

Again, I saw the silver outline of the moon burning behind the clouds as Morris and I left Wolf's *Lonesome Café*. While I was there, he was here. While I headed home everyone else gathered for a party. Maybe even those girls with their whorehouse-stinking flowers. I pivoted and then forced myself to turn back and then pivoted away again. Shit. Embarrassed. Hurt. I wanted to know why I'd been left out, but I refused to ask. Instead I tried to be flippant.

News to me, I said.

Because you live over here.

I waited for that welcoming sign, the open flower of a dish pointing toward a future. But it remained closed. He could have said it, I'll let you know next time.

With this newssheet, all of Lousetown would soon know I could be trusted with the secret of the garden. All the printers including Vincent already knew I hadn't published anything about their rooftop dish. So why not tell me about the parties? Was I, once again, being punished for that foolish announcement? For his rude and cruel treatment by that wretched deputy? I wouldn't ask. I pictured me night after night alone upstairs, staring out the windows and sitting at a table set for one. Feeling sorry for myself, then, and now, seeking out Parker as a source of company. Occasionally, Morris. Two-Gun, as he called himself, now. I supposed he was there as well, went back after seeing me home. Shit. I would not cry over this.

It happens all of a sudden, he continued. The winds shift, the moon climbs higher. And bang, there it is.

When he said the word *bang* he slammed a hand onto the counter and I jumped, my hand leaping at my side, my nerves were that stretched.

I waited for him to say more. Come by more often and you'll hear it, you'll see it.

Instead, he said, Your rose. It's turning blue.

True enough, the bud had unfurled, the delicate veins of each petal ink-stained from drawing at the cloudy tap water. I recalled the abandoned house and the blue rose growing in the tall grass. Not so rare, after all.

By late afternoon the prep work was done, Vincent had left and the newssheet copies were handed out. I was walking back up Zero, admiring the opera tents that glowed like lampshades. I couldn't write about the garden but I still had the performance. In this place so dependent on arrivals, it made a good lead story. The whole town was excited. It wasn't so much newsbreaking as a break from the usual. We all need that from time to time.

Morris stepped onto the street, then, glowing almost as brightly as the tents. I hurried ahead to confront him. About the party. About the fact that he was standing on the corner near the bank, hands in pockets, forcing the sides of his white jacket behind his arms like coattails, exhibiting his pistols for the whole world to see, and after telling me it wasn't prudent to show them.

He seemed lost in thought, and when he saw me he leapt out of his reverie like this time I was the one who'd popped out of a black hole.

My dear! Let me buy you a drink, he said, though I wasn't the one who needed calming.

I could have raised my point then about his contradictory behaviour with his guns, but the thought of his long-winded explanation suddenly exhausted me. And it was seldom anyone invited me out for a drink. Indeed, he was the only one who ever had, and I didn't want to be alone after hearing about those parties.

This would be an opportunity for me to finally see *The Saloon*, but he said he wanted something fancier for me.

We stopped for my mail first, then settled at a table amongst the familiar ferns and tusks.

Your strongest brew! Morris ordered. And he winked.

You'll have to drink from a teacup, I warned.

I'd drink out of an old boot if I had to.

It really was quite pleasant in *The Bombay Room*, where I could pretend I was in a foreign country, especially now that I had the desperado Two-Gun with me, and needn't argue with Ed for a drink. I was being mean, but at least I kept the comment to myself.

I dropped the mail onto the table and opened my newspaper bag to make room for it all.

What's that? He asked. *The Edmonton Journal?*

Yes, I've been ordering different newspapers from all over, to see what they look like. But they keep disappearing. I had this one sent again by post to make sure I got it.

May I? And he snatched it up.

I suppose you'd like to brush up on the news business, too, I said. I just handed out our last newssheet. Did you see it?

They were remarks made hopefully, as a way of bringing up our partnership, but his nose was in *The Edmonton Journal*.

You can have it when I'm done, I said. You can keep it then.

No need. I have a brother living there. I like to keep up. But there's not much here. Ah, he said, fumbling around in his jacket pocket as his eyes darted about the room. Then he handed back the newspaper.

What news were you looking for?

Immediately I regretted my question, and braced for the long answer. There was an awkward break in our conversation then. He rolled his eyes upward as though the tin ceiling could provide the answer, then to each side, as though it were lurking in the potted palms and ferns.

At last, he said, Anything that might affect his tailoring business. That's what you were considering, once.

Yes. He seeks my counsel from time to time. Fabrics. Threads. Colour—

We had our teacups now and he finished his in two gulps, raised a finger to order another.

Look inside, he advised.

I pulled my teacup closer, but he tilted his head toward the *Journal*.

For what? I opened it, and stopped asking. Inside *The Edmonton Journal* was a gaping envelope, thick with bills.

I slapped it closed as Ed leaned across the table to take the cup and saucer to the bar.

I waited until he returned it, and we were alone again. Morris! I whispered. How much is in here?

Hundreds, he said. I know, I know. Hundreds more owing, but—

No, this is, well, this is good. Quite honestly it's more than I was expecting at once, more than I ever thought I'd see. We struck that deal some time ago.

Three weeks ago. Well, now you can tell the whole world. Here's Two-Gun Cohen, my partner. Two-Gun Cohen, publisher. Just don't wrinkle up that freckled nose of yours when you say it.

It's not freckled, I said. Two-Gun, I added. Partner.

Two-Gun Cohen, Esq.

His words fought for my full attention. The things I could buy with that money! I could pay off much of the loan. Pay for supplies. Most importantly, pay Vincent. That would improve things between us.

While I considered, his focus had drifted toward the window.

This whole place, he said, looks like a battlefield.

You enlisted?

Indeed. I was a sergeant in the Canadian Railway Troops.

My brothers were with the expeditionary forces. All four of them. That made me think of Will, and I shifted my focus.

But, earlier you claimed—insisted—that this place was no different than Manhattan or London. Why a battlefield, now?

I hadn't yet seen the other side, he explained.

Where we were shooting, I said, nodding. But this side as well, the place where you surprised me by popping out of that hole. The trees nothing but black limbs. Odd, isn't it, an orchard on either side of the mountain?

Then he said the most extraordinary thing.

It looks to me that those are coal leavings, dug out of the mine and dumped into the orchard. That's the black mountain, he explained. It covers everything in the middle and spoils much of what remained, creating two orchards at the same time that it killed them both.

I should have guessed that. It all made sense. More of a hill than a mountain, and filthy, but I assumed the town exaggerated its size to inflate its own sense of self, and that the filthy surface was nothing more than the coal dust that covered everything else, here.

We finished our drinks.

I was glad, now, that I had asked him to accompany me to the opera.

He knew about mines, true. But he had also seen action, as had my dear brothers, and his money was pleasantly heavy in my bag.

The bank was about to close when I arrived, but my bag of money convinced them to stay open a few minutes longer. I kept a few bills for myself, as well as some for Vincent's wages. On my way back to the shop, both load and spirits lightened by the deposit, my eyes were drawn once more to the glowing opera tents, and I stopped in.

You are just in time for an impromptu rehearsal, Ben said. Have a seat.

And he shoved over to give me room on the clothes trunk.

The tent flaps had been pinned back to form a stage. We were seated just outside the tent, next to a fire that crackled. Again, a memory of smoke and heat and flame, though in this setting even the strike of a match would have ignited the sulfuric vision of that day in my schoolhouse back home. The players before me, half-nude as they struggled in and of costume, rounded out the recollection, and that drink, still warm in my guts, became a perfect lubricant for musing: working late, attempting to finish some ponderous marking, surprised at the heavy heat. A snapping sound that at first I did not connect to flames, until I smelled smoke. I bolted out the back door to see that the schoolhouse steps had been set on fire and there, just beyond the flames, a group of men and women in a state of rapture, arms upraised, voices rising, naked. Freedomites. Large and lumpy, rail thin and sinewy, their flesh licked orange.

I don't know why they chose my schoolhouse. It wasn't on Doukhobor land, and usually they targeted their own: retribution for those who had drifted from tradition. Perhaps it was because I taught a couple of students whose families had left the community. Or maybe my schoolhouse was conveniently in their path. Briefly, I was spellbound, and then I raced back inside.

This was one protest that never made the newspaper, because no one else knew of it. The bucket of water intended to scrub the desks easily extinguished the flames. Next, at least half of the tin of paint meant for whitewashing the walls went onto the steps, wet as they were. I worked furiously, determined to cover up their actions. For John, for what he had once meant to me, for what my father would have said. This was the very thing people in town complained about: Those Dukes! Yet I had never witnessed anything so strangely beautiful, a passion that transcended our sense of decorum and decency. They had a purpose, a conviction, and they didn't care what we thought. They wanted us to stop forcing our style of education upon their children, whose futures required knowledge of farming methods, not literature. And there I'd been, daydreaming about hot summers and time off at last from a tiresome year of teaching, a year that had lacked all sense of passion.

I handed in my notice the next day.

The players before me were clothed, now. I had lost track of what was going on.

What do you think? Ben asked, turning on the trunk to look at me.

Caught off-guard, I improvised.

Such passion, I said. Beautiful.

With great satisfaction he slapped me on the knee with one of my own newssheets.

The shop was silent the next morning when I came downstairs, the press, still. I passed the sink quickly, not bothering with the calendar. I was well aware it was the 26th and that we had three days to complete work on the first edition before we printed up all the pages. Vincent should be here.

I called out his name and indeed found him, straightening his collar in the metal mirror. I must have hurried right past him on my way to the press.

Why are you dressed up? I asked. Aren't we going to run the inside pages?

We. I meant him.

No time, now, Vincent said. He's here.

I swivelled around. Who? Morris?

No, he said. There was an edge to his voice, but he explained, Our leader. Everyone's going to see him, to hear his speech.

The awkwardness of the last few days vanished as I contemplated this great event.

Take me with you!

He shook his head. He's here to ask for support. Last month he had to escape to Shanghai, again. From the warlords.

I grabbed his arm. I remembered him speaking of warlords.

I should go, too, I said, don't you see? I've read his book. Now I want to hear him with my own ears.

His gaze locked onto my hand on his arm, and I pulled it back.

I'll only print what you agree to have printed. I'll check with you this time.

Uncle would never have consented to that, but I was determined to see this famous man under whatever conditions Vincent required. It meant him taking me to Lousetown, but no one there would object to seeing us together.

I waited for him to answer. I knew that Two-Gun would eventually introduce me to the leader. I had his money now. So this would not change our deal. All I wanted today was a glimpse, an opportunity to hear the man, to further familiarize myself with his beliefs and with his followers. If I listened now, I could ask informed questions, later. I could dig deeper.

I said some of this in a rush, and then I added, I saw someone, a dark figure in a long coat.

Again, I hoped this would improve my chances of going.

Where? he asked.

One of the alleys just off Zero. A couple of times, actually.

I expected him to refuse me, but as I'd hoped, my luck had risen with this information.

You can't go like that.

If he had let me slip from his grasp before, he was reaching out again, and I, left dangling all this time, was scrambling up once more, grabbing hold with all my might as I rushed to the back of the room near the sink to step out of my coveralls. This time it was not a disaster that was bringing us together but a political event, an extraordinary one, and I was ready for it.

With a quick snap I straightened the coveralls and hung them on a hook. The cotton summer dress I had worn underneath was plain—and yes, blue flowers over a background of blue polka dots, which gave it a grayish look, but with a white collar, which I would point out to Morris if he were here—still, it was a good enough dress for a meeting. I stepped out, ready to leave.

Vincent said, I have another idea.

I reached up and touched where he looked, at the silver pin I used to hold my wild hair in place, my one feminine indulgence in the work shop. I could have pulled it out, but then my brown frizz would have come tumbling down and I'd look even more the part of what, I realized now, must have concerned him most: a woman, and a white one.

We hurried along the narrow streets between the shacks. This was a different route from any I'd taken before. The paths even narrower. More twisted. Dark as night, reek of urine, damp and cold in the deepest shadow of the crowded buildings. He slid a bolt and a door opened.

There were many reasons why a woman shouldn't be here. A man's room, an employee at that, and, as much as this woman might tell herself it didn't matter, a Chinese. And yet, this was Lousetown. Even the taxi drivers wouldn't come here. There would be no one from town to point a finger or ask, no one to stop me from stepping inside.

The space was so tiny I was ashamed of all my complaints about the bachelor room above the press, the tub sitting in the middle of the room, the missing sink. Here, there was just a narrow bed, a wooden pole suspended above the head of the bed, hung with shirts, trousers, jackets. A tiny window, cut in half by a curtained wall, let in a blade of grey light. On the other side of the curtain was an identical space, he said, on the other side of it, another, and then another. For now, unoccupied. The residents must be on their way to the meeting.

He pulled items from the pole, handed them to me, then stepped behind the curtain.

I pulled my dress over my head, rolled it into a ball and left it on the bed. The trousers were too tight in the hips, too large in the waist. But the jacket was long and hid the ill fit, while its looseness over the baggy shirt helped to flatten my chest. In his old clothes, I was wrapped in the odour that was him. Soap. Tobacco. A faint trace of solvent. And—? His skin. I breathed in deeply, then looked down at my footwear, a simple pair of heels that matched the dress. I had slipped into them before we left, a moment of vanity.

Shoes? I whispered.

He emerged, smiling slowly at my appearance. A pair of beaten boots from under his bed matched my look. They were too large, and he gave me an extra pair of thick socks.

Now your hair, he said, and put an old black hat over it.

We continued to talk in whispers, should anyone return.

It was my pop's, he said. For special occasions, Chinese ones.

And he grinned.

In the mirror, a bowler hat with a false queue dangling from the back, and my own hair that glowed beneath the brim.

Let's shave it.

His fingers grazed my to show me.

I shook my head.

Not much, he promised. Not like mine. A roll at the back, he said, like the French.

His fingers traced through the air a route along my jaw line to the nape of my neck.

I liked that. I pictured a French roll, the sides low enough to hide the shaved temples. And I felt his fingertips along my jaw, then pulling my hair into a knot, even though he was rummaging in a drawer, then sharpening a long razor on a strop nailed to the corner of the bureau. I watched, intent on the details that must be part of his daily routine, as though I were there with him first thing in the morning. A mug with cake of soap still damp from his shave, the same brush he must have used, whipping the soap to a foam.

He told me, Outside, keep your face down. This might help.

He pressed his thumbs against my cheeks, rubbed them with the coal dust that collects on every surface in this town, readily available for my unusual make-up.

I sat on the edge of the bed and then he came around and sat behind me, unpinning my hair, running his comb through the strands, leaving the scent of his hair tonic. He held the mug with one hand, brush in the other, and dabbed along my temples.

Hold still, he said.

I didn't know why he agreed to do this. I didn't care why. The long razor scratched and strands fell into my lap. He breathed evenly, his hands steady. I closed my eyes and wished I could stay here, never mind the famous man and his big speech. Right here, this was the story.

We darted through cramped alleys and skirted along fences until we reached a clearing already filled with men, all Chinese. Head bent, I followed Vincent to the very back where I could watch and not be seen.

An old motorcycle pulled into the clearing, towing a wagon in which a man stood, waving to the crowd. I elbowed Vincent. This wasn't so different from the new motorcycles and sidecars on the other side of town, only this driver wore no helmet or goggles and was Chinese. So was the man in the wagon. An *ahhhh* rippled across the crowd as the vehicle came to a stop and the elegant man in black suit and hat stepped down, his polished shoes gleaming in the dust.

From under the worn brim of the old man's hat I scanned the crowd, the stage, looking for Two-Gun. Where was this friend of the Chinese, now? But all I saw was the famous man—spare, trimmed moustache, languid, lidded eyes, modern haircut—making his way to a quickly erected stage of boards and crates. Two aides took an elbow each and helped him up the steps.

In his suit and hat and shiny shoes he looked like an Englishman. He was as pale as one. His first line of greeting was in English and I smiled as though he had aimed it at me, My thanks to all of you for coming out today.

Then he began speaking in Chinese.

Vincent's gaze shot around the gathering.

What's wrong? I asked, careful to lower my voice.

Not their dialect. I don't know, maybe they get it.

I whispered, Tell me.

He leaned in close. You remember this one, he said. The British treat nations as the silkworm farmer treats his worms; as long as they produce silk, he cares for them; when they stop, he sets them on fire, he feeds them to the fish.

It caught my breath to hear them said aloud, the very words I had read in that book.

At the sound of Vincent's English, though, a man in front of us turned around and stared.

Vincent said something in Chinese, and the man turned back, again. I hadn't heard him speak anything but English or French since that first time I glimpsed him in the fog with another man, digging through the cargo pile. It was unsettling, as though standing beside me was someone I had never met before. But he returned to English.

I had a notebook up one sleeve, pencil cupped inside the other. I brought my sleeves together and wrote without looking. My blind scrawl covered the whole page. I thumbed the sheet over for the next quotes.

A railroad, Vincent whispered, his words buzzing about my ears. That's what we need to make China modern, like North America. And an army to fight the warlords.

I already knew this from what Vincent had told me before, and from what I had read, but the men around us began grumbling.

Trains are old, one said in English. Air travel is modern.

Loud Mouth Sun! someone shouted.

No Gun Sun! another cried out. Where is this army?

All shouted in English. Sun was dressed like an Englishman, and their English was full of insults. No wonder the man in front had stared at us.

Another voice called out, Where are your weapons, eh? In answer, someone threw a stick. It sailed in the air and landed flat on the ground, short of the stage. It was followed by a hail of chopsticks, and laughter. So. They had come here prepared to heckle the leader.

Vincent shouldered his way forward. I grabbed his arm with a grubby hand, hissing, Vincent!

It's okay, he said. I can translate.

My grip tightened as my thoughts skittered. I had meant me. Alone, in this crowd When just a few minutes ago we sat together in his room...

Look, he said, and pried my fingers loose to free himself. I have to. Sorry.

My anger was so keen it tasted like metal shavings on my tongue, and then I realized I had bitten my lip until it bled.

In the sudden silence that fell with his appearance on stage, his queue swinging out as he turned to speak to the modern man, the crowd did not notice this small man in hat and false queue who slid along the wall, feeling for an escape. Others rushed forward, seeming to see only that the small man's departure made room for more.

Up on the stage, Vincent lifted his arms. He spoke a line after each line spoken by Sun, translating, his voice growing louder, more confident with each line, again like someone I had never met before, while the famous man smiled, nodding at his new friend. I stood with my back against the wall, no exit in sight, watching my printer's transformation.

That's when I heard the roar of motors, several of them. First there were no motorcycles in Lousetown and now they were coming straight at us. At once the gathering broke apart and men began running. I ran with them. Too late. The thin walls of wood and tin broke apart and fell, and the motorbikes burst into the clearing, fumes turning the grey air bluish, the bikes wheeling erratically, chasing us, their tires spraying an arc of dirt and rocks into our faces, deputies leaning from the sidecars, armed with clubs, swinging. Us, dodging and darting, in and out between the bikes and the deputies and each other. Them, black and shiny in the grey-blue light.

Vincent—I needed his help. But he was gone. So was his leader. A door at the back of the stage hung open. They had escaped, leaving me to fend for myself.

The smell of fuel was in my mouth and nose, along with damp wool and dirty skin, that same odour from back home of dead ducks about to be plucked, as I was shoved, arms jabbing my ribs, heels against my shins, a red burning sting as an elbow hit my nose, a shoulder clipped my ear.

My hat. I gripped the brim with both hands, the queue over my cheek, and twisted it until it hung down the back, again. My own fingertips raked my temples to pull up my hair.

But a deputy saw and cried out, White man! Over there!

Silver had taken the leader's place on the stage and for the moment the bark of a metal megaphone snagged the deputy's attention. I plunged back into the crowd.

Silver boomed into the speaking horn, This is an illegal assembly! Residents of Lousetown are forbidden from gathering in public places. This is a warning! All who disregard this law will be punished.

All the while the bikes circled, menacing. I took a large rock to the throat and it winded me. I fell back and then rolled over, crawling under the steps of the platform to avoid the stomping feet and spinning wheels. With the walls down now I could see, between the boards of the steps, a man standing on one of the hills, spectral in the gloom of fog and fumes and dust, the mine owner himself, clearly the owner Mr. Drummond in his dark, three-piece suit, surveying the raid and all it uncovered, as someone looking at new land from a ship. Silver had said he only showed up for special occasions. From this perch could he see the solar dish or the garden or me?

A man grabbed my shoulder and pulled me out, shouting, Move your ass, China Man!

It was that horrible deputy, his hair still dirty and hanging in strings. Did he never wash? He knocked my hat off when he pulled me out. I tugged my hair over my shaved temples.

What've we got here? he bellowed.

He recognized me at once, of course.

Silver had left the stage and now forced his way through the jostling crowd to join the deputy. I trusted in his fondness for me. I shook my hair free, let its brown strands fall redly against the jet black of the coat. I might as well have been shaking my tail feathers in a barnyard, hoping to attract a rooster. I should have been ashamed but I wasn't. I would do whatever was needed to be free of this deputy, and to keep my shaved temples hidden.

The deputy's face soured with disgust as he held up the hat with the false queue, and said, She even dresses like one of 'em.

I snatched the hat back from him.

I'm here to report on the speech, I told Silver. I had turned so that

I addressed him only.

Why the get-up? he asked.

Because they don't want me here any more than you do.

My voice shook with the truth of this statement. Where was Vincent now? Where was Two-Gun? All I had to protect me was my hair, and I would use it. Damn them all to hell, I would bloody-well use it. I tossed my hair, carefully, and let its copper light shimmer about my shoulders, fingers at my temples to check that they were covered.

His eyes followed the strands. Then he turned, in a hesitant jerk or two, to consult with the figure on the hill. I couldn't see any signal from the man, but when Silver turned back he said, Mr. Drummond wishes to see you.

Good, I said. I'd like to see him, too. You can take me there right now.

Deputy, Silver said.

I meant you, I said. I'll go with you.

You'll be fine, Silver said. And then he turned to the dirty deputy and repeated it, She'll be fine. You make sure of that.

And he left.

I was prodded from the clearing by the deputy's billy stick, much as Two-Gun had been that first time I glimpsed him, much as the miner and that girl had been. I wrapped the black coat about my ribs and hugged them, the brim of the hat dangling from my fingers, as I stumbled along in my big shoes.

At the pithead, just across from my own shop, we climbed metal steps into a shed of an office where I was seated against a corrugated wall.

Make yourself presentable, the deputy said.

I faltered.

Wash your face, he said, then pointed an elbow toward a door.

I had forgotten about my black make-up.

The door led to a water closet meant for just men. No mirror, a tap running cold water, a board with a hole in it. I washed my face and rubbed it dry with my sleeve. I combed my fingers through my hair, satisfied that it hung straight down over my temples, pulled the hairpin from my pocket and pushed it into place. Then I returned to my chair.

Don't bother sittin', the deputy said. He'll see you now.

He opened another door and this room was larger, with the same bare look except for an oriental rug beneath an oak desk, and next to it, a table set for two. Behind the table were windows looking out onto the blackness of the pithead and the yard, as well as my back porch.

The deputy indicated with a jerk of his filthy thumb that I should sit at the table. He stepped to the side and stood, arms crossed, in the corner. A back door swung open, from a sitting room or a bedroom, where the women from *The Saloon* had conducted their negotiations, I presumed. A man with a bald patch framed in grey hair entered the room.

Miss Sinclair, he said, flipping his suit tails behind him, and sat opposite me. I'm sure I need no introduction.

Mr. Drummond, I replied.

Dine with me while we talk.

I told him I wasn't hungry but he replied, Indulge me.

I watched his hands moving toward a silver bucket of ice beside the table. He pulled a bottle from it and poured wine into my glass.

You've been writing about my coal mine.

I have, I said. I've been wanting to interview you about it.

I'll be doing the interviewing, he said. Drink.

I obliged with a small sip. It was crisp and refreshing and I was thirsty, but I put the glass down right away.

Are you agitating for a union?

I'm reporting what I see and hear, I replied. There are few safety regulations. If miners are injured or in danger of drowning there is no rescue plan in place. And yes, no shop steward, either. I saw a young woman—

You, he interrupted, would have Lousetowners treated as equals, is that right?

—of course, I began.

The Chinese are a group you are especially fond of?

I stared to the side and the windows that looked out on my back porch and door, and thought of the comings and goings he might have seen from here. I turned back to answer yes, then thought better of it. The man was eyeing me with the same contempt the deputy had, my outfit and the bowler with braid that I had set on the table, too. My get-up, Silver had called it. I slid the hat onto my knee.

I have it on good authority, he said, that these Chinese are not to be trusted. They are rebels wanted in their own country for acts of anarchy. This man making the speeches. The government would like it if he never returned.

I lifted my chin and said, The warlords, you mean. He is the government.

The door opened and one of Drummond's staff appeared with a tray from which he produced two large silver soup spoons.

You are familiar with Chinese cuisine? Drummond asked.

Somewhat, I replied.

I had a dish made especially for you, he said. A delicacy I understand.

I nodded my thanks as the attendant left to fetch it.

Where's your printer? Drummond asked.

This time I made sure not to look at my back door.

I wish I knew, I replied.

He's a ring leader of some sort.

I simply laughed.

In my mind, Vincent was guilty of many things, but not of that.

I would check my sense of humour if I were you. There's something going on. If those Chinese get fired up by this emperor as you call him and do anything to jeopardize the operations of this mine—

He's not an emperor, I said. That's the whole point.

Drummond couldn't know how rude the crowd had been earlier. The Chinese weren't following the famous man anywhere.

Drummond ignored my interruption and continued. Your printer translates for him.

My heart leapt to hear that. He knew too much.

We saw it all, he said. Thank you for the warning: Revolution comes to Black Mountain.

My thoughts were rocking with opposing emotions. Regret, once again, for that stupid, thoughtless notice, anger, next, for being left to defend myself, and chagrin, to realize the full extent of that notice. I had caused the raid.

We were ready for it, he continued. There were far too many of them heading off from the mine in the same direction, today, chitter-chattering together. Then some rust-heap pulling a rice wagon. We got suspicious and followed. Any public assembling of Lousetowners is illegal. We break them up. And we found them all, together, plotting and speech-making.

What makes you think they were plotting? You don't know their language.

That's what I hear.

I assumed that was another dig at me and my article, but he was smiling mysteriously.

I said, You have spies, you mean.

I'm not about to tell the newspaper publisher if we do or if we don't.

Neither was I about to tell him that I knew there were Chinese who wanted Sun dead, and that I had seen mysterious figures about town.

Your printer, he repeated.

I repeated, I don't know where he is. He's free to come and go as he pleases.

A little too free if you ask me. Ah, he added, here it is.

Two bowls were placed on the table, the lids removed at once. I fought to stay composed, to keep my eyes from widening, my mouth from opening, my face from flaming. I took measured breaths.

It was fish head soup, with the severed head set just so, its eyes aimed at mine, its mangled mouth gaping, its skin blistered. Prepared just for me, to remind me of the fish on my doormat and the fish nailed to my door, of what all of these meant, this one in particular, that I had employed a Chinese, had followed one to a meeting attended by many more, had done so dressed in one's clothes, had written about their dead. The increasing violence of each fish's appearance, from simply dead, to nailed, to decapitated, was a message for me.

From beneath my lashes I could see the deputy moving. He stood in the corner behind Drummond's back, rounding his lips and opening his mouth like a fish, his hands in his pockets, jiggling. That again.

I raised my face to Drummond and said, As I told you, not hungry, thank you.

I knew my cheeks were on fire but I held his gaze. At last he scraped his chair back and called over his shoulder as he stood to leave, Deputy. Escort her home.

He looked directly at me next, said, Just remember, I can shut you down any time I like. I own this town.

Drummond closed the door behind him without looking back.

I told the deputy, I can make my own way back.

I was about to push my chair away from the table when his dirty-hair smell swamped me.

Nothing scares you, that right? Not even this?

Not the one nailed to my door, either.

I turned my head to stare him down.

He was standing beside my right shoulder, undoing his trousers, the stink of him up my nose. This time he got the reaction he was after. I made a sound that wasn't a word, a gargle of a scream matched by the table and chair legs scraping on the floor where my face landed next when I fell in my haste to leave. He roared with delight as I crawled out from under the table and ran to the door, checking over my shoulder to see if he was following me.

His meaty paw scooped up the fish head. Run all you like, he called. Dressed like a fucking fish. I'd rather hump this.

I wrenched the door open. I ran past Silver who stood, startled, as though about to enter the room, ran, across the office and down the stairs, though I knew from his words the deputy wouldn't be following, could see with my eyes that he wasn't, ran anyway, along the filthy creek, cursing Vincent with each step, his lousy loyalty to that leader, because yes of course he had to protect him, but did that have to mean abandoning me during the speech, during the raid, leaving me to this, this! I ran and stumbled, and hid, in the shed behind the newspaper shop, hid though there was really no need but hid until it grew dark and no one could see me from those windows, until I could creep up the stairs to my rooms, undetected, wash and strip myself free of the whole day, of Vincent's clothes, his comb, his scent. Him.

RIFLES FIRING AT ONCE

I found my dress at the foot of the stairs, neatly folded inside a wrapping of newsprint. *The Chinese Times*. He must have dropped it off, and then left. I kept telling myself he'd had no choice but to help his leader, yet still my face and neck flamed with indignation over yesterday's events. That horrible man and then before him, the raid, the speech. Sun. The same name as that great orb in the sky, the thing that never shines in this place.

When I scored through 27 on the calendar, I pressed so hard I tore the page.

All morning I had wondered what I would say to Vincent when he arrived, but it seemed he had wondered the same. He hadn't stayed. I left his jacket and trousers folded on a stool beside the press, his socks, boots and his father's hat on top. Then I scribbled a few words and tore the page from my notebook: *Careful. We must speak. L.* I might be upset but I wouldn't want to see him hurt. Drummond seemed far too interested in him—my printer. And my news coverage had led to the raid. I couldn't forget that.

I tucked the note under the hat.

I stepped out the door, prepared to seek out Silver and lodge a complaint against the deputy. Was I hurt? No. Did he touch me? No. And yet I was, he had. I left the place humiliated, crawling like a bug, robbed of all dignity, and with his ragged laughter in my ears.

I had no sooner turned the key in the lock and spun around, than I found myself staring at the spectacle of an outhouse propped over top of what was one of the town's many black holes. Nailed to the door was a newspaper clipping. I knew what it was even from here because its headline cried out:

An urgent need for
public facilities

Well, damn them all to hell if they think that's funny. I'd rather see a man pissing against a pole than this.

I heard the jangle of keys from the store behind me and, knowing it was Parker, composed myself before turning.

Afternoon, I said.

'Noon! he replied.

Locking up for a late lunch?

Nope!

Of course he wouldn't elaborate, and of course I wouldn't say what was really on my mind. I didn't give a damn about his lunch. But I refused to address the thing that riled me, though it squatted directly in our path. Out of pure contrariness, it seemed, neither would he.

I felt the air stirring, then, as agitated as my thoughts, and lifted my eyes to a sky that was growing brighter.

Parker, I said. Look! But he had already seen, and had slipped on sunglasses beneath his visor.

Atmospheric disturbances! he said. See? I told you! Now the wind's going to blow up the inlet and if we're lucky we'll get the sun.

I don't think I'd seen him smile before that moment. It was a grin, wide and giddy.

Just for a short while, he added, but we'll have sun.

And he began to scuttle along the buildings in a half-run.

Where are you going? I cried.

To the shore!

Parker hurried ahead, melting into the growing crowd. I followed. The wind was roaring up the inlet and already the fog had thinned. I had to shade my eyes with a hand against the unfamiliarity of brightness. A scattering of clouds ran like a filthy stream overhead and in the breaks we saw, sure enough, blasts of sunlight. Each brilliant beam caused an *ohhhh* across the crowd. Each time the light faded so did the exclamations. My hair was yanked one way and then another. Tin walls creaked and came loose, cart-wheeling across the street. All light disappeared then, and hailstones drummed on the tin roofs.

I stepped into a doorway, exhilarated, waiting for the fall of gentler rain. And then I heard the drone of motors, bleating and choking amid the building wind.

A crack of lightning lit up the sky, a yellowish grey, and then cries rose from the crowd. I couldn't see, but I could hear what they were saying: The airship!

It was the 27th, the day it was scheduled to arrive, but hours too early to attach itself to the midnight ship. It would have to be the coal hulk.

I could feel the lead plate in my hand, with its promise of tours for the modern traveller, the bullet shape pressing insistently into my palm that I should be one of them. I ran where they ran, arm flung over brow to protect my eyes from flying debris.

The rain was so heavy now I was soaked and so were they but still we ran to where the river met the ocean, a slice of gravel and rotted logs, ink-stained where the wind picked up the murky water and stirred it into the air. Above, a torpedo shape slipped in and out of the clouds, growing larger as it neared.

I stood on my toes and spotted Parker, off to the left, in his sunglasses and visor pulled low, standing alone. Everyone else packed together for the best view from the middle of the gravel. I waved but his eyes were on the sky.

A voice in my ear, then, What does that look like to you, darling?

It was Ben, come to gloat. I remembered what he'd said about airships: Nothing between you and death but a thin sheet of silver held up by wooden ribs.

Still, I leaned over to him and shouted, A crop-duster strapped to the belly of a whale!

He looked immensely pleased for a moment, then his face slackened. You just watch, he said. This is all wrong.

He was right. The storm had driven it here too soon for the midnight ship and too close in for the coal hulk that was filling its belly on the other side of the point.

I wondered, Why doesn't it turn back? But I could imagine what Parker would say to that: How? Through the storm?

In the molten horizon a shot of flame as the tail end of the airship bucked and swung around, then dipped itself into the sea, dousing the fire but dragging its full grey length along the water's surface, then along the shore, its belly sliding over us, hanging so close I found myself ducking, the whole sky above us black with it, and then into the rocks on the far shore. Its ribs cracked on impact, a sound like rifles firing at once, and its sides deflated, collapsing in a spray of steam.

The rain stopped and the wind, in one final gust, cleared away the last of the clouds. Sunlight swamped the sky and reflected painfully off the water, a floodlight onto the sack of skin, withered, grey, on the tiny shore. Someone in the crowd cried out that it looked like a dead elephant. I'd never seen one. But I had a childhood recollection of a trip to the coast, all details lost but for the vivid image of a beached whale, ribs jutting out of the carcass, skin sagging between each rung, a filthy corset. And I was seeing it again.

I could hear men and women sobbing. Others ran toward the craft with ropes and nets. Passengers and then crew members emerged one by one, alive if not unhurt.

The outhouse, an afterthought of the storm, skidded past me on its side, the door wrenched loose by the wind, the three remaining sides wobbling violently until, at last, they collapsed flat into the dirt. And yet I felt no better at seeing the prank, made at my expense, crushed like this.

Parker and Ben and the rest of the crowd had swept along the gravel toward the crash site. I could see the women from *The Saloon* gathering, too, sheets and towels bundled in their arms, because who else in town had a constant supply, and I could hear the tearing of fabric, could see Doctor moving amongst them, tying the white strips into bandages about heads and arms and hands. I knew that I should move in closer rather than observe from afar. But to what end? No one had died. A single paragraph was all this would merit. What more could I offer? Those who wanted more were here to see for themselves.

I felt my throat swelling, and wished I could join in the sobbing. It was like seeing the future collapse in front of me, that's what I wanted to write about. Are we not modern, after all? Are we not *avant-garde*? It was a future of cocktail parties and opera gowns and a solar dish that could capture the precious rays and print the words, a place where for four hours a day I could feel the sun on my skin and I could grow food and flowers and be accepted as one of them, a place for me and maybe even for a modern couple, but with this crash a doubt that had been spreading for weeks was confirmed. Even before Sun's arrival, his words had Vincent reconsidering, shifting, examining. Each time I felt him draw near, he quickly pulled back, as though someone were whispering in his ear, counselling him, questioning whether this is how a good son of the revolution should behave.

The followers would now claim that the leader's words, calling for arms and railways, traditional things of substance, grounded in the earth, not frail and floating in the sky, had predicted this crash.

Gloom filled me, spreading much as the clouds above had, returning to streak across the weakening sun, cooling the air and filling the sky, further darkened by the plume of smoke rising from the burnt craft.

Even without the crash, this moment was worse than if the sunlight had never appeared at all. The light was taken back too quickly and its sudden absence, replaced at once by darkness and rot, offended my senses as only the mutilated fish and that indecent deputy had offended them before. And now an utter sense of loss. I had no one to share the thought with. I stood on the beach, alone, the lines in my notebook blurring as I wrote.

III—La Fanciulla

Manchurian and Mustached

Mr. Bones delivered my dress early in the afternoon, sliding the box onto the counter. Tonight was the opera, the last story I would cover for our first edition tomorrow. One day left. I was alone, working on the copy, as I had been for much of the time since the crash two days ago and the ugly incident with the deputy the day before that. Was I the sort of woman who could be healed of such trauma by the sight of a black and white striped box tied with a silver ribbon? Apparently so. I couldn't pull my eyes from it, and didn't fully hear what Mr. Bones had started to say.

Riot, you should have seen the miners' riot. It was something. The regulars marching up Zero Avenue to the mine, the Lousetowners marching down, Silver and his deputies in the middle, waiting for them at the pithead. There was an agitator and he got the miners into a fury about Lousetowners working for less. Lousetowners were in a fury themselves that regulars got more and still complained. And then there were persons like myself who are neither of them, not mine workers of any sort, but we joined the crowd of gawkers because we knew that something of importance was about to happen. Your uncle was there, too.

Reporting on it, I said, though it's no secret that he sided with unions.

Mr. Bones paused, tapping his fingers on the counter. Your uncle, he finally said. He was the one who told me about the agitator. He was neither for a union nor against one. He didn't like their attitude about the Lousetowners. For obvious reasons.

By then he had turned to leave and paused, the door ajar, his face tilted.

The two groups clashed, he said, with boards and pipes and whatever they could find. Fists flying, too. What a sound, wet, like mother pounding dough for *roti*. The sheriff and his deputies came in with bats swinging to break it up. When the two sides drew back your uncle was found lying on the ground.

Air out my lungs like a head butt from Pete.

I was told it was a heart attack, I said.

It was. Brought on by the riot. He collapsed and then got trampled. Each side felt bad. Each side blamed the other. Still do. He was liked by many, though his choice of, ah, company, did not agree with all. Some have felt that your coming here would stir things up, again. That you would point fingers.

You knew him well.

Not as well as some. But yes.

-*===0

I thought about his words during and after a long soak in the tub, and my near-success at removing ink stains from my knuckles and nails. Trampled. No one mentioned it. Not here. Not back home.

It took two attempts to gather my hair into a French roll. In the end I decided that a loose sweep of strands actually hid the shaved edges nicely. I checked the sides in the closet mirror, and pushed the hairpin in place.

I tossed the box onto my bed and walked around it, still thinking. For obvious reasons, he said. What did that mean? I stopped pacing and leaned over, pulled the bow, lifted the lid and parted the layers of tissue.

Oh-h. I said it softly though there was no one to hear. Vincent had been by to pick up his clothes, and to run the inside pages and slice them from the roll of newsprint with his knife, but I had missed the event, missed him. I had been at Meena's for last-minute fittings for this very gown.

I lifted the dress by the shoulders, and the frothy hem tumbled down. I laid it out on the bed and looked at it, trying to imagine myself in anything so fine.

She had thought of everything. Gloves, chemise, garters. Even heels that I had carried home myself that last day.

I left my plaid housecoat in a puddle at my feet, slipped into the silks and then sat on the bed to pull on my stockings, snapping their tops into the garters. The sheath slipped over my head and fell into place when I stood. My stockinged heels slid into the pale shoes, the fit snug, perfect. I climbed onto the chair. In the closet mirror I saw a woman of style from Paris who fastened the side hooks and smoothed the skirt with the palms of her hands.

Carefully, I climbed down. I wriggled my fingers into the gloves, dark as the deep blue of the dress. I took up a rectangle of sheer material in the same blue-black, wrapped it around my shoulders. My mother's beaded bag on my wrist, just large enough to contain keys, invitation, notebook and pencil, I descended the steps.

⊷══◦

At six o'clock a motorcycle and sidecar pulled up, a two-seater. It would be dark at evening's end and my escort and I would have to walk back, but for now my gown would remain pristine. Even so, I insisted that I ride in front, risking the wind and dust in my face. The driver revved the engine and we tore around the newspaper building and back onto the road. Two blocks of high speed exhilaration. The wind forced my mouth open, blasting down my throat. Morris clapped a hand onto my shoulder and shouted, That's my girl! I twisted my head around, beaming at his words. I didn't even mind the grit, though I almost lost my silver hairpin.

We arrived just as the musicians were jostling for room in their orchestra pit behind the bar. Sweet strains of the violin floated over the heads of the gathering. Tables were set with linen and silver. Guests sipped from glasses of champagne and chatted.

My gown rustled pleasantly as I walked among the guests. I was a flawed Parisian, but the drape of the hem covered my stitched leg, and about my ears the curls of hair that I could feel had sprung loose from the hairpin would help to further mask the shaved edges.

I felt the scratch of the razor, still, as we sat on his bed, felt as well the prickling of new growth that would soon disguise all evidence of that day.

My date was by my side only briefly, elbowing his way over to a table to shake hands and talk. I greeted those around me: the Scot, San Francisco, Silver. My stomach lurched and every nerve in me twitched at the expectation of that deputy appearing by his side. He would have to wash up for the occasion and maybe that was too much for him because no amount of scanning the room produced him. My eyes had found Drummond, though, standing by a wall, observing. I had words for him, too. In time. By then I saw where my escort was headed: to Vincent's leader, the famous man I have been desperate to interview.

I whipped my head around to see if Drummond had noticed. He had. He stared intently at Sun while Silver moved over to his side and they whispered.

So this was to be a stand-off. Sun and his people were untouchable here. This was no illegal gathering of Lousetowners but a dinner and opera for the residents of both Lousetown and Black Mountain. Miners at work right now could attend the matinee tomorrow. Anyone else who could afford a ticket was here tonight. Wolf lifted his chin when he saw me, and folded his arms. Parker seemed oblivious but maybe he didn't recognize me in such an outfit. Doctor/Mr. Bones, who was there in the capacity of neither healer nor stitcher but audience member, flashed his glasses appreciatively at my gown, his creation. The women of *The Saloon*, in every lewd colour from tropical pink to bright orange, had indeed taken the evening off—why not, their customers were here as well—and were already settled into a table by the stage. Dee half-rose and dipped her head at me in greeting. I had once held unkind thoughts about her and the others and their boudoir-smelling roses. I had been a cow, really. But I had come to terms with those feelings. I had been ill-treated by the very deputy I had warned her about, and all because I had been abandoned by the very man I had been jealous about. My anger had been used up on them. I raised my glass to her and she raised hers, wincing as she did so. I recalled now that she hadn't joined the other women of *The Saloon* after the mine explosion. One of them said she wasn't well. Was she still ill? I didn't see how. Not only was she drinking, but she downed hers in one go. She was joined by a couple of miners, then, clean and dressed but with the visible residue of coal about their hands and necks, and they bent their heads in conversation. Good. I had other business tonight.

I took up my skirts and, trying not to expose my stitches, hurried over to Morris. I was certain he would have already introduced himself as Two-Gun.

A horrible tragedy, he was saying as I approached. I saw the crash from a nearby window. Trains, he continued. I agree with you wholeheartedly. A rail line running right into the heartland, a ribbon of iron that will form the backbone of an industrialized nation. You'll need guards on the trains, experienced gunmen to fight off the train robbers. We've had our share of those scoundrels in the west.

Two-Gun's bulk was blocking my view of the leader. All I could see was one thin shoulder and then skeletal fingers tracing a map of China in the air, or so it seemed. I could imagine a scalpel in his hand. Not a labourer, this one. I could hear his voice, the measured pace and rounded vowels next to Morris' harsh Cockney gallop. A man such as yourself, he said, and then something about a valued addition.

He couldn't know that this Two-Gun had no right to even mouth the word scoundrel in reference to anyone but himself, who had his charms, yes, but what about getting into fights and lying and consorting with someone named Cold-Ass Marie? It would have been tempting to mention the posse and his time in jail, too, but I was after an introduction.

I wedged myself beside Two-Gun at last, only to hear the dinner bells chime. He tore himself away from the cluster, amazingly swift when food was the draw.

The shit. This had been the deal: an introduction to Sun in exchange for partial ownership of my newspaper.

Morris! I called out, sharply. Two-Gun! But already he was back at the table.

I decided I would introduce myself. The leader, however, had melted into the circle of aides who folded their arms and would not let me through.

I told them who I was but they wouldn't budge. How, I asked them, is he supposed to get his word to the people when you won't let him talk to the press?

They stood their ground in silence.

As I neared my date I heard gasps from surrounding tables, and I enjoyed them. An *ooo* sound that could be simply in appreciation: *soup*, but more likely, *Jew*. There seemed to be some chatter about diamonds, too, and exploration. Not surprising, given the mining interests in the crowd. I heard *The Bullet* named, as well. So they were reading it. Good.

Silver shook his head as I passed by. Him! he said.

Silver might have expected me to ask him to be my guest, instead. I smiled as sweet a smile as I could muster before thoughts of his deputy took hold.

There you are, I said tartly, and took my seat next to my date. You were supposed to introduce me. Remember?

He leaned over and admitted, Yes. But I didn't want to scare him off by saying you were with the press.

Oh, I said, realizing I had done just that.

There, there, he said, patting my gloved hand. There'll be another opportunity. We got along famously, as I knew we would.

Meena arrived late and was seated at our table, joined shortly after by her escort who had been supervising operations in the kitchen, and was now free. I was both pleased and startled. It was Marcel. I tensed, wondering how this throng would respond. But he didn't inspire the hoots that Two-Gun had. He was our chef, and men rose from their seats when he passed, women fluttered and gushed. Even Bugle Boy, too drunk to stand, tipped his head and smiled.

Mademoiselle, Marcel said, and kissed my hand.

Chère, he said to Meena.

He drew out his chair and sat next to her, whispering something in her ear that had her laughing.

From here I had a good view of the side table and the leader, Sun. Surrounding him was his entourage and beneath their jackets I spied the bulky outlines of what were certainly pistols.

A figure darted behind the backdrop of Paris. The sharp voices told me he wasn't one of the players, and wasn't wanted back there where they were dressing and putting on make-up. It was the only reason for the painted background. There was no Eiffel Tower in a story set in the West.

I shot a glance at Drummond and noted how his eyes flicked from Sun to where the figure had been, and then back to Sun.

At the table on the other side of us was the Scot, who half-rose in his seat and blasted, Cook boy! This soup is cold.

Cook Boy trotted out from the kitchen with a steaming bowl of soup on a tray.

I gasped so loudly that everyone at my table turned to look. Only my date guessed what was wrong.

Is he—

I tried to look away. But Vincent saw me. Of course he saw me. I was sitting there in plain view.

His expression seemed to ask the question I had not even considered until that moment: Why Morris? Two-Gun was pure business, my business partner in fact, which he knew very well. But this was one place where Vincent and I could have shown up together, just as Meena and Marcel had. Is that what his look meant? I had spent days, weeks, working next to him, telling stories, eating lunch, talking about opera, this very opera, and yes, even sitting in his room, his razor tracing my temples . . . but no, not long after that he had fled with his leader. So why not Morris? And I had to admit that his queue, his most handsome attribute in the intimacy of my shop and his room, looked suddenly out-of-place here, out-of-time.

He had stood for too long. Now everyone was staring where he stared. At me. My only consolation was that he didn't look at the man who made the speeches. Not once.

Moonlighting! Two-Gun cried. By Christ it's your fucking printer! Vincenzo, my man!

Attention from the surrounding diners switched in an instant from my printer and me to my escort and his language. A drone of disapproval.

Two-Gun half-stood to apologize, somewhat off balance in his haste to right the situation, backside tipping his chair onto its rear legs and belly shoving the table forward.

Humblest, humblest apologies, he offered, then fell back into his chair, which slammed loudly onto its front legs. By the time I raised my hot face, Vincent was gone, a steaming bowl placed before the Scot.

A roast pig with an apple in its mouth was carried out and placed on the bar. I didn't need to wonder where either had come from.

Two-Gun whispered coarsely in my ear that it was a lot of bacon even for him.

My dear girl, has no one considered hunting in the back hills for game? There's a story for you.

I had thought the same but it was better coming from him. I could quote him.

Marcel got up from our table and stepped forward to carve up the cooked beast with great flourishes of a large fork and knife. Waiters, none of them Vincent, bustled around him serving plates of sliced pork with tinned peas and Yorkshire pudding. Women first. Dessert was baked apple with tinned cream. The locals must have thought Marcel special-ordered a crate of apples just for this dinner.

After the meal, which I pushed around my plate, the tables were cleared and dancing began. I wasn't in the mood but relented, Two-Gun insisting rightfully that it was a waste of a pretty frock if I didn't.

It's your colour, he whispered hoarsely.

It is not.

I thought of the burnt orange I was supposed to be wearing, what a jolt of colour that would have been.

There's nothing grey about it, I insisted.

Exactly, he said, pulling his head back to look me in the eyes. And then he winked.

I couldn't help but laugh, then.

Still, with each twirl around the room I turned my head toward the kitchen door. Other waiters scurried in and out. But none of them was Vincent.

The lights were dimmed and we returned to our seats. Each of us was handed a folded programme at the door, and I read it quickly. As Ben had said, the setting was a saloon, and the lights returned to shine on our *Saloon* dressed up with the Parisian tarp. A group of extras that formed the production's bar patrons were all Chinese, giving that backdrop of Paris the look of Shanghai, though that city wasn't in the story, either.

I watched as the Diva in scarlet rolled out on stage to play the slender young Minnie. She was in love with the dashing young Johnson, played by Ben's old friend. The opera's sheriff was played by the other actor who tugged off his green tights in the tent that time, brandishing them high. Their real names were in the programme, but it stayed folded in my hands because, as the action moved along and the players began to sing, I began to forget who they really were. I could see why it wasn't Vincent's favourite, it had none of the urgency of the ones I'd heard on the gramophone. But it took little time to believe the drama's premise, that Johnson was, in fact, the outlaw Ramerrez, and that young Minnie didn't know this as she danced with him.

At intermission there were waiters with trays held high, balancing more glasses of champagne. My eyes darted around the room, but no Vincent.

I wanted to push the evening forward, away from my discomfort, my guilt. I was determined to look as though nothing was wrong. The men stepped outside to smoke and I stood, too.

Z-z-z-z-t, Meena said, an utterance that needed no explanation once she reached over and yanked at my hem.

I thanked her, and strode after them. I would be outrageous I decided, I would be *avant-garde* and ask my date for a cigar.

Isn't she something, gentlemen? he said. He struck a match for me and added, I think I'm going to marry her.

Morris, I said. Really.

It was an awkward moment as my appearance seemed to kill the conversation. I didn't know if that was because I was a woman or the newspaper publisher or the so-called future Mrs. Two-Gun, for God's sake. I smoked the cigar, anyway.

Back inside, Minnie told Johnson about her life. I wished she wouldn't sing it, but I could see what Puccini was trying to do. They might as well have been leaning against a printing press, sharing stories over lunch.

Was he watching from the kitchen doors?

There was a sudden scurrying on stage and then a pistol aimed at Ramerrez/Johnson. I gripped my handbag so tightly a bead popped free and rolled across the floor like a stray bullet, and then a bang sounded as the young man was shot.

Several audience members scrambled to their feet: Two-Gun, Sun and his entire entourage, Silver and Drummond, and two figures this time, their long coats flapping like sails as they dashed from the room.

Their faces, Manchurian and mustached. I couldn't quite tell, they moved so quickly. But the way they moved was familiar.

It's them! I said. The ones I saw before!

Imperial troops! Two-Gun shouted. They're after our leader!

And he was out the door, too, Drummond and then Silver behind him, shouting, Deputies!

My lungs and guts tensed to hear that.

Ben bellowed from the stage, *Intermezzo!* And the band behind the bar began blasting a tune.

The famous man must have ducked out the back door, again—Vincent, too. I imagined he shed his kitchen clothes to become, once more, aide and translator to the great leader. Two of the entourage were left at the table, standing nervously, palms pressed at hip level over their guns. Watching.

I grabbed my beaded bag and headed out into the street. A black horse bearing a white backside and legs thundered past me and I leapt aside as its rider shouted, Humblest apologies, my dearest darling!

Take me with you! I shouted back.

I waited for him to ride back. I could throw myself onto the saddle behind him. I'd done that many times before. I'd tear the dress doing so, but damn the dress. I wanted to follow the action. If nothing else I didn't want to be left standing alone. That despicable deputy could come by, and there I'd be dressed in a gown tight as a corset, forcing my breasts up like an offering. I had lost the protection of the suit and old man's hat.

But Two-Gun rode away without me.

A cluster of motorcycles buzzed past, in each sidecar a pair of men with guns pointed up the street. Deputies, none of them filthy. I waved dramatically but they, too, kept going. At the far end of Zero I heard shooting, and then the drone of idling machines. I peered into the blue-grey air, the murk of dark, moving shapes. And I heard it, I am certain, the clopping of hooves over the scrabble of one of the hills. The motorcycles weren't built for that, and it was too dark. They'd have to turn back.

A horse in this place. I pictured a hoof caught on the edge of a hole, a tear in its flesh just like my own. Its screams as the bone snapped and burst through.

Had Morris leapt into the role of bodyguard just now, become Two-Gun once and for all? Did he think there was no better way of showing he was capable of apprehending train robbers than to appear on a horse like a western gunman?

The horse. I saw it delivered and only once allowed memory of it to fly across my brain, quickly lost in a stampede of facts about cowboys and leather boots and gamblers and Cold-Ass Marie. The delivery man's voice, so clear to me now in recollection without the distraction of whisky and Morris' stories, called out a name not familiar to me then, Twooooooguunnnn, as he led the horse from the dock. Why did we walk all the way to Lousetown that night? And with those pigs about. We would have been safe up there in the saddle. I should have asked right then and there about the horse but the fleeting thought hadn't returned until now.

I was losing my mind. He was right. I was bushed.

I should hire my own taxi. I should grab one and drive it myself. There was a story in all this but whose was it? Who should I follow? I wanted to follow the horse and lead it to safety. Imperial troops? Ridiculous. I didn't think there were any left. The leader's revolution had returned the country to the people. Or tried to. Maybe they were spies working with the warlords in the north, the ones hired by Drummond to work his cause as well. Yes, that would make sense. Spies who were here to find out what the famous man was up to, and then to sell their information to Silver and Drummond while they were at it. I had many things to ask them. Vincent as well, if I could find him. Or the leader, himself. And Two-Gun—he was always up to something and especially now would merit following. But if they'd headed for the labyrinths of Lousetown, and I was certain they had, I'd never find my way, not on my own. And he'd be much faster on that poor horse—if it had survived the holes. My thoughts turned and turned until I felt dizzy and sick.

A single motorcycle approached from the opposite direction, heading toward the docks. Was this my chance, at last? I might be able to get it to turn around.

I began to flag it, then snatched my hand back, hoping the driver hadn't seen. In the sidecar was a sight I had been dreading all evening, the deputy. They wheeled within inches of me yet he refused to look my way. In a suit and no longer dirty but scrubbed pink, he looked almost more vulgar. Exposed. He stared straight ahead, one hand gripping the handle of a leather suitcase stuffed beside him. He was going away. He was leaving on the midnight ship.

I bent to take up my dress, mindful that in so doing I provided full exposure of my twin offerings. So what, the sound of the motorcycle was growing faint, its human cargo gone for good. I climbed the steps back up onto the veranda, and returned to *The Saloon*.

The band was playing furiously, men and women fanning themselves with programmes and turning nervously as the saloon doors swung open at my entry. The commotion had spoiled the opera. Ben was pacing across the stage, waiting for enough of us to return to resume the production, now running late.

More champagne, waiters scurrying from table to table, every waiter except Vincent. And now my escort was gone, too, and if not for Meena I'd be sitting alone. Marcel had disappeared as well. I threw myself into my chair and accepted two glasses of champagne, one for my date and one for me. I downed them both, and wiped my mouth with the back of my satin-gloved hand.

I nodded to the empty chair beside her. Back in the kitchen? I asked.

No, he has gone back to our place in Lousetown, to make sure there is no damage.

I worked the words over in my mind: our place.

You don't live over here?

With him? That would never be allowed.

We had to take the programme's word for it that Minnie nursed the wounded Ramerrez back to health, and that he was subsequently arrested. We'd lost time with all the commotion, and had to skip ahead.

Hands cuffed with raw rope, Ramerrez fell on his knees before the noose.

Meena whispered excitedly, This is where he says don't tell her. Let her think I've gone away.

The Chinese extras gathered round to mourn the imminent hanging of Ramerrez whose voice, deeply and convincingly that of the handsome outlaw, began to sing, *Ch'ella mi Creda*.

It was singing I had never expected from this opera, nor from Ben's old friend. Had Vincent come back and was he listening on the other side of the door? I hoped so. Hoped he would hear what I heard in the deep bass, barges on a river and the moan of fog horns, lungs exhaling wearily as workers pushed on poles that guided the junks and sampans along the harbour's edge. Couples strolling along the Bund, just as he described them to me, the gardens heavy with pale pink azaleas and roses. Even the low blast of the approaching midnight ship, signalling that the deputy would soon be gone, folded itself into the sounds of the opera.

My thoughts drifted back to the other Shanghai. I lifted the programme to my nose, the programme that his shop had printed, smelled the green of warm air rubbing against water, of sulfur-yellow flowers struggling up from cracked concrete, of poverty.

He'd asked, *Crazy, isn't it? To drag the worst of Shanghai here, to Black Mountain.*

They hadn't of course. They had brought people like him. Why hadn't I ever told him that?

Next to me, Meena let a single tear slide down her cheek. A sob climbed up my throat. And something more welling up inside. Each draw of the bow across the cello's strings was the razor shaving my scalp, was a blade between my ribs. I couldn't breathe. I stood, chair scraping noisily as I bolted for the door.

THAT PISTOL-PACKING FOOL

We'd practised this day and become so efficient it took just a few hours. I wrote the opera story, set the type, Vincent inked the press, ran the final pages through. This would have been the second time he brought the knife with its enormous blade, but it was the first time I had seen it used in my shop, the metal flashing each time he raised it and sliced the printed paper, cleanly and neatly, a constant arc of action. I took stacks of the sliced pages to the table, folded each sheet in half, swiping the crease flat with the bone, then inserting the inside pages he'd printed previously, making eight-paged copies of our newspaper.

Our first edition, right on time, September 30, the very last day of the month. I paused by the calendar, but moved away without touching the pencil. The day was not over, not yet.

We worked in silence.

I supposed I should be grateful he showed up at all. I went over all the reasons why he had. He had to run the big press, of course, though he could have walked away from it. Then there was my promise to show him my coverage of his leader's speech before the article was set, but he could have looked when I wasn't here. I would have simply asked him why he had, but he might have said, For the money, what else?

Well, and why not? Who was I to criticize him for that. Money. It had obsessed me since I arrived here and found the printing machine in a rusted heap. It is the reason I agreed to a business deal with Morris, the reason I set up that unsavory appointment at the bank. Without it I had nothing to pay for supplies or Vincent's wages, or yes, even to buy a gown for the opera. Somehow, I had found the funds for that. So who was I to judge him? He couldn't let his leader be dragged away by Drummond and the deputies. What would I have thought of him, then? Political passion was something I valued, to the point of finding another wanting for having had none.

And yet the fact was I was abandoned, left alone dressed in men's clothes. I was stuck on that point.

I could imagine his argument: That's why. You were in disguise. You were safe.

Safe? I was a sitting target. Even that pistol-packing fool of a partner was nowhere to be found.

You can handle yourself, he'd say. Isn't that what you're always saying? And you made it home okay, didn't you?

But with that thought came the deputy and my head filled with such raw emotion I felt the top of it might explode.

As we were finishing up, Doctor came by to take out my stitches. Why not yesterday or two days ago so that I wouldn't have worried each time I sat or stood at the opera that I would be exposing that tarantula of a stitching job? Meena had buzzed in my ear about it, even leaned over that time and gave a yank at the hem.

I could have taken Doctor upstairs, or into the back room. But I wanted Vincent to see. I was hoping for sympathy, to get him talking to me, again.

I pulled off my coveralls and stood in my blue-flowered dress, the same one Vincent had brought back to me, wrapped in paper. Doctor had me climb onto a chair and then he snipped each knot.

Steady, he said, and pulled the thread all the way through and then out, a nauseating sensation, as though the thread had been strung between my legs and up and out my navel. It brought tears to my eyes, and I wiped them away with the back of my hand.

I looked up just as Vincent looked away.

I handed Doctor an envelope that contained his payment, along with a freshly printed copy of the first issue. It was only as I closed the door that I heard him say something about Uncle. Your uncle would be pleased, or proud. Something like that.

I climbed back into my coveralls and by late morning we were done cutting and folding the last copies, and still not a word between us.

He began cleaning up. I paused in the doorway, and finally spoke.

I won't be long, I said.

And then I headed straight out into the arsenic gloom of midday, canvas sacks slung like saddle bags across each shoulder, to deliver the newspapers.

I expected some hand-shaking with the townsfolk, another crowd of them outside my door requesting copies. But there was no one to greet me. I supposed a newssheet was no different to them than this first edition, but I was proud, and reviewed the headlines as I slipped the front page behind the framed glass, and then stepped down from the veranda.

**Ch'ella mi creda
highlight of
La Fanciulla**

**Gunshot
spoils
opera
night**

**Sun Yat-sen
speaks of hope
in Lousetown**

Below it, a sub-headline:

**Raid
ends
talk**

and finally,

**Coal heap
chokes
orchard**

These front page stories continued onto the second page, filling it, along with an index listing the paper's contents.

Parker's was the largest order, but he had a sign on his door: *Back in 5 minutes.* So I dropped a bundle on his doormat and felt the load across my shoulders lighten immediately. I headed down Zero, walking briskly as I considered the third page of news items.

Wind storm
brings
blast of
light

And next to it:

Future
dreams
crash
with
airship

These, along with several ads, filled page three. I'd written a small editorial to follow up that previous news item on strange fish:

Foul stream
Runs through
Black Mtn

and a larger one that trumpeted the new, full-sized newspaper, with plans for upcoming issues:

Bringing
news on a
regular
basis

How regular remained to be seen. I hoped the next issue wouldn't take a month. We might have to run just six pages to make sure of that.

These editorials, along with more ads, left room for a small announcement on page four. I had thought long about this one, deciding in the end that this was business and was the right thing to do.

2-Gun
backs
Bullet

I was going to call him by his last name. That is proper newspaper style. But *Cohen* isn't a name that immediately conjured his visage, not to me. *Two-Gun* did, and its close proximity to *Bullet* amused me with its play on words. However, there wasn't room for six letters and a hyphen. That's when I struck on the idea of using the numeral 2. I was quite pleased with myself for my inventiveness, though Vincent merely nodded. I gathered he had seen many such headlines in his work in Shanghai.

Then there were all the smaller items that filled the remaining pages, such as the holes in the ground. Parker was always ruminating on them.

Black holes
in the road
a danger

and Morris had suggested hunting as an alternative to roast pig:

Hunting
for game
proposed
in the wilds
beyond
Black Mountain

and then a small item:

Healing
properties
of leeches
and tea

To fill a hole, once more I carried forward the subject of the front page story about the airship crash. This time it ran as a separate piece on the last page.

Women
of the Saloon
donate
yards of linen
— making
bandages for
the wounded

It was a first edition that would make a second hard to follow. Only eight pages but what news in them, more than I could have imagined a small town capable of producing. And again, so much more that I couldn't include: the *Lonesome* and its fresh food, the garden where the food came from, the press run by sunlight.

Meena's shop was closed, so I fed a slender bundle of six copies through the mail slot and returned to the street.

There were more ads and items on those back pages but the specifics left my mind quickly. Something was going on. There were few people on the street, but the faces of those I passed looked stricken, half laughter and half horror, which wasn't all that unusual in this town. But was there another strike?

I left a stack of papers behind the bar of *The Bombay Room*, as arranged. It was empty. Next, the opera tent. I left a bundle on the dressing table.

I dropped several copies through the mail slot of the bank's double doors.

We had fulfilled our part of the deal, the bank, at least, would be pleased. But with September over, now, what next? I came to an abrupt halt in the middle of the street. I had never thought beyond this deadline. The money from Morris had paid supplies and wages and reimbursed the bank, leaving but a few dollars. Had I simply earned the right to keep the business and borrow yet more money?

Up ahead I saw Meena, and I ran, calling to her.

Lila! she said, turning to greet me. Thank goodness you must help me.

What's going on? Where is everyone?

I don't know, she said, but I need your help.

I've got just a few more copies to deliver.

It can wait, she said. I'll explain.

She hooked my arm in hers and yanked me off Zero and down two rows of metal shacks that were the miners' quarters. Three shacks in, she took my canvas sacks and handed me the bucket.

Fill it. The cleanest water you can find. And hurry!

She ducked into the doorway. The very foul-looking sludge of a stream that I'd written about slid past the shacks. Just ahead was a tap coming out the back of either *The Saloon* or the shop next to it, the taxi garage. It would be the same grey water that flowed into my bathtub, but it would have to do. I filled the bucket and counted the doors back to the third shack.

Inside, dark as you would expect a tin shack to be. Against the far wall, that same girl from the mine who had fought with the women from *The Saloon*. She was on her back on a cot, that same gaping dress yanked up, a gruesome view of a sea creature opening up between her legs.

I felt the horror inch across my face as Meena watched me.

She isn't due for another three months, she said. I'm the closest we have to a midwife, here. Not much call for it. Put the bucket on the stove, over there. We need it hot.

What about Doctor? Can he help?

Her eyes smiled until I remembered.

Perhaps later, if any stitching is needed.

My scar twitched where he'd pulled the thread out. And then I recalled the dress he had helped to sew, and had then delivered, and how he made that curious comment about my uncle not liking the general attitude about Lousetowners: For obvious reasons.

He knew my uncle, I told her. Did you?

She didn't answer. Her slender hand and then her arm up to her elbow had disappeared inside the girl. I lost my footing for a moment.

The look on Meena's face said something was terribly wrong but she told the girl, Easy now, breathe, I'm just turning the baby around. Head down.

To me she said, I need you to go see Deirdre.

You mean Dee?

I need to borrow back a bottle of medicine. I got it from Mr. Bones— Doctor—and gave it to her. She'll know what you mean. Hurry.

You mean above *The Saloon*?

Oh, yes, the matinee is still in progress. Go the back way. No one will see you. Hurry, she repeated. See if she'll come back with you.

⋆⟹

I ran across the alley and up the wooden backstairs and knocked at the door, winded, considering as I did that the town and neighbouring Lousetown were too small for a library or a school, yet managed to support a bank and three drinking establishments, one with a whorehouse.

When no one answered the door I grabbed the handle and pushed, sticking only my foot and head into the opening. My eyes were met with a room that pulsed with red wallpaper, lush, burgundy sofas, cream-coloured lampshades on crystal stands, a large carpet with roses on a black background. I was so busy staring I didn't see a girl approach.

Hello, she said.

It was the one whose shoes were too large, and her eyes were round and sad.

I explained why I was there.

Just a minute, she said. Have a seat.

Before you go, I said, If you don't mind me asking, are you happy here?

What do you mean?

I mean is this where you want to be, to stay?

Where else could I stay?

No, I said, never mind. Thank you.

The problem was me. I wasn't putting the question right. I sat on a large sofa, then considered how many liaisons might have occurred there. Swiftly I stood, and moved to a single chair next to a side table, with a vase filled with pale pink roses. Indeed the boudoir stench was everywhere. I sighed deeply. I hadn't come to terms with those feelings, after all.

Miss?

The girl had returned.

She'll see you.

And she indicated the second door on her left. I crossed the floor and entered a room as lush as the sitting room, only in copper tones not unlike the dress I never got to wear.

Dee was lying back against cushions on her bed, her legs akimbo beneath a gold satin quilt that climbed to her bare shoulders, sucking on a plum, juice dribbling onto her skin.

Hand me that cloth, she said.

Hello, I replied.

I didn't want to touch the folded cotton. It swam in a basin of water beside the bed and alluded to other purposes. She had been entertaining a client, and I had interrupted. And most disconcerting of all was another vase of pale pink blooms next to the bowl.

I pinched the edge of the cloth between two ragged fingernails and passed it to her. I'm here on an emergency, I said. Meena sent me.

Meena? She sat upright, cotton in one hand, satin in the other, barely covering her bosom.

She said she gave you a bottle of medicine, and she needs it now.

She looked at me quizzically.

The girl from the mine, she's giving birth.

Is she! The little tart. Well, I still need it, too. Did Meena tell you that?

I shook my head.

Then let me tell you because it was that deputy from the mine you warned me about. I wouldn't have been there if it wasn't for that—girl. But that was the deal to settle the strike.

I know, I said.

Yes and that filthy scum of a deputy was—well, in an unsatisfied state. He blamed Lousetowners for it. Said they had contaminated us and there was only one thing to do with fish.

She dropped the satin quilt to expose a breast, its nipple bruised the colour of blackberries where it had been pierced with a fish hook.

I felt my stomach rise, my womb throb.

He got his satisfaction, then, she said. I'd never seen a man so quickly satisfied as when he stuck that thing in me. I screamed, God, I screamed, and Suzie, she finally pulled him off me. But we couldn't pull out the hook. It's got those things.

Barbs, I said thickly.

She'd closed her robe, but I was still seeing it.

He's left town, I told her.

I know.

She then reached under the nightstand and brought out a long, silver bottle.

Here. Pour some out into that teacup over there. You can have the rest. Bring it over here, will you?

Encouraged by this sign of generosity, I added, Meena also thought you might come back with me.

Her grip tightened on the bottle and she called the girl a worse term than a sluice box. I had hoped she would show more grace, but it seemed she had grown coarser since we first met in the dress shop. It was the deputy's doing, though I had a role in creating that strike, in bringing about the confrontation with the girl. I worried she might even change her mind about sharing the medicine.

This, I said to her, taking the bottle by the neck, tugging it gently, this alone is generous of you, considering.

And I nodded toward her bruised nipple.

Yes, it is, she agreed, and let go.

I poured some of the cloudy liquid into the cup, pushed it towards her, and dropped the bottle into my pocket. I asked her then what I had been anxious to ask since I saw the pale blossoms.

Who, from Lousetown? And I pointed my chin at the vase.

Her eyes narrowed for a minute.

I heard there was a fuss about your printer, she said. I can't speak for the other girls, but he ain't one of mine.

I breathed out, not aware until then that I had been holding my breath.

I'm sorry about that, and I nodded again at her breast.

I'm stuck with it, I guess. But it's healing over. Some of the gents even ask for me because of it. I'm in demand, now.

Her pride in her new notoriety saddened me. Still, I left her boudoir satisfied that at least one man wasn't asking.

I crossed the alley and pushed through the door of the metal hut. Dead silence. And a peculiar smell of meat.

Hello, I called.

In the gloom I finally made out the form of Meena, in the corner, and I crossed the floor to her, silver bottle in my outstretched hand.

Here you are, I said.

She had tipped her chair back and, looking up at the metal ceiling, said, I knew your uncle, yes.

I had forgotten I'd even asked her.

Oh?

Before Marcel, she explained, letting the chair fall forward.

She looked at me until I understood.

The same place I live in, now, she said. Near the café.

I tried to control my face. For obvious reasons. That was what Mr. Bones had meant. To Uncle, Lousetown was Meena. No wonder his room above the press looked so empty. He didn't live there. I thought of the brass plate on the press. "B" for *Bluebell*.

He said to me once, *It isn't easy, loving someone from another world.* He was thinking of himself as much as me. He was married to his business because he couldn't bring a woman like Meena home, not to our family, not to Black Mountain. I fumbled for the right response. If Meena thought I was shocked, she was correct. I had always thought I was my uncle's niece and here was proof: We had both looked for love in Lousetown. Yet it hurt to know that he had not only looked for it but had found it, and I hadn't. And I wanted to ask her how she could love another man so quickly, a man who was younger, more handsome. Darker. Was that the reason? Would I be replaced as quickly? And I was also thinking, wasn't it greedy of her to have two when I had none.

The medicine, I said at last, and dropped the bottle into her lap.

Not necessary now. But thank you.

She slipped it into her apron pocket.

Thank goodness she has lost consciousness again, she said. I've never seen anything like this. Barely a pound. Put it by the door. Mr. Bones will see to burying it.

She slid a box across the floor. I took it up, and forced myself to look inside. Small, glistening, grey-green.

Malformed, Meena said, like a fish.

Where she saw fins I saw wings, but bug or not, the tiny creature was not a human shape.

Poor child, I said.

Meena nodded sympathetically at the wooden box.

I mean her, I said, and looked at the bed. It's just as well, I added. She's in no position to be a mother.

I was seeing that wretched miner, and her with him.

Meena shook her head. She is a mother, already. A little girl and a little boy. Why do you think she does what she does? To feed them.

Where are they now?

Being looked after by others.

I haven't seen any children here, I said. Just in Lousetown.

They were born somewhere else. But it is curious, you know. I have delivered only a few babies here, and all of them on the Lousetown side. Nothing like this.

I set the box by the door. Already, I was composing headlines: Giving birth/To death

No, it was more than death. Somehow, its natural development had been corrupted. Silver should hear about this. He was the law, and I felt that a law of some sort was being broken.

For the first time since I began working on the paper I realized we needed photographs. I could have used a camera for the airship crash, but I relied instead on my words. This was different. This required more than description. This required proof. I didn't even know how to begin. How to take photographs, how to make images and how those in turn would be printed onto the newspaper page. I've read enough about them to know there is a process, and that big city papers use them, such as that photograph of Shanghai that looked like Lousetown. We needed photographs here. We needed evidence.

Vincent would know.

Parker said Uncle liked things the way they were. But am I not the one who said she was eager for change, who'd otherwise be happy to hand-crank newssheets and let that beast of a press fossilize in front of me? Change would mean a modern press, cameras, darkroom equipment.

The thought of crates of fragile equipment being dropped onto the wharf, though. I'd have to accompany them, safeguard them from being broken. Vincent could join me. A trip out of town. Together. A break from here, I could say. I'd proved my point. I could produce a newspaper.

I could put up a notice just as Uncle might have: *Closed for the fall.*

I took up my newspaper sacks and left Meena with the girl. Outside, I stood for a moment, frozen, wondering whether to return to the shop or go looking for Silver. Night had fallen. I decided on the sheriff. If Vincent had a camera I'd have seen it by now, and I needed to plan my wording carefully. I needed time for that.

Ten Minutes Past
Seven O'Clock

I was walking past the front of *The Saloon* when I saw Silver inside. The matinée was over, and it seemed a town meeting had been called. He was surrounded by citizens, many of them talking heatedly. I pushed through the swinging doors, dropped the sacks with the rest of my papers onto a table behind me, pulled out my watch to check the time, and sat, taking notes.

I paused to glance up at the staircase and railing that ran above, across the length of the room. Behind that railing was a waiting room in luscious reds, another room in copper-golden satin, and Dee, with that fish hook. I should have taken a few copies of the newspaper to her. I wouldn't be going back, now.

Chairs had been arranged in rows for the meeting. The tables we had dined upon at the opera last night were shoved to the side. The air rustled with the opening, folding and closing of newspapers. A drone of voices, too, commenting. While no one had been around when I was delivering the papers, these citizens had returned, in the time that I had been with Meena, to pick them up and read them, and bring them here.

One voice rose above the others. Something about diamonds found in the old tunnels.

Another voice shouted, That's exactly what he told me!

I leaned over to Bugle Boy. What's going on?

Ha, he quipped and turned so I couldn't read his notes. You missed it all, he said. It's almost over.

And with that, still hugging his notes to his chest, he gathered himself up and scuffled out, taking the reek of booze with him.

Someone two rows up cried out, For one hundred dollars you get a piece of the Black Diamond Mines. That's what he told us. The evidence is everywhere!

I sat up high to see who it was. Ed. He turned and pointed at me. There you are! he said. You wrote all about it in your paper.

Me? I reached back for a paper but I didn't need to read it. I knew what I'd written and that item was in the last newssheet.

That was in South Africa, I countered, and rose to my feet to defend myself.

In the far corner stood that damn Mr. Mooney, arms folded as he listened.

I was quoting the travel experiences of someone else, I said.

And then I realized my mistake. I hadn't sought corroboration. I had taken one man's word for it, and what a wretch of a man. It was an error Uncle never would have made. He would have been very unhappy with me. There was no corroborating a story about South Africa, not unless I could track down someone else who had been there. That was unlikely. It was equally unlikely Two-Gun had even been there. The fact is I shouldn't have run the story at all. I was too eager to fill pages.

My eyes scanned the turned faces, all angry, and tried again. You're saying diamonds were found here?

That's what your partner said.

I wished I could deny our connection, but they were reading the very newspaper that announced:

2-Gun

Backs

Bullet

which meant not only were we partners, but partners because of his money.

Fakes! another added. Courtesy of Two-Gun.

I recalled his great white rump as he rooted around in the dirt. You dropped something, I told him. Yes, and he had been planting it until I came along. A piece of glass, most likely, and not a diamond.

The Saloon had grown hot. The air itself seemed to glow with the rows and rows of reddened faces. Then, one by one, the angry citizens stood, and their faces loomed higher, their voices shouting at once: You owe us! We want our money back! We'll have you thrown in jail!

And they rushed at me, shaking my own newspaper at me, mouths still open and moving, their words now incomprehensible as each accusation gobbled up the one before.

Surely they were not saying that because of what I wrote—and what they found—what he planted—that I…

And then I realized what they meant and how he had earned the money he gave me. One hundred dollars for a full share. It was *their* money he gave me. How many of them had bought a share or gone in on one together? How many people in this saloon had been duped into putting their money into his scheme, money that he, in turn, put into my paper? That's how he backed the *Bullet*. I should have asked him, but I was too busy planning how to spend it. So busy I never wondered why he wanted to invest in a paper that was struggling. To hide money, why else?

That conniving, corrupting two-faced—he had used me. He used my paper to pull a scam, even used my copy of *The Edmonton Journal* to hide what he was handing me, an envelope fat with their money. In no time he'd be trying to steal it back. Why else give it to me?

And not a single sign of him since the opera.

I was too shocked for tears. I began to stammer and stutter. I could not be held responsible.

Could I?

They dropped my papers, stepped all over them as they surged, hands reaching out to grab a piece of me, my collar, my shoulder, my hands. And Mr. Mooney right there watching the whole show.

Silver took my arm to hustle me out of the room.

No, I said, yanking my elbow from his grip. I do need to talk to you, but this first.

I called out to the crowd, Please! I tried again. Please tell me what he took.

The roar was instant. Silver produced a whistle and blew one long blast until all noise subsumed to his. Then he shouted, The lady has something to say.

I flipped open my notebook.

Tell me your name and what he took from you, I said. I'll write it down. I'll get the money back to you, somehow.

Mr. Mooney turned on his heel while Silver barked, One at a time. Line up.

And they did, shuffling up to me with their names, Jessup, Marcus, fifty dollars, Martini, Anna, twenty-five, Anders, Lars, a full one hundred dollars on behalf of his family.

For twenty minutes I wrote names and recorded numbers, until the last person had left.

Silver walked to the door and said, C'mon. Patrons will be wanting in, now.

The canvas sacks were almost empty. I slung both over one shoulder and followed him to the jail where, finally, I conducted my interview.

It was my first time in any jail and it was smaller than I expected, with just two cages of black bars set into the room, with no wall separating them from the front door. The bars were the first site to greet me, and both cages were empty. Also unexpected.

We sat across from each other at his desk. I hoped he had a bottle in the drawer, and would offer me a drink. I needed one. I was so upset I was shaking, and at one point had to tuck my writing hand under the weight of my thigh to steady it. But he didn't even offer me a glass of water. My intended interview, about the birth, was brief, given the sudden turn of events.

No, he hadn't yet heard about the child but said no good could have come from such evil doings in the mines. He completely mistook my meaning, which was that something about this place caused the malformation. He blamed it on blasphemous fornication.

I moved the discussion along to Two-Gun, who had become a more pressing subject to me since I stumbled into that meeting and heard myself and my paper slandered.

Silver was curt about it. I brought your friend in here for questioning, he said, same day that airship crashed. We watched it through the bars.

Well, he's not—

Business partner, then. And your guest at the opera. I let him go. I had him promise to stay in town in case I needed to question him further. He said he had no intention of leaving because he had that date with you. Wouldn't miss it for anything, he said.

Date! I said.

Silver shot me a look not unlike the look he gave me at the opera. I had mistaken suspicion for jealousy. He was onto Two-Gun by then.

I'm the law, he said, but I figured there's not much we can do about fools who part with their money so easily. There was no proof there were diamonds in that seam. A couple of people insisted they saw gems in the ground that looked like diamonds. I said who's to say Cohen put them there?

I opened my mouth to say what I had seen, but Silver wasn't stopping.

And don't they know that diamonds don't come out of the ground looking like diamonds on a ring? he said.

My face grew hot, because I had thought they did. Silver was sharper than I had first thought.

They have to be cut and polished, he said. And don't you think they misunderstood his use of the term black diamond, which anyone knows is a fancy name for anthracite, the fanciest of coal? I'm not saying he's innocent. It's not my first run-in with him. He cheated at cards and a group was going to string him up.

I saw that! I said. When I first got here.

They roughed him up and I said that was warning enough. I figured he wouldn't do it, again.

But he did.

Yes, a different group altogether. The first was just passing through, drifters just like your Morris Two-Gun. The second lived here. One didn't know t'other, so there was no advance warning.

I listened as Silver talked. He could have warned them. Maybe he was in on the scheme with Two-Gun. I might have said so, but I had finally found my own defence, people drew conclusions I hadn't intended.

Exactly. Can any of us help it if people are so willing to be convinced? Even you. Well, in a town rich with ore deposits, who would question a new mineral find? Your friend mimicked their success and acquired their legitimacy. You should have seen his evening of cigars and brandy. I'm surprised you weren't there.

My face burned hotter. Was I invited? Not exactly, but I set the type for the notice. I helped him write it. Maybe he thought that was invitation enough. Or maybe he wanted to keep me away.

That soirée, Silver continued, was full of the sort of person that deserved to be swindled. One of them turned to me and said, I don't normally like his kind—a Jew he meant—all the while swilling his drink and gobbling his shrimp on toast.

I appreciated that about Silver. Still, by now I was even more certain that he had conspired with Two-Gun. He had such a deep level of understanding, of admiration, almost, for the man.

If you knew what Two-Gun was up to, why didn't you warn me?

Figured you knew, being the newspaper publisher and all. He must have done this before.

I thought of his eagerness to take my *Edmonton Journal*, probably looking to see if other parts of the country were onto him.

Silver nodded at my newspaper sacks. So, he said, your printer returned.

I was filled with the need to hurry back. I had intended to ask about that dirty deputy, and whether it was Silver who had sent him away, but the evening's events had taken my thoughts in new directions. I had to get back to the shop. I had left that note, though with the opera and then our silence over the first edition, I still hadn't explained the note's contents. I needed to warn him, but with the deputy gone was there a need? Drummond. Yes.

It was well into the evening, now. Vincent might be wondering where I'd got to, if he was even still there. I hoped so. There was the business to discuss, photographs, a trip to purchase equipment. And while I had every reason to feel glum and uncertain about my reputation, now, the promise of that second edition, or a trip, or both, lightened my step.

HALF-PAST EIGHT O'CLOCK

The troupe was dismantling the tents, their shouts less exuberant, now, as I rushed past. The players had a few days yet before their next performance in another town. Their pace had become leisurely. I noted the flashes of flesh between robes, their knickers as they bent to pull up trousers. All seemed as usual, except for Ben who stood aside, peering into a wicker basket.

I hated to see them go, and I stopped, briefly, to tell him so.

He shook his head. The matinee is over, he said, our work is done, so it's time we left. What a contagion of a place. Some sort of mining swindle—and you heard about that child? Everyone's talking about it.

Yes—

Yes, well, not just the child, he said. And he offered the basket.

I had checked my watch repeatedly since leaving Meena. I felt as though I was in one of those dreams where, no matter how you tried to hurry, to move, you might as well have been wading through sludge, or glue, each step forward a struggle. I wanted to tell him I would look later. I had things to do. But he was leaving soon and his expression, a mixture of disgust and horror, made me hesitate.

A quick look, then, I decided, followed by a hasty exit. I lifted the top and peered inside. I lowered the lid.

It was a twin to the fish that had sailed belly-up beside me as I walked along the stream, that I found across my doormat and nailed to my door, and finally, floating, in my bowl of soup.

I know, I said. I've seen this before. I wrote about it in the paper, too. Didn't you see it? *Strange Fish*, I called it.

You didn't say it was this strange.

Something—I grasped for what possibly could have created the horned snout and blistered skin on this fish and the others.

I've poked around that creek more than once, he said. It's full of them. I brought this one back for you to see.

The entire creek? I asked.

I pictured the lovely vegetables, the hidden garden, watered by that creek.

No, he said. I was at Wolf's the other night and the fish there looked fine. It has to be something down here. What sort of sorcery is going on in this place? You saw that child. Now this. Which is why we're not sad to go, he said. Nice to meet you, darling. But we're leaving in a couple of hours. I suppose you'll be leaving, too.

I don't think so, I replied.

In truth I had just been thinking about it, a trip to get equipment. But I wasn't so sure anymore, not with all this news going on.

I said, Vincent and I have just produced our first issue. We'll have another to get out, now. All this to write about, and the girl—

I didn't know her name, something I would have to take care of right away, and I was about to tell Ben this, but he took off his bowler, twirled it, then replanted it over his ears, clearly in preparation of speaking.

I saw you at the dinner, he said, the way your printer looked at you, the way you looked back. Pure opera.

Opera?

I could feel my ears burning. What had my face or my words given away? Too much.

Yes, he said, him leaving and all.

Leaving? When?

Oh, my dear, opera indeed.

I didn't hear what else he said. I was running up the street.

A QUARTER PAST
NINE O'CLOCK

From fifty paces I could see the light burning in the shop. This had been a day that had dragged on and I was relieved to be nearing its end, nearing home. He would want to stay when he heard my plans. Why didn't I think of this sooner? A partnership. A real one this time. The sort of connection that would permit a future. We could put all awkwardness behind us, and who knows, who knows? If I wasn't running I might have been able to freeze those thoughts, analyze them. Or maybe I preferred them floating, elusive, inviting any number of possibilities.

I burst into the pressroom, and dropped the newspaper sacks where I stood.

Vincent was staring into the metal mirror. One hand tugged his queue to the side, the other gripped the large blade we had used to cut the newspapers. It took me a moment to realize what he was about to do, and as the metal flashed I cried, No!

I had startled him, and the knife cut just one twist of braid that now sprang loose like the straws of a broom.

If I hadn't taken so long to get here, if I hadn't helped Meena or stopped at the meeting and stayed to interview Silver, if I hadn't talked to Ben, I might have got here sooner.

He reeled around at the sound of my voice. What?

The word stung like a slap. I wanted to say I never minded, but I had, really, at the opera dinner when his queue looked suddenly out of place, wrong. So why would I care if it was gone?

And yet I did care, and in place of logic I felt anger swell, and along with it, all the words I had held back when we were printing the paper. I walked around him, circling him as though I were a schoolyard bully, taunting him, the words spilling freely.

That deputy would love it, you cutting your hair. That crowd would be cheering you right now. This is your grand leader's idea. Isn't it?

You're leaving with him and he needs you to look the part.

He held the blade high, across his chest, as though that could stop me. With each revolution, me circling him, and with him following me, I was backing us closer to the press, the machine that had been the focus of our work here, week after week.

I tried a safer question next. And what about Paris? Montreal? That's not important anymore, he said. I'm going back.

I took a risk with the next question, Is it because of the opera? His lip turned further down.

This is about China's future. No nationalism, and what have we got? More years under the rule of alien interests—

I'm not asking as the newspaper publisher!

I hadn't meant to shout it. Hadn't meant to admit that, either. But it was out now, and I breathed deeply before continuing.

It was in that role precisely, as a newspaperwoman, that I asked Morris to the opera. He knew about mines and he was my business partner—all right, don't look at me like that, I was wrong. But he was your friend. Maybe I wouldn't have trusted him so much if he wasn't your friend.

It was a low thing to say, putting the blame on him, but desperation had poisoned all sense of dignity. Now I paced back and forth in front of the press that steamed and rumbled through a cleaning of the rollers. Vincent didn't move.

Soon's this is done, he said, I'm off.

Morris will be leaving, too, you know. Pardon me. Two-Gun. He wants to be Sun's bodyguard.

And then I told him how Two-Gun had paid for his investment in the paper. I watched Vincent. I hoped this fact would bring him to my side. I blurted my idea of photography and a future partnership, a real one, this time.

I can't run the business on my own. What am I supposed to do, now? Sell it? Who'd buy it?

The only person I could think of was Parker, out of sheer proximity, and he didn't know a blasted thing about the news business. No, the bank would take it. Mr. Mooney was probably still rubbing his hands after what he heard at that meeting.

I pointed at Vincent's lopsided hair, ridiculously touching.

What about your father? What would he think of what you've just done?

But I knew the answer. If I'd listened to him at all these weeks, I knew it. He had worn the queue to please his father and infuriate the western bosses, but now he had his own concerns, his own politics. To make certain I understood this, he raised the knife and stared, a stare meant to hurt me, as he hacked through the rest of the queue. It fell to the floor while the rest of his hair, freed, hung raggedly like an Indian's.

He'd have to go to a barber now, have it all cut away. Neat. Parted down the middle.

I can also be cruel. I hurled the words at him, Now you'll look like every other man!

I was angry, he was angry, there was no way to fix it, too much said, now, far too much and I was done with talking.

I snatched the knife from his hand before I knew what I was going to do with it, and in one motion that eliminated the awkward metal buttons of my coveralls, grabbed up a shoulder and slit the grey cloth from collar to waist, the dress beneath it as well, even scraping my throat in my haste. Let him see me as a woman, for a change, not a newspaperwoman, not a printer's helper, let him see me as he saw me that time before, on the floor in this same thin chemise. He was going away, what would it matter to him what happened, now? No one could do anything to him, he'd be gone.

He tried to take the blade back but I held on until I could feel the copper eye of the machine pressing against my spine and his weight against me, the iron tangle of wheels and bolts and bars rising above us, around us, daring us, right there against the machine, hissing steam and shuddering, his weight on me and my hands full of him. I didn't hear the blade hit the floor, how could I, overcome by the shaking of the machine, of me, and the sound of his voice, as though he had been saying it all along, *Lila!*, his teeth on my neck, nipple, rib. I ran a hand down his spine, fingers playing each bump as though they were the nubs of braided hair, gone now, as was the man who once wore it. And I could have lost myself right there, allowed myself to sink into swirling grief and regret at that realization, could even have lost the very thing I had sought for so long, and was about to have, and what a fool would I have been then? And so I let go, fingers sprung free from his spine and its rosary of reminders, reached behind instead and gripped an iron limb in each fist, held on tight as he took me, yes, right there against the machine, braced myself to be loved for the first time in my twenty-nine years.

NEARING ELEVEN O'CLOCK

The door had closed and I was on the floor. Scattered about me were the leavings of our love, blade, blood, torn cloth of blue flowers, a severed queue. I stared up at the beast that had shook to life so recently. Vincent was gone, now, and in his absence both of us were stilled. His last act was to shut off the machine, the cleaning done. His hand had lingered by the switch for several moments, his back to me, and then he left.

I tugged at the straps of my chemise, straightened my linens, then rose and climbed into the coveralls that flapped open where they were slit. Only then did I see it, dangling long and finger-like from that switch: the spare key to my shop. And I knew for certain then that he was gone. I stuffed my dress into my pocket, picked up the queue and pressed it to my chest, still sore.

At my desk I pulled out my own set of keys and unlocked the top drawer and laid the braid of hair inside it, next to the two notebooks, their edges worn and pages thick with my notes. There, my head so heavy I could barely lift it, I dragged my eyes over the first book, remembering my first days here. How hopeful I had been, then, and how sorry for myself I felt, now, at moments pathetically boastful, forcing him into an act that at last proved that I had been right, he had wanted me, and then bereft, more at a loss now than I had been before, to know it was over.

As determined as I had been to do what I set out to do, run this newspaper and yes, perhaps, even run the machine that produced it, the fact remained that I would have left with him had he asked me to, without a second thought I would have followed him.

But he didn't ask, it was as simple as that.

I snapped the cover closed, and locked the desk. I could still smell him on my skin when I climbed the steps to my room upstairs, peeled back the coveralls. A bath would fix that, but I didn't want it fixed. I pulled the coveralls back on. I didn't have the heart to search for another outfit. I stuffed the torn dress into the bottom of the closet and then sat by the open window.

JUNE HUTTON | 222

What now? I could go off by myself to the city to buy photographic equipment. There must be a book or an operating manual that goes with it. I could learn.

Would anyone in this strange town notice the strangeness of a woman working long hours into the night, red light glowing behind a closed door, the reek of vinegar and acid as photographic images bloomed beneath the liquid surface, ghastly images that would become her sole contentment, until she could decide what else to do?

A flickering of light, then. Flames leapt orange and yellow in the black night, and I shot forward, enlivened, head out the open window, craning my neck. The sight kindled no recollections this time. My head was too full of the present. I smelled the clouds of exhaust and felt the glass trembling and realized that for the second time in the month recorded in my notebooks, motorcycles were roaring around in the dead of night.

They were after Vincent's leader, still.

Vincent—I forgot to warn him. Again.

I leapt up, dug through my jewel box for a simple brooch, and found it in my brother's army pin, jabbed it into my coveralls to close the slit. I fastened a leather belt high up around my middle as further security. I knew without looking that my hair would be askew. Good. Well-loved, that's how I must look. With the spine of my notebook knocking against my knee, I charged down the stairs, pausing only to take up the blade, again, a weapon should one be needed, shoved it into the back of my belt, then out the door.

Citizens were stepping out from alleys and doorways to stand wide-legged in the street, head-lamped and holding blazing torches high. This was an organized search, unlike the mad chase the night of the opera that had brought them no satisfaction. They had learned from that mistake. This time, torches marked the holes in the ground, and I could only assume this was so that the motorcycles could avoid them and continue the chase into the night.

Engines roared from the direction of Lousetown, and I ran around to the back of my building. I had forgotten my headlamp inside, but no matter. More citizens with torches lighted the route. The motorcycles had already reached the pithead and now raced past me, some with headlamps slung over the handlebars for extra illumination, all of them looping around the crackling torches, with men cradling shotguns in the sidecars, their hats fixed as well with miner's lamps, glowing, their tin badges blinking dully from their deputized chests. As each whipped past, my head snapped around to check. But no Vincent. No Sun. Not in the sidecars with guns trained on their temples, not stumbling after, their hands tied, sticks prodding their backs. The posse hadn't found them in Lousetown.

Now the bikes veered toward the cramped roads that housed the miners, where there were any number of hiding places. I followed with the crowd. The motorcycles roared down each alley and looped back onto Zero, then back again down the narrow roads, searching. I soon gave up. Vincent must be leaving with the opera boat. How else had Ben known about his plans?

I raced back onto Zero, dodging the crowds and the holes and the crossing bikes, I ran just as I had run when the airship crashed, this time in the dark of night with torches helping to light my way.

I was almost at the shore. The blaze of torches made the mist a mere veil. I could see the opera troupe's tramp steamer, scraped and varnished, could hear its newly fixed motor rumbling. On deck, Ben, in his brown pin-striped suit, paced, stopped to pull out his pocket watch, then paced some more. Up ahead, the Diva squeezed through the crowd and lumbered down the pier and up the ramp. Immediately behind her trooped Ben's old friend, along with the actor who played the sheriff, and a number of musicians, distinctive in their old black suits and with their black hair slicked back from their foreheads. The womanly curves of the cello in its case, followed by the violin, were carefully passed from player to player and then below decks, followed by the four musicians themselves.

I couldn't see Vincent at all.

A motorcycle pulled up in the swirling mist and Silver leapt out of the sidecar. I called his name and he turned, consternation all over his face at having to stop.

I've been meaning to thank you, I said.

For what?

For sending that foul deputy away. It was you, wasn't it? I was going to lodge a complaint about the man.

I was trying to stall Silver, and it worked. He accepted my thanks, and explained his actions, I saw you come flying out of that room, and I went in, and there he was, undone, and saying that about a fish head, Chrissakes. I threatened to fire him and thought that would be the end of it. But no. You're not the only one he tried to vulgarize.

I blinked at the odd turn of phrase, as well as at the comparison, especially now with me standing before him, unwashed, in my torn coveralls.

You mean Dee, I said. That happened long before. At the strike.

I know that now, but didn't at the time. I was elsewhere. Busy.

I didn't need to ask where.

So, he said, I ran him out of town.

It seemed to me the man left on his own, but perhaps Silver had done something to convince him.

As I was saying, I can't thank you enough for that.

Then his silver ant head snapped around. Chinese miners and maybe even extras from the opera, masses of them illuminated by the torches, burst through the grey and converged onto the beach, shouting and running, through the crowd and onto the pier, toward the boat.

Silver pushed past me and ran after them, shouting, What the hell you think you're doing?

They continued to bunch, so many of them that several were tipped off the edge of the wharf, a funnel of white spray against black as each body struck the surface, a sound of logs tumbling from skids into the water. I shoved past shoulders and knocked a couple of hats askew, their miner's lamps bobbing crazily, in my attempt to get closer so I could see. The Chinese, their soaked hair standing in dark spikes, waded their way knee-deep back to shore, wave upon wave of them. But Vincent was not among them, and neither was his leader.

Silver stormed back down the boards, boots pounding, and then onto the gravel beach, crunching over to me, again.

More of your friends, he shouted, arm flapping behind him to indicate the Chinese. Stupid bastards, he said, what are they trying to do?

I shook my head. I really had no idea.

They'll sink the boat, he cried, there's too many of 'em. And me, I'll catch bloody hell from Drummond if they don't show up for their shift.

He called out to two deputies and ordered them onto the wharf. He pointed at the Chinese. Don't let any of 'em get on board, he said.

He cupped his hands around his mouth and yelled, Cast off! Right now!

The crew of the opera boat scurried to pull in ropes and push off from the wharf.

A musician had re-appeared from below deck. He leaned on the steamer's railing to watch as pandemonium broke out on the pier and on the shore, deputies pushing Chinese and Chinese pushing back. A punch, a board broken from a railing, swung hard into a head, making the same pulpy sound as boys booting a pumpkin down a lane. Screams, then, and more boards torn free, more punches and kicks, whistles piercing the gilded air. I backed out of the way, up against a warehouse wall, my spine wedged into its corrugated ruts.

Silver climbed into a sidecar and two motorcycles kicked up gravel, herding the crowd away from the water and up the street, disappearing into a fog broken by tongues of flame. Motors roared, deputies and citizens ran back and forth, Lousetowners and regulars alike, shouts for torches in this direction and that.

Meanwhile, the little vessel inched away from the dock, steaming lustily, while another rose darkly behind it, larger and larger as it drew closer to shore. The midnight ship.

A breeze stirred over the water and the musician at the opera boat's railing stood taller and lifted his face. The tramp steamer was strung with lights and his face, paler than Ben's, was awash with the glow of the yellow bulbs, rendered featureless in the distance. Still, I could tell now, by the cut of his suit and hair and his English bearing, that he was no musician.

I breathed out my discovery in a long gasp to myself: It was their leader, Sun.

There had been an extra musician, I had noted that, four not three, but the significance of the fact had not sunk in. Who else recognized him? I swung around, but all eyes were on the approaching ship and the need to stop anyone from boarding it. I swivelled back again to watch the little boat, still listing to one side despite repairs. Sun stood alone at the railing, erect, calm, observing the struggle on shore while the little tramp steamer wobbled further up the inlet.

The struggle on shore was for him. They were causing a scene so that he could get away. What I wouldn't give to be standing beside him right now, recording his words in my notebook. He had achieved it at last, his people acting as one, and they were doing it for him.

I stepped forward, away from the building and onto the gravel, and then, on impulse, raised a forlorn hand and waved good-bye. It was my final attempt at communication with the leader, and it was successful. He waved back.

The midnight ship would dock soon. What of the one I had been waiting for? He, who from this moment onward I refused to name, for so many reasons but mostly for giving me all that I had wanted, and then leaving, and who, for all I knew, might have a Chinese name as well for me to decline. He had never said. I had never asked. Slowly, I lowered my hand.

A dislocation of air struck with the force of a cannonball. It was coming right at me. The clatter of hooves on stones, the ripe sweat of an overworked horse. The only one in town with a horse was Two-Gun, and I had words for him. I put a hand to my back, and waited.

It exploded through the fog, big and black and muscled, nostrils wide as craters, teeth a demonic grin, and thundered round me with each squeeze on its ribs from a pair of thick, white-trousered thighs.

You! I cried.

A long tail lashed the beast's haunches and my cheeks on passing. I stepped back, out of the way of the pounding iron shoes, then forward again, hand ready.

Now, now, Two-Gun pleaded.

Swirling fog rendered him headless, but I knew he lifted his white hat imploringly. He, however, did not know what my hand touched, tucked between spine and belt. I could kill him right here. Wound him, anyway. One throw.

But I let go and pointed toward the wharf and better revenge.

You missed it, I shouted. The opera troupe left without you. On that.

I know, Two-Gun huffed, coming into view for a moment. It was on purpose, trust me.

Ha. I saw who was with them.

Exactly. So you should have. No time to explain, my lovely. But I will, I will.

He jerked the reins and the horse reared up, turned, charged back into the mist.

Come back here, I yelled.

But he was gone. Cries erupted from the grey as he galloped through, and I heard the whoosh of torches waved to keep their bearers from being trampled.

The mists parted again, and there it was. The midnight ship slammed against the dock and reversed its engines, a roar that challenged the clamour of voices on land.

A rope was tied hastily while the crew flung crates onto the boards below. In minutes, the delivery complete, the midnight ship dipped and groaned under the advancing boots of the deputies who took up positions, and waited. I knew what they did not, that there were more than opera players on the tramp steamer that just left.

The navigator's grizzled head appeared at the ship's railing and shouted down at anyone interested that departure would be delayed by three hours. No boarding allowed before then.

The one I was waiting for would also have to wait.

I spotted my bundle of newspapers at the edge of the cargo pile, grabbed it by the rope and dragged it all the way up the dirt road to my shop. Once inside, I heaved the papers onto the wooden table and sat, wrists nudging the edges.

The bundles have arrived irregularly and never yet contained the magic I sought, the clue or set of clues that might have charmed him, through my sudden knowledge of newspapering, or of foreign places. I was a fool, of course. Even now, I delayed reading them, putting off the disappointment for a few moments, enjoying, for those same moments, even the slightest chance, until at last curiosity compelled me to reach behind my back for the knife. Metal sang through air as I dropped the blade into the rope, chopping it in two. A sigh, a groan, the papers gave like a corset opening, their folds an accordion of possibilities: a street, a scene, a scent, all things that I might still have absorbed and, in making them part of me, further bound him to me. I was a fool, indeed.

I flattened the stack of curling pages with the hardened heels of both hands, blackening them, and found amongst the headlines and printed type a map of China. With a lazy finger already stained with printer's ink, I traced along the coastline, drawing first over Canton, further east, Macao, and then Hong Kong, drifting back again and then northward, past Swatow, Amoy, Foochow, Ningpo, finally coming to rest on the city he loved more than any other, more than me, the city that never quite accepted him, with doors that remained closed to him: that perfumed *femme* of concessions, that flower boat of a settlement. Shanghai.

I gazed at the wall above. Familiarity told me there were pencils dangling by strings, shelves with slots of type, wooden frames, tins of ink and solvent. None of it registered, though, as I tried to imagine, instead, couples strolling along the treed streets, the gardens heavy with pale pink roses and azaleas, the women in gauzy dresses, the business-men with glasses of brandy in smoky bars, the horse races and the cafés with their pastries and cups of chocolate, and the riverfront, a brace of banks and trading offices transplanted from Europe's finest cities, with pillars of stone and arched windows, brass doorways and chandeliers.

And my thoughts sank once more into that other Shanghai.

I lifted the newspaper to my nose, again smelling the green of warm air rubbing against water, the stink of cabbage churning from gutters where something as precious as leaves of cabbage would never be tossed, and my imagination ripened. Entrails from butchered hens.

Bare-footed boys pissing behind market stalls. Old beggars trembling with dysentery. Raw boards dropped over putrid waters, creaking with each footstep, releasing into the mix its own smell of oil and rotting wood. Even that place had touched him as I never could.

FINALE

Three hours was more than enough time to skim through the stack of newspapers. There were many items about the ongoing battles with warlords, but no mention of the leader's absence, or of his presence here in North America. They had kept the secret better than I had. And now he had sailed off on the opera boat.

The body had left without the bodyguard, though, and just as well. Still, Two-Gun seemed strangely unconcerned. Was the leader not his reason for being here?

Two-Gun and Sun. Side-kick and hero. A thief who filled his pockets at people's expense; a politician who filled people's ears with words, intent on raising funds for his dreams of a Republic. Two-Gun & Sun, to me a single corrupting entity, two rotten peas in a festering pod, fouling everything they came in contact with. The town—and one that needed no further corruption. My newspaper. Him, whose scent was still on my skin and in my hair. Because of them, I had lost everything.

I drew the notebook from my pocket and began to record the events of this long and exhausting day, all the while my thoughts drifting to the other two books. Each time I turned their pages I saw wisps of thoughts forgotten these past days, sometimes best forgotten, and yet I knew I would return to them for comfort, for assurance.

A knocking at the door stopped me before I was done writing.

I didn't need to ask who it was because a raw voice sounded below my window: Are you up there, my dear girl? I'm here at last.

I sprouted wings, the wings of a bat, and flew down the stairs.

You! I cried, the door banging open into his white bulk. This is your idea of soon? Where have you been for three hours?

My dearest—

I could have sliced you with one throw!

I grabbed the blade from the back of my belt this time, and swiped at the air, hoping to make contact. But he was agile and pranced back.

And where is your horse, now? You rode off without a word of explanation. Left me standing at the docks, wondering, shouting into the fog for you to come back! Just like you did at the opera.

I have much to explain, granted.

Yes you do!

I came here as soon as I could—what on earth happened to your camouflage suit? A printing mishap?

Yes.

My dear, there isn't much time. The midnight ship is cleared to leave, now.

And you plan to be on it?

I said it hotly and with no suggestion that I would miss him. I wouldn't.

But to my amazement he replied, Come with me.

Of all people—I began.

I threw my hands into the air, one still brandishing the blade, my hair sticking out in ten directions, if the prickling of my scalp was any indication. Of all the cheek, of all the bloody nerve.

And I blasted at him, Why would I?

He tossed his hat onto the counter and said matter-of-factly, Because I promised you an interview with our leader and you shall have it.

Hah! I was there when the opera boat left and I saw him on deck, dressed as a musician. I wasn't fooled like the rest. I saw him leave.

He ran his hands through his hair.

I need a drink, he concluded. What do you have?

I shoved the blade into the back of my belt and grabbed the bottle from under the counter. I needed one, as well. There were perhaps three inches left in it from that night of the mine explosion when *he* and I worked all night on the press. I polished two grimy glasses on my sleeve and poured. Two-Gun raised his glass to me and then downed it.

In different circumstances I might have asked him to sit, but I was furious. I left him shuffling from foot to foot. This meant I had to stand, too, and I was tired. I eased an elbow onto the counter for support.

That wasn't him, he said at last. Our leader.

What do you mean? I saw him. He took his hat off and lifted his face and I could see clearly that he was Chinese—

The air turned orange about the edges, and then black. I sat, hard, right down onto the shop floor, as though I had been expecting a chair and someone had pulled it out from under me.

Excellent, my dear. This is exactly the effect we were attempting with our ruse. I took him to the Lousetown barber and asked for a cut just like our leader's. He needed it tidied up anyway after cutting off that damn queue.

I thought I might be sick right there on the floor. He did indeed look like everyone else, now, even his leader. I had bid him a final farewell without knowing it.

Two-Gun reached for my hand but I pulled myself back up to the counter and asked, Where is he then, your leader?

What makes you think he was *ever* here?

Because I saw him with my own eyes. Heard him, too.

Again I ask, how do you know *that* was him?

Because he took me there, my printer—

Even though you had written about the leader, which warned everyone in town that he was coming—

The cruelty of the man, to add to my grief. I could blame myself well enough without his help.

What are you saying? I had his name in my headlines!

I'm saying my dear, that for all you know someone took on his identity once before, to protect him, knowing full well that there would be a raid.

But at the opera, you spoke to the leader yourself.

I met a man. We had a chat.

Oh, I don't believe you! Why not have the imposter ride off on the opera boat, then?

Perhaps he left right after the opera on the midnight ship. Dressed as one of the extras.

Two-Gun held out his glass but I poured the rest into mine. Dressed as an extra. It seemed too outrageous to be fabricated.

The raid that was meant to stop his speech, he said, turned the tide for the cause, and won the people's sympathy. The sight of the deputies storming their meeting! The instant those walls fell he had their support. Everyone is saying so.

The imposter had, you mean.

I drained the glass. I had heard his speech, recognized phrases from his writings. Any actor could memorize the lines, true. I asked Two-Gun, Did they know it wasn't really their leader?

Who's to say what one man knows and another believes? And does it matter? Look at them this very evening, my girl, running interference while his double sails away. They support the cause.

Once again we were thinking alike, but I was especially annoyed that this time I wouldn't be able to at least quote him, as I had when he suggested a hunt for fresh meat. I had no printer, no paper.

My dear, he said, taking my arm in that way of his, two hundred pounds of stubborn insistence, forcing me to walk with him. I have much to tell you. Come. We will transfer to a ship bound for Hawaii.

Not Shanghai?

Hawaii, first. Sandy beaches. Maidens in grass skirts.

The change of destination had only a temporary effect on my mood. I took back my arm and pulled out the notebook I had been scribbling in when he arrived, and shook it at him.

I've recorded the names of everyone you swindled. I've written down how much it cost them, how much you owe them.

Good, good, he said. I'm glad to hear that. I'm a changed man, my dearest. This damn foolery of mine. I'm getting too old for it. Our leader is promising change, a future. The events of these past days have put a spark in me, given me a cause worth following. I'm going to China.

You owe me money, first, I said. I'm not paying those people back by myself. You're responsible.

I stuffed the book back in my pocket.

I'm selling the horse.

Really.

I am ashamed to admit it was to be my means of escape, on a moment's notice. But my intentions, my whole purpose shifted when that gun fired at the opera. In that instant, as I leaped onto that beast, I became our leader's bodyguard.

To hear my thoughts parroted back at me yet again stretched my patience. I raised the glass and then dropped it down, annoyed. It was empty.

I'll have no need of the creature, now. Lila, my dear, why not come with me? What an adventure, the two of us on our way to China.

He had a point. It was the only reason I bothered to listen to him. I'd already come to the conclusion that, on my own, the best I could do was crank out single newssheets. Would they be enough to pay my expenses? Mr. Mooney would seize the business, otherwise. But leave with Two-Gun? I walked to the staircase. He followed, talking some more—my God, the man could talk—while I pondered the life of a woman who had lost her lover and was married to her business, reduced as it was.

I've been promising to introduce you to the leader. Allow me to do so, my dear, in China. It is my gift to you, my way of compensating for every wrong I've done to you.

I needed time to think, I told him, and slipped past. I grabbed the railing and left him at the bottom of the stairs.

He called up after me, I'll wait right here. But don't be long!

⊸≡

I paused by the globe to give it a spin, my fingers stopping it at China, the heel of my hand on Australia, all the marvellous places between them nestled under my palm: Malaya, Indonesia, Siam, the Philippines. And between there and here, Hawaii.

Perhaps I deserved this. Instead of *him*, it was Two-Gun, that windbag of a wheedler, cheat, liar and thief, reformed all of a sudden he said, as unpredictable and untrustworthy a travel companion as anyone could be cursed with, who waited patiently downstairs for my answer, on the very slimmest possibility, one that grew slimmer the longer he waited, and yet one that, having sprung from his offer and his willingness to wait, did, in its very act of simple decency, move me.

Oh, he could make me laugh. He could also make my eyeballs smoke in their sockets.

I considered my closet of clothes, all the items I might pack for a trip, the outfit I might step into right now, that would seal my decision one way or another.

The black dress was slit up the sides after the pig attack, the hem torn off. The blue flowered one, slit down the front this very night. I had few outfits left. The lavender-grey hung poorly but would travel well. I could imagine what he might say as I descended the steps in it.

My darling girl. I'll get the captain to perform the ceremony on the boat. It's your colour, well, yes, a bit grey, but with a diamond or two, here and there, perfect. When we get to Shanghai we will get you dresses for every occasion. They know fashion better than any of them in Paris. Until then, my lovely, why not pack your opera gown, my sentimental favourite. It will be perfect should the captain invite us to his table.

Or I could simply stay as I was, in my pinned coveralls.

I clomped down the stairs, depressed with my decision.

My dear girl, he said when I rounded the bottom of the staircase. I thought this might be your choice, but in truth I expected no less of you. Pride. It is your most endearing quality. Unless—No, no, don't say another word. I embrace your intentions as though they were my own. A perfect ruse. Take my arm. In this outfit no one would guess that you are not just walking me to the docks but are about to board the ship with me. On to Victoria, and then Seattle and then Honolulu. Plenty of dress shops along the way. Thank you, my darling. You are the only woman I know who could save me from certain moral decay on those flower boats of temptation that await in Shanghai. You trump a hundred Plum Blossoms and Lotus Buds. And I in turn will save you from this place. Give me that notebook of yours. I see it peeking from your pocket. Allow me. Enough business for one day. The hour approaches. Come with me—on the open seas, the wind in your hair, exactly as you like it. Rest assured I will become the leader's trusted bodyguard. I will introduce you. Tut, tut, not another word. Listen! I hear the ship's whistle. The future awaits, as do your hosts, *messieurs* Two-Gun *et* Sun.

I folded my arms.

No? Well then, I will say my *adieus* and hope that we will meet another time.

He took my hand and kissed the back of my wrist.

From the shop window I watched his white bulk fade into the mist.

Really, a horse was not enough to pay back the rest he owed the townspeople. What did he take me for? I had it all here. I reached for my notebook to look over the figures, and found my pocket empty. It took a moment to recall that Two-Gun had plucked the notebook from me, and failed to return it.

The thieving, scheming snake of a man.

I'd shoot him dead myself.

I'd have him arrested.

The ship's whistle sounded again. It was nearing three hours past midnight. The month had ended on its own without me noticing, without me scoring through that last number. It was all over. And what now?

I wrenched open the door and stood on the veranda. Motorbikes zoomed past, lifting strands of hair from my face and neck. A throng parted to let them through, then closed up again to surge down the street. I took in the dizzying sounds of roaring engines, shouting voices, crackling flames, all of it cloaked in a veil of grey. I understood in that chaotic moment that I had a choice, a choice very different from deciding to teach, to prove I could provide for myself and to thumb my nose at another's beliefs, or to take on a business that was someone else's creation, and inherit all its problems, or especially to take on a dubious deal intended to save such a business. No, this time it was a choice that was mine alone to make.

I could flag a taxi. Or I could walk. I checked my watch. Or run. Two-Gun would be approaching the pier. I would grab his sleeve and demand my notebook back. And then? I could leave with him. Or I could arrange to meet at some future time and place. I could head to another place entirely. Malaya, Bali, Siam. I could catch the next day's sailing, or the one after that. Because now or next day, it really didn't matter. Once you've contemplated leaving a place, there was no staying, not for long.

I slammed the door behind me and I called across to Parker, who was also locking up, Catch!

I tossed him the keys to my shop, and then, on further thought, my pocket watch. He caught the first but dropped the second.

No time to explain, I shouted to him. I'll send word!

I could send for my things, too, whatever things I deemed worth sending, broken watch included. I could put a note in the post to Meena, asking for her assistance. She would do that for me.

I stepped into the road to flag a taxi.

The driver pulled over long enough to plant a black leather boot on the ground and tell me what I could see for myself. He was full, with two deputies in the sidecar. But I could climb on behind him if I was desperate.

I was.

By the time he lifted his boot I was already walking around to the back of the bike.

Shove forward, I said.

I didn't wait for him to brake at the wharf. The ship had eased from the dock. I slid off the back and ran until my boots hit the boards. The women from *The Saloon* had arrived, belatedly as always, pulling at their clothes from recent assignations, and were gathered to see what was going on. They turned, still tugging and yawning, when they heard me, heels hammering the boards, and drew to the sides, forming a phalanx to let me through.

The wind was in my hair and my thoughts were racing. I stopped, hopped on one foot, seeing yet again those two notebooks in my desk, along with a rope of a man's hair, bristling where it was chopped, still raw with the anger of it. I dug a toe into a heel to peel the boot from my foot, no time to untie the laces, then switched to the other foot.

The third and last of my notebooks was on that ship, with several pages waiting to be filled. They were like three acts of an opera, swollen with my first moments in this town, and the month of moments that followed. A month in the late summer of my twenty-ninth year, a year that swung on the hinges of possibilities, a squawk of metal on rust that said, Now, or not at all.

I wriggled out of my coveralls, easy enough given the slit down the side, blade and belt clattering onto the boards. I jabbed the pin into one strap of my skivvies, slipped the silver hairpin onto the other, then continued to run, bare feet pounding along the pier.

All the while the ship steamed mightily away from the docks.

I didn't want a bath before. Well, too bad, I was going to get one, now. At the edge of the pier I stomped the ball of my foot against the wood and sailed off the end in an arc whose trajectory was aimed directly at the ship. It would be an easy swim compared to the west arm of the lake.

I could hear shouts and screams behind me along with a warning blast from the dock, followed by the ship's low bellow in reply. Then I exploded into the water, gliding in green silence below the surface, until I curved upward and skimmed the top, gasping, and heard more shouting, saw a rope ladder dropped down the side of the ship, a white sleeve hanging over it, big hand waving. My arms sliced one after the other, repeatedly, into the freezing chop of the inlet, each stroke exposing my face to the stinging waves, bringing me closer to the rusted hull.

This chemise was going to be as sheer as the water that soaked it by the time I climbed the ladder, exposing every detail from neck to knees. Well, let the passengers and crew see me, then, let the whole blasted world see me. Water up my nose and down my throat, nipples like lug nuts from the cold, who cared, who bloody well cared. I had lived long enough in small towns on the edge of nowhere to know what it was to want more. I'd had a glimpse, now, a taste, of what could be: adventure, passion, love. It's all in that notebook, not just numbers and news, but my life, my opera—and I will have it back.

ACKNOWLEDGEMENTS

This is a work of fiction and while the titular characters are the historical figures Morris Two-Gun Cohen and Sun Yat-sen, the events as described in my novel, along with the newspaperwoman who writes them down and the pressman who prints them, have come from my own imagination—with a few facts thrown in. Cohen would approve. He not only led a wild and marvellous life, but he told wild and marvellous tales. I am indebted to Daniel S. Levy's *Two-Gun Cohen, a Biography* for revealng the discrepancies. Cohen's stories were widely published in newspapers as the truth because they were a tantalizing tangle of real and imagined. My story does not try to separate one from the other, but, in the true spirit of fiction, revels in the snarls, and then contributes a few more in the process.

Many people have supported me in the writing of *Two-Gun & Sun* and to them I am sincerely grateful:

Agent extraordinaire John Pearce of Westwood Creative Artists, publisher Vici Johnstone who leads the fine team at Caitlin Press, editor Marnie (Doc) Woodrow for exquisite nips and tucks.

SPiN writing group pals Mary Novik and Jen Sookfong Lee for their constant encouragement; Terri Brandmueller and Tony Wanless for courageous readings.

Barbara Pulling for insightful feedback, Paul Taunton for embracing my "otherworldly Western"; Anthony De Sa for his friendship and his counsel.

Hal Wake, Jenny Niven, Alexis Lefranc and Jenny Tasker who coordinated the many and complicated connections for my reading at the Suzhou Bookworm; Ben Potter, Worm chef and unofficial tour guide; Paul French for The Glamour Bar on The Bund, Shanghai; and all those who made our stay in Hong Kong a delight: Alice Eni Jungclaus and family, Myrna Holm, Wyng Chow, Peter and Idy Comparelli.

Maxie Von Schwerin and vintage clothing collector Ivan Sayers for their 1920s fashion advice, Mary Beth Sullivan for those tickets to *La Fanciulla del West*, Andrea Polz for her operatic voice.

Co-workers and students at SFU, The Writer's Studio Online, UBC's Writing Centre and Langara Continuing Studies for feeding my writing habit.

Paul Erlam, former *Whitehorse Star* pressman, who read over the mechanical details and tried his best to fix what I had broken; Rusty Erlam, former Star owner, who told me about Cold-Ass Marie; Nick Russell, journalism mentor, who taught me never to mix fact with fiction, and whose forgiveness I seek.

Garth Erlam who, along with Terri, put the steam punk in *Two-Gun & Sun*; Joni Erlam for tech support; and the boys, Liam, Merrick, Morgan and Mason, who brought so much sudden joy into our lives.

The Canada Council for the Arts for making the development of this novel possible.